ANTON CHEKHOV WAS NEVER IN CHARLOTTETOWN

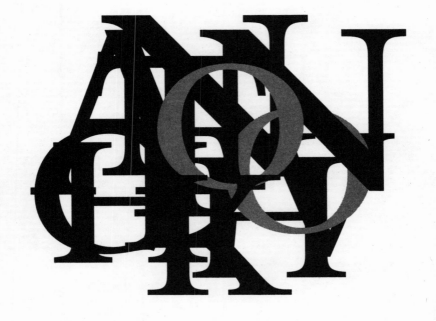

ANTON CHEKHOV WAS NEVER IN CHARLOTTETOWN

A
T
N
O
C H
K
E

ANTON CHEKHOV WAS NEVER IN CHARLOTTETOWN

STORIES BY J.J. STEINFELD

GASPEREAU PRESS
WOLFVILLE, NOVA SCOTIA

*Dedicated to the memory of
Pamela and Moncrieff Williamson*

*For Sandra and Hugh MacDonald,
and for Brenda, as always*

CONTENTS

ANTON CHEKHOV
WAS NEVER IN CHARLOTTETOWN

Stone walls do not a prison make,
Nor iron bars a cage ...
– "To Althea, from Prison"
by Richard Lovelace (1618-1657)

I TOLD HER IT WAS A DOUBLE-BAR-
relled accomplishment that I made it into the new century *and*
managed to last a half-century on the planet. What kind of accomplishment is that? she asked me, then insisted that the twenty-first
century actually starts in 2001, not 2000. I was trying to put things
into perspective. We had been shouting at each other over the
phone. And what was the argument over? *Star Trek*, of all things.
Star Trek and Anton Chekhov. I told my woman friend that I don't
give a shit if more people would say *Star Trek* if you said Chekhov.
Chekhov to me is Anton Chekhov ... I told her she could have
her Ensign Pavel Andreivich Chekov, and I'll have my Anton
Pavlovich Chekhov ... He's my friend, I shouted, and she shouts
back that my friend never came to Charlottetown. So the fuck what
if Anton Chekhov was never in Charlottetown? I acted in *The
Seagull*. She never believed me.

I don't watch *Star Trek* anymore. I don't even have a TV. I gave
my TV away a year ago. To a bartender. And my onerous bar tab
miraculously disappeared. I admit, I've seen every episode of the
original *Star Trek* TV series, more than once, but I've hardly seen
any of the subsequent ones. I'm not a purist, nothing like that. I
got tired of watching them. I've seen a couple of *Star Trek* full-
length movies, but because of her. The woman I had the horrible
argument with. She has life-size cardboard figures of the *Star Trek*
characters in her apartment. The woman's forty and she's a Trekkie.
I drew a moustache on one of the cardboard figures, and she got
annoyed. I got a little drunk, and kicked one over, and she got furious. I got a lot drunk, and tried to mate two of them, and she

went ballistic. When I wasn't drunk, I told her she was in love with pop culture. That her reality is a product of pop culture. She asked me to define pop culture and I said anything she liked was pop culture. After that argument I bought her a huge one-volume encyclopaedia of pop culture, as a forgive-me present. She loved it. Started looking up whatever popped into her mind. The irony of that gift was lost on her. I should have written in big capital letters on the title page, THIS IS AN IRONIC GIFT. Of course her favourite *Star Trek* characters were listed. Ensign Chekov, spelled without a second *h*. My Chekhov is spelled with a second *h*. She started to read some of the entries out loud, an inspired performance. We have other problems. It would be idiotic to blame our problems on differing opinions over *Star Trek*. Or on irony. She cannot comprehend why I have to have Anton Chekhov in Charlottetown for the play I'm writing. She has lectured me about Russia. What can I do about Russian politics? Chekhov transcends, I told her, *transcends*. Current events in Russia don't concern me. Anton Chekhov concerns me. She gave me a lecture and a half about that statement. Told me the Soviet Union/USSR is no more. As if I needed a history lesson. I told her Chekhov died in 1904, *before* there was a Soviet Union. Chekhov knew there were big changes on the horizon. The old order was fading ... passing ... The new order arrived ... faded ... passed ... And there will be more fadings, more passings. What is it they say: The only constant is change, or some simplistic platitude like that. The basic problem, I think, was that I was cheating on her.

I had two women who loved me, and now I don't think I have any. Is that a blues song, or what? When I get my computer fixed ... We communicate electronically. The other woman and I. She won't meet me. She won't send me a picture. I don't even know her real name. I know her code name: Mata Hari. But I've never been more intimate with another human being ... That will teach me to buy a computer from a smiling B & E punk. He smiled like his teeth were trying to leave his mouth. No warranty where I purchased my computer ... If you could see what Mata Hari says to me on the computer. I get very daring with her. And she gets more daring. If you could get pregnant with words, we'd have about twenty kids.

I have a bedroom, but I use it pretty much as a storage room. Not that I have an abundance of things to store. I usually keep the bedroom door shut. I like to maintain the mood of this room and the bedroom would only change my reality. Not that it's that easy to change my reality, but I do have moods to maintain when I'm working on my play or just dealing with life. I live and sleep and write in the living room ... It does look somewhat old-fashioned. Except for the computer. And my two posters of the Canadian Rockies. I have a maquette. It's a model of the set of the play I am trying with all my heart to finish. It's an imaginary theatre I have in Charlottetown, and the play takes place from 1902 to the present, in four acts. The theatre gets renamed during the play, and it becomes the Anton Chekhov Theatre. I paid a carpenter to make the model, according to my specifications.

I 5

Except for the posters of the Rockies I have on my walls, I decorated my living room to look like Konstantin Trepliov's study, in Act Four of *The Seagull*. It's the drawing-room in his uncle's house – nice old-fashioned term, drawing-room – and Trepliov is using it as his study. But it's only my living room that's really old-fashioned. The rest of my place is a regular, dreary one-bedroom apartment. I don't know if the porch is considered part of the apartment, technically that is. I have a bathroom, the door of which I also keep closed when not in use.

I can see a fair number of seagulls from my window. You can see them in the parking lots of fast-food joints. At Victoria Park. Any place the eats are good. But seagulls to me ... seagulls remind me of *The Seagull*. By Anton Chekhov. He was an incredible writer. His short stories and his plays ... I didn't have much of an acting career, but playing Trepliov in *The Seagull* was definitely the highlight. No way you can categorize Chekhov's work as pop culture. Maybe if you gave people a choice between seeing a *Star Trek* movie or a Chekhov play, the movie would win hands down. That doesn't prove anything. I'm not trying to prove anything anyway. Chekhov and *The Seagull* happen to have importance in my life. In a different time and place, *The Seagull* could enter the realm of pop culture.

Pop culture will consume nearly anything, given the right circumstances. Pop culture, I can take it or leave it. That's not denying it's all around us. Even in my head. A little in this room. It encrusts civilization. I like that phrase. *Encrusts civilization.* The Rockies themselves aren't pop culture ... The posters sort of fall into that realm. I like to have a few reminders in my living room of the world out there. Beyond the front door or the porch door. There are four doors in my humble apartment. Seems like quite a few in such a small area. Bedroom door. Porch door. Bathroom door. Front door. Lots of doors around me, and right now they are all closed.

I 6

    I was talking to a man at a coffee shop a few weeks back, and he was wearing a seagull cap, with a big splotch of white you-know-what on it. Interesting character. He has four doughnuts, two muffins, and five cups of coffee, with sugar no cream, each and every morning. Been doing it for years, he told me. I calculated on a napkin how many doughnuts, muffins, and coffees he has per week, per month, and per year. I joked, and told him his eating habits could turn him into a pillar of sugar. He told me he hasn't had a cold or a headache or any other health problem in over two years. I was getting over a bad cold at the time, and he prescribed lots of doughnuts and coffees, a dozen of each if I could handle it. He told me the muffins were optional. He acknowledged that his doughnut-and-coffee prescription was strong medicine, but he assured me it would be a long time before any cold germs got into my system. Another customer, a table away, on his third tea of the morning, no sweetie confections for that guy, said he hadn't had any big health problems since 1972. He knew it was September 1972 because he was in the hospital then, recovering from abdominal surgery, when he watched the Canada-USSR hockey series, flat on his back, and Paul Henderson scored his famous goal. Then another customer stood up and asked where was I in '72 when Henderson scored that goal. He started to yell that question in the coffee shop. I mean really yell, at the top of his lungs. At me, at the other customers, at the counter people, at the walls ... *Where were you in '72 when Henderson electrified the country?* He screamed it at the cops when they came. I tried to intercede – ain't that a big-league irony – but the management and staff wanted him out of the coffee shop. Barred forever, if possible. Exiled to another coffee shop. I think he might have varied his normal nerves-soothing hot chocolate intake that morning. He was into dipping his dough-nuts good and soggy into hot chocolate. Messy, drooling eater. It took a while for the place to settle down after that mid-morning pandemonium, and I thought about Henderson's eighth game, tri-umphant goal, where I was. I got to see game three of the series in person. It was in Winnipeg. A 4 - 4 tie. By the time game eight rolled around, in Moscow, I was in jail ... Hence the aforemen-tioned reference to big-league irony when I was talking about law enforcement officers. Lots of ironies in my life.

My woman friend, lover, whatever – the woman I was talking to earlier – she accused me of being more honest to a stranger in a coffee shop than to her. What's wrong with being honest with strangers? Oh, we did have some horrendous arguments. A month ago, while we were watching TV, she said she lost the baby – it was an inadvertent pregnancy, but she was starting to warm to the idea of motherhood – and I said, *Where did you lose it?* She called me some horrible names. I've called myself worse. I apologized, but that didn't help. Not that time. It was ending before that. Before my attacks on her *Star Trek* life-size cardboard figures. I said her cardboard figures were hollow effigies, and she came right back and said I was hollow. That word *hollow* came out like some vile spit from her mouth ... I smiled, and she got angrier, asked me what I was smirking about. I asked her if she thought the world was going to end with a bang or a whimper. She got even angrier, thinking I was being a real smart aleck.

You called me hollow, I told her ... a hollow man, and that reminded me of "The Hollow Men," by T. S. Eliot. Playing the English prof, I explained to her that the poem finishes with the declaration that the world ends with a whimper and not with a bang. I remember how impressed I was when I first read that poem, how much I liked the last stanza. Then I asked her if she wanted her world to end with a whimper or with a bang, her personal world, not the planet. Do we have a choice? she said to me, not impressed by my probing of her psyche. I said that you have to have a choice. What's life without choices. I think she started pressing her remote control right then, zipping through the channels. Choose, she said, the channels zooming by like flickering comets. *Choose* ... I told her our argument had degenerated and she shut off the TV. I read T. S. Eliot when I was in Germany. That's another story. I'm an avid reader. A voracious reader ... A habit I developed in prison. What's wrong, I don't sound like someone who read avidly, voraciously in prison? If you were here you could see all the books I have. And on the top bookshelf is a superb wooden carving. I picked it up at a flea market in Winnipeg. When I still had two arms. It's the only possession I still have from those two-armed days. I'll get to all that in due course. I'm not going to keep any secrets from you. But what's the rush?

I do terrible things, which I will reveal shortly. On the surface, most of my actions seem random or senseless, but everything in my life fits, waiting to be deciphered, like the cryptic writing on the wall of a long-buried tomb. Entombment, that's a nice image for me, but you'll see that for yourself soon enough. You can be the archaeologists who do the deciphering. It's the middle of winter, as good a time as any to meet a new friend.

What detail should I disclose first? Would you prefer a titillating morsel or a trivial fact? What little secrets or dark thoughts? That he masturbated daily as a boy or couldn't stand the chiding voices of his teachers might be interesting, but those drab tidbits stand miles from the contours of the soul. Souls are what we should be interested in. If it were possible, I would display my soul on a platter, like a rump roast on supermarket special. Not that I like supermarkets. I go when they're not too crowded. Actually, one specific supermarket downtown. I don't like to wander too far. I've been all over the world, and for now a radius of a half-mile or so is good enough for me. Supermarket, coffee shop, library – oh, I love that library – what more do I need.

For starters, I'll throw a few cold facts at you: I've been in prisons and I've been in mental institutions. But what does that say? A transgression here, an anti-social act there, unable to meet some official's definition of acceptable behaviour. Perhaps loathing or contempt is beginning to stir in your heart. A criminal! A maniac! you may condemn. Go ahead, start to enumerate the advantages to an

orderly society of having the death penalty. Sidle up to the executioner and whisper into the executioner's ear that you want your
crime-ridden streets swept clean. But don't be too hasty or blood-
thirsty: jails and nut houses, nothing more than a few bricks and
some metal bars. Remember, poetic souls, "Stone walls do not a
prison make, Nor iron bars a cage ..." That's not "The Hollow
Men." Richard Lovelace, "To Althea, from Prison." So far I've given
you only silly scraps of biographical rubbish, yet better to start cautiously and not irretrievably alienate your sensibilities. Without you,
I do not fully exist; confessions require ears, even if they're unsympathetic ears.

19

Let me tell you about my contribution to NATO and the safe-
guarding of Western democracy a few years back. Cold War days.
Remember those days? We need enemies, don't we? Big enemies,
little enemies, concrete enemies, invisible enemies, we need enemies
... I like to bring up that me-making-a-contribution-to-NATO story
for its dramatic effect. Unbelievable as it sounds, I tried the military. I was a hard-bitten eighteen when a judge in Ontario gave
me the choice: six months in the can or, if I *voluntarily* enlisted,
freedom in the Canadian Armed Forces, building my character, spit-
and-polishing my soul. I served my six months and then some, pun-
ishment for ten lifetimes, saluting and prancing around in ridiculous uniforms, but at least I saw Germany. That was way before
the Berlin Wall came tumblin' down.

Ah Deutschland, ah my troubled youth. In Deutschland I made
love to a woman who claimed to have been hugged as a little girl
by Hitler. Der Führer came right into her classroom and she was
the lucky one he nestled in his arms. How that German woman's
excitement grew when she described the event of her life. The embraced schoolgirl grown into a beautiful German woman talked
about that experience for almost thirty minutes, me sitting there
in my military-issue boxer shorts and twiddling my thumbs to her
ecstasy. Der Führer this, Der Führer that, here a Führer, there a
Führer, everywhere a Führer, Führer ... Her knowledge of history,
I must emphasize, was sadly deficient, but she had the loveliest rose
petals for lips and legs that were smoother than silk. I traced out-
lines of the Rockies over and over on her legs, offering lessons on

Canadian geography and describing the indescribable Rockies. All in all, it wasn't a wasted evening. I learned a little more German from her and pretended to be loved. I paid the beautiful woman and left, but to this day I see that Fräulein in my mind being bounced up and down by the bounce-crazed Führer. She must be in her seventies by now. I wonder if she still tells the story with the same fervour. In all honesty, I met more than one person over there who had some affection for Hitler, and that confused me back then. Later, during my first stay in a mental institution, twenty-seven years ago, when I was barely twenty-three – quick calculation, that makes me fifty – I met a flipped-out character who claimed to have been Hitler's lover, but he couldn't have been more than two or three years older than I was.

We're talking a lot of years under the bridge, and under the bridge is a lot of booze and a lot of medication. German women, on the whole, were good to me, especially if I lied and told them I was a Canadian rabbi's son. But that heart-scarring, brain-rattling soldiering sure wasn't for me. I followed orders most of the time. But that wasn't good enough. I'd start to recite T. S. Eliot poems at the strangest times. Not too many officers appreciate a poetry recitation when they're giving you some hut-one-two-three order or another. Whimper-bang, whimper-bang, whimper-bang … Hut-one-two-three, hut-one-two-three, hut-one-two-three … Attention! Attention! Attentionnnnnnn!!! When all else failed, that was my response: a few lines from T. S. Eliot. As well, my sense of humour got me into a few scrapes. Perhaps you're starting to get a taste of my sense of humour. Perhaps a whiff. Bit on the dark side. But not benighted, I hope.

But you know who has become my favourite poet? Milton Acorn. That's right, the People's Poet. I'd read some Milton Acorn before I moved to the Island, in anthologies, but I didn't really get into his poetry until I moved here. I don't know if Milton Acorn liked Anton Chekhov, or ever watched *Star Trek*. I never met Milton Acorn, but I've talked to people who knew him. The Milton Acorn stories there are. Talk about a legend. I tried to work Milton Acorn into my play about Chekhov in Charlottetown, but I had all sorts of problems. It was as though Milton didn't want to be in my play.

There are a lot of Acorn poems that would fit into the play. But Milton started raging at Anton too much, so we had to come to an arrangement. I read the poems for inspiration, hear his poetic voice, and he doesn't take over my play. Still, Milton would be a powerful character on stage.

Maybe a little of the physical will be helpful to flesh out my portrait. I'm not a vain man, but I've become distressed over these red blood vessels that have started appearing on my nose. My damn snout is swollen, growing redder by the day, and I find myself lingering in front of the bathroom mirror, wondering what affliction is overcoming me. I figure it's some allergy or too much boozing. Lyebedev, a character in *Ivanov*, another one of Chekhov's plays – don't I know my Chekhov – goes on about having a red nose from imbibing too much, but he's more of a vodka man, and beer is my weakness. I try taking all kinds of vitamins and drinking jugs of orange juice, but my nose isn't impressed by the treatments. I'd go to a doctor, but I don't trust them. I wouldn't mind going to Chekhov, he was a doctor, but I don't think medicare would remit payment to Dr. Anton Pavlovich Chekhov, even if he was currently practising medicine on Prince Edward Island. There's a doctor in *The Seagull*, Dr. Dorn, Yevgheniy Serghyeevich Dorn, but what kind of medical treatment can you get from a fictional character? No, I don't trust doctors. Not since one of the chop-mince-and-dice wizards amputated my left arm, and me being a natural lefty. Nothing to do with the one-armed man in *The Fugitive*. See, more pop culture. Hard to get away from. And there was the one-armed character in *Bad Day at Black Rock*, played by Spencer Tracy, a really great movie. I was a confused adolescent when *The Fugitive* series was on TV. One of my foster fathers really liked that show. Drank beer and watched *The Fugitive*, that was the life for him. I'll get to the whole foster parents subject later. I did see the movie of *The Fugitive*, with Harrison Ford trying to track down the one-armed man. The things they can do with special effects. No special effects in my apartment. I can turn the lights on and off. The heat up and down. I consider my dishwasher pretty special. Named my dishwasher Socrates. That's not pop culture. That's classical. But Socrates had two arms and I have one, and I shouldn't switch sub-

jects left and right. *Discursive* is the word. A shrink calling you discursive is a lot better than a shrink calling you pathological. I'm
not that, I don't think. Doesn't mean someone can't call me pathological. You can call anyone anything. Try it. Pick someone out on
the street and give them a label. Not now, next time you're on the
street. I don't care if it's a relative or a friend or a stranger. Best if
it's a stranger. But it doesn't matter. See if you think he or she is
pathological. Sociopathic? How about schizoid? Sneaky? Peculiar?
Odd? Not to worry about it presently. I have to explain why I have
one arm, and as I said it has nothing to do with *The Fugitive*, the
original weekly TV series with David Janssen as Dr. Richard Kimble
or the blockbuster movie with Harrison Ford playing Doc Kimble.
Losing my left arm has nothing to do with pop culture. Unless
you consider Winnipeg a hotbed of pop culture.

22

I liked Winnipeg, the nearly three years I spent there off and
on, even if I did do some time there, in jail and in a mental-health
facility. After my second stay in jail, I was working on a small farm
outside Winnipeg and stuck my damn hand into a contraption I
didn't have the slightest idea what it was used for. The kicker in
the whole bloody fiasco was that the dumb cat I tried to free got
away without even losing any fur. The cat probably wasn't dumb
at all. Speaking of cats. T. S. Eliot's *Old Possum's Book of Practical
Cats*. Mega-spectacular hit musical *Cats*. See the connection? *Cats*
is pop culture, at least in my estimation. It's theatre, sure, but it's
also pop culture. T-shirts. *Cats* T-shirts, that's a sure sign of pop
culture. Once they put something or someone on a T-shirt, and
sell it, that's pop culture as far as I'm concerned. Put the most revered historical personage on a poster, blow it up, and that's pop
culture. Posters and T-shirts, the cornerstones of pop culture. Hell,
they'll put anything on a poster or a T-shirt to make a buck. But
back to the events leading to the operating room ... Before I went
senseless, still in possession of my shredded arm, I heard the cat
meowing, almost laughing. If you knew me, a farm was the last
place you would expect to find my big-city ass, but I needed the
work and fresh air so I signed on. For a month, only a month, I
told myself, a stupid shot at rehabilitation. When I was coming out
of the anaesthetic, before the explanations and dry condolences, I

heard someone joke that "the farm hand lost his hand" and I tried to punch the voice with a left hook, but my punching hand was already in some garbage bag. The next day, to salvage a little self-respect, I gave the doctor a solid sucker punch right. I was transferred quick as hell to another ward and afterward, whenever I got a fighting look in my eyes, a nurse or a doctor simply drugged me silly.

Missing an arm doesn't bother me now, but it sure did then. I was only twenty-four and thought my bra-unfastening days were over. But I've managed to become perfectly right-handed, like most of the people in the world, just that I had to wait twenty-four years to become that category of normal. I used to have a very lovely artificial left arm but it's probably floating somewhere in the Atlantic Ocean now. Given the currents, it could be anywhere. Maybe it got eaten and it's inside a whale, an inanimate Jonah artificial arm. I don't know what I got so mad at. I only hurt myself. I heaved the arm into Charlottetown Harbour. That was months ago, before the winter. I have an appointment for a fitting today but I don't know if I'll make it. I've missed three appointments already. I broke another artificial arm years ago. That was in a fight. The fight wasn't over anything important, but it was a vicious fight, as if we were battling life-or-death about the existence of the world. If I could only have channelled that hostility into loftier pursuits. I do need a new prosthesis. It was summer when I lost my arm. A very hot summer. Whenever there's a really hot day, I think of meowing cats, and whenever I hear a little pussycat meow, I think of a hot summer day. Hey, but it's winter, right? Winter as I'm writing. Winter in my soul.

So, in your mind's eye you have a one-armed creep with a big red nose. Some sight, eh? But I don't think I'm bad-looking, even with the missing part and overripe trunk. I got a certain way about me the ladies like, a Humphrey Bogart swagger or something you might call animalistic. Yes, Humphrey Bogart does qualify as pop culture. Pop icon. Posters. T-shirts. Nostalgia film festivals. But he was a solid actor. I like old Humphrey Bogart movies. *The African Queen*, with Katharine Hepburn. That scene with the leeches. Still gives me the willies thinking about it. I saw it again on TV, when I

2 3

was at my woman friend's house. My ex-friend. I should give her a name, because she'll be coming up from time to time during my heartfelt outpourings. We were in love ... Love, the hardest of words to define accurately. Harder to define than pathological, if you ask me. I don't want to use her real name. Call her Ann, without an *e*. My Ann, my former Ann, not to be confused with the world-famous Anne with an *e*. Remember, Ensign Chekov, spelled without a second *h*, and my Chekhov spelled with a second *h*. A connection! Well, a variation-on-spelling connection. Without an *e*, with an *e*, without a second *h*, with a second *h*.

24   I don't think you have to know my name. Look, we've made it this far without me identifying myself. I could be Everyman. Or Everyperson. Or No one ... Aliases ... pseudonyms ... nom de plumes ... Why do you need to know my name anyway? What is this, a sanity hearing? You assessing my fitness for — For what? Do I need a name to tell my story? There was a time in my life when aliases were highly advantageous, and phony IDs real important to my economic well-being. There are people who are downright artistic making phony IDs ... Call up Ann and ask her my name.

We had a turbulent relationship, to put it mildly. Turbulence does not preclude love, or love preclude arguing over cardboard life-size *Star Trek* characters. Ann was very much into watching TV, and when I was over at her place we used to watch all sorts of programs. Sometimes we'd have really good discussions about what we were watching. I'd tend to lean more toward the sarcastic about most of the shows, and she more toward infusing TV things with more worth than they merited. Pop culture is important ... pervasive, fucking ubiquitous, all that shit. I'm not trying to say otherwise. But this is a big planet and we, I mean as a species, have been stumbling around for a few thousand years, and we can't use pop culture to describe and summarize and deal with everything. Yet the physical isn't all that important. More details are what you need.

I can't recall a great deal about the fifteen foster homes I passed through on the way to the joys of adulthood, but I can manage at least some vague recollection of each "mother" and "father." About a year ago I tried to make a list of the names of all my foster mothers and fathers, the way an ordinary person might make a list of friends to invite to a party. My memory party. I came up with eleven foster-mother names and eight foster-father names, including the old lady who was dying of cancer when I was in her house. Even when she was real sick she didn't want to send me to another home. Eventually I was taken out of her house, and that did bother me. It also bothered me that no one informed me of her death. I only found out when I went back to her house, with a bag of candies for her birthday. I remembered her birthday for some reason, and I bought her favourite kind of sweets. I got myself a haircut and put on as good clothes as I had, and hitchhiked across town to see her. Her husband, who didn't have the soft heart his wife did, opened the door and asked me what I wanted. Those words don't get erased easily: "What the hell do you want?" The cringing look he had, like I wanted to trash the place. He didn't invite me in. Then I hitchhiked all the way to the social worker's office, and dumped the candies on her desk. As she was lecturing me, I was spinning the candies. I bet she had a good time updating my file. All those foster mothers and fathers tried to sell me on being a good boy, making something out of myself. As I got older, I thought about the straight and narrow path, buying into the system, getting married and settling down, but that scene was as impossible for me then as growing a new arm now. For the most part, I liked the loose way I lived. I seriously thought about getting married only once – Ann and I never talked marriage, even when she was pregnant, and me wanting to marry my code-named Mata Hari computer lover doesn't count in the conventional sense – and that one time was because of five-hundred bucks and some rotten-luck idiot getting his throat cut in jail. I might as well tell you about that now, not that it's going to change anything.

I got the money for helping a friend settle things with a business partner of his who had ripped him off badly on a drug deal. I knew the partner and the woman he lived with pretty well. In fact, I used to have a thing for the woman before she settled down in the suburbs. I didn't think too much about what I'd done – I wasn't quite twenty-seven then – and spent the five hundred in two straight days of partying. The guy we framed got killed his first week in jail over some nonsense no one can remember now. I started looking at what had happened as getting a lousy five-hundred dollars for his life. I went to see the woman six months after her boyfriend was killed and gave her three-hundred-and-fifty dollars, all I had left from cashing a forged cheque a week earlier, telling her how I owed the money to her boyfriend before he was arrested. I had to make it good, I told her, my conscience and that kind of crap. At her kitchen table she just kept smoking cigarettes and crying and playing with a big steak knife she had used to cut me a piece of fresh cheesecake. She told me she hadn't made love since her boyfriend was killed, and asked me to sleep with her. I wanted to tell her what I'd done. I wanted to believe that I never rationalize or bullshit about what I do. I may have spent most of my life hustling and stealing, but I didn't want to go around indulging in any kind of self-deception. I told her it wouldn't be right, us sleeping together, but I couldn't tell her the truth. She talked about needing to make love, about forgetting, about getting on with her life, about not losing her mind ... As I listened to the woman, I wanted her to stab me, even for her to cut off my good arm. Insane as this might sound, I wanted there to be some sort of justice. One second I desired to marry her, to take care of the woman whose boyfriend got his throat cut because I had set him up to do time, and the next second I wanted her to kill me. If she had been able to admit the satisfaction of seeing me bleed to death, I would have saluted her with my last smile. But most people wouldn't be honest about such a horrifying emotion. It borders on being god-like, being so honest with yourself and creating a death. *Creating a death,* funny choice of words, but they make sense to me. Perhaps I should have been an intoxicated tightrope walker; perhaps I should have climbed mountains or parachuted out of airplanes, but that stuff was never my style. They're too much out in the open and I'm a person comfortable in alleys and darkened rooms. Not that this room is dark.

But don't write me off yet, even with these homely snippets from my life. You need me. Think it over: you need me to dump on, to feel superior to, to fear like children fear the bogeyman in the dark. If I were politically correct, I'd call it a bogeymonster.

2 6

Gender neutral. But it was the bogey*man* when I was a kid. I love words. I want people to understand what the fuck I'm talking about.

Sometimes, in more reflective moments, I consider my life worthless, flailing at myself with scathing thoughts. Maybe I shouldn't burden you with these remarks, but psychological insights are important, as important as hair colour – mine being dusty blond and getting thinner all the time. I often feel like a cornered Peter Lorre in *M* – if you ever saw that old film about a hunted child-murderer – or Shakespeare's Shylock or the spat-upon, ridiculed hunchback in a short story I once read in prison. What a trinity, Peter Lorre in *M*, Shylock, hunchback, all of them anxious to explain, to be understood, embedded instead in their deformities and the vileness others see in their faces no matter how they act or plead. Other times I feel more heroic, but I know that persona is a lie. I can entertain the heroic fantasy only briefly; it shatters of its own weight. But I believe it's more important how I see myself. The world has been wrong about its outcasts innumerable times before. So, this said, what self-images do I latch onto and clutch as if they were the only self-images imaginable: *criminal* and *one-armed loser.*

My creativity – yes, I'm creative – flows from these detestable images. You notice how I hold back revealing certain things, then just toss them into the air? Well, I have referred to working on a play about Anton Chekhov in Charlottetown, but you probably thought that was an empty dream.

I do want you to know about me, but I think detailing a life in a chronological fashion, itemizing character traits in an orderly, perhaps alphabetical manner – antagonistic, belligerent, contentious, destructive, so on and so forth … you don't want me to give you twenty-six character traits – clouds more than illuminates. Most of the professionals who have dealt with me over the years might not agree – they'd probably have four or five words for each letter, along with a daily catalogue of my uncooperativeness, but they have better things to do now than discuss a long-ago case. I create out of my own failures and the hope for recognition, willing to trade personal dross for the brass ring. My mind, disengaged from logic or common sense, must imagine I will be redeemed or purified if I become famous. A mindless crustacean regenerating his claw, fame and fortune the restorative potion, the world eager to embrace its crustaceans. Even with a few more beers the image of me succeeding falters. It scares me when I reach for a beer bottle with my left hand. I've had many fucking years not to do that, but invariably I will try to use the phantom hand. Hell, I am a criminal and a loser, even if I embark on a saintly pilgrimage for the rest of my one-armed days.

And how do I conduct my days, besides struggling to create? I try to read at least one book a day and I keep journals that make Mackenzie King seem like a half-hearted diarist. These aspects of my life must seem odd to you, given my erratic background and less than exemplary behaviour. But then, I'm full of contradictions. If I wanted, I could pass myself off in high-class society, as long as you put up the money and clothes, but the thought of that charade sickens me. I'd rather parade the streets in drag, blowing kisses at all the hypocrites. I make the point about my chameleon social skills only to demonstrate my versatility and underline that things are rarely what they appear to be. I want you to understand me, but not too much. That I read a great deal; that I've travelled all over the world and have slept with women in ten different countries; that I now live in the Cradle of Confederation; that I can feel paralysed by shyness and then bare my ass to some pompous matron just to hear her shriek – perhaps these details tell you a lot or nothing at all, I really don't know. I should have some profound statement tattooed on my behind, something like "Behold the Wisdom of the Ages" or "Truth in Flatulence," to make mooning a little more meaningful.

You know what I do have tattoos of? Three of them. On my right arm I have ... a left arm. A tattoo of my deleted left arm. Not the greatest tattoo, but I wanted it badly at the time. About a year after the real one was deleted. I have a couple of other tattoos, much more artistic ones. A seagull. Bet you guessed that one. And what do you think the third tattoo is of? The Rockies. The majestic, awe-inspiring Rockies are on my chest. Got the Rockies put on a couple of days after I got out of jail, the second time. But you know, I've never been incarcerated on the Island. I've had some close calls, a held-breath away from apprehension a few times, but no being locked up in any kind of government-funded institutional facility on the Island. I find that almost incomprehensibly amazing.

I spend too much time analysing myself, trying to convince myself I'm not crazy. Numbed senses, buried feelings, endless rationalization, that's insane, but who the hell is going to lock you up for being obedient or quietly living a lie or refusing to rage when Death – my apologies to Dylan Thomas – comes to seal your tomb. So I can't honestly take this sane or insane business seriously. Except when some psychiatrist got his tentacles around me and said with a straight face that for my own good I should be locked away and treated. Tentacles, what a screwy image. You wouldn't know how screwy. I have this dream every so often. About me being an octopus. Living in the sea and swimming any damn place I want. No, it has nothing to do with the Beatles' song about an octopus's garden. The first movie I ever remember seeing had an octopus as its star, a gigantic, horrifying octopus. *It Came from Beneath the Sea*. One of my foster fathers took me after I promised to be a good little boy. He slapped me good and hard the next day when he caught me drawing a picture of a giant octopus on a wall in the house … The Beatles, *It Came from Beneath the Sea*, what am I rambling on about? Pop culture gets its tentacles around me even when I'm discussing my octopus dream. Sometimes I have eight arms in the dream. Other times eighty arms. Or eight-hundred arms. How would you interpret that dream? Arm envy? Tentacle envy? I never told that dream to a shrink, but I've told it to you. When I did talk to shrinks about dreams, most of the time I made them up, not finding my actual dreams worth talking about.

The shrink who called me discursive wasn't too bad. He wasn't as big on medication as some of the others. He told me he was taught to diagnose and prescribe, but he liked pills as a last resort. However, he did have to visit that resort more often than he liked, and I think I was causing him to stretch his metaphor. During one of our sessions, he took some samples out of his drawer, and showed me how he could juggle four pill bottles at once. As he juggled,

29

he told me this great story about Freud and Jung meeting in Heaven and believing it was Hell because no one had any psychological problems, and I laughed my head off, and he tossed me one of the pill bottles, and I caught it in my hand, having good reflexes. Free sample, he said. I couldn't juggle four bottles of pills if my life depended on it, even when I had two arms. I didn't mind going to that guy, the juggling psychiatrist, but one day I showed up for my appointment – I had a great made-up dream to tell him about, an erotic dream – and his receptionist was sitting there crying, saying her boss, the juggling psychiatrist, had left the psychiatric profession. I bet you're waiting for me to say that he left to join the circus, being a juggling psychiatrist, but it wasn't like that. I could lie, and say it was like that. But there's enough bullshit in the world without me adding to the pile. Making up dreams because your dreams aren't good enough, that I don't count as bullshit. Prevarication, certainly, but not bullshit, which is messier and uglier. I found out later that he went sailing around the world. He was a dedicated sailor. His boat was never found. Neither was he. I think of him at the bottom of Davy Jones's locker, analysing the fish and eight-hundred-tentacled octopuses. Maybe I should have told him about my octopus dream. Great juggler. Good shrink. Not an altogether happy man. My next psychiatrist couldn't juggle, but he also had a boat. A yacht, he called it. Weekends only. I'm an inept juggler. What do you want from me? You try juggling with one arm. You think people would pay to watch a psychiatrist stand on stage and juggle bottles of pills? Maybe if the psychiatrist was nude. I don't think the pop-culture-saturated public is too jaded for that. Anyone who wants to run with the idea, be my guest. If you're a budding impresario, start your career with a nude juggling psychiatrist. Then you can work your way up – or down, depending on your value system – to nude somersaulting lawyers, nude sword-swallowing bankers, nude fire-eating prison wardens ...

I really should go to my prosthesis-fitting appointment. But I'd rather work on my play. If I'm able to work on it. I remember when I first got the idea for the play, while I was rereading *The Seagull*. I was trying to get out of a depression by reading *The Seagull* out loud, performing all the roles, using different voices. Then I could almost see Chekhov in front of me, in this living room. I can't describe how exhilarated and inspired and excited I was. I wrote all night and part of the next morning, Anton Chekhov starting to take up residence in Charlottetown. That was two winters ago, around this time.

Today the weather is mild and the sun is perched up there pleased to be so generous, smiling in a most grandfatherly way. Or grandmotherly. I have no problem with that kind of gender balance. No problem at all. Not like bogeymonster. Grandfatherly or grandmotherly. Seems natural to personify the sun, even for a criminal who loves the dark, and never knew his real grandparents ... or parents. It's been dreadfully cold lately, so this mild spell is most welcome. Looking out my second-floor window, I can see a Coast Guard icebreaker docked by the wharf and a helicopter hovering over it, preparing to land on the wharf. I love the scene. The whole operation is mechanical and smooth and each time I view it I can't help but think that life does manage to work, on the mechanical level at least. I once saw a seagull fly right into a helicopter's blades and split into countless pieces as if God had detonated the bird. But that was during my second week on Prince Edward Island and I haven't seen anything like it since. Yet the image sticks with me, becomes important, acquires layers of meaning far in excess of the pathetic event. If this were the play *Miss Saigon*, I could bring the helicopter into the apartment. But do I really need a helicopter messing this room up? Besides, Chekhov would turn over in his grave if a whirlybird disturbed Trepliov's study. I'd take a seagull over a helicopter any day. In *The Seagull* it's a stuffed seagull. The white seagull that Trepliov shoots in Act Two, turns up stuffed near the end of the play. I wonder if anyone has a line of stuffed seagull dolls ... You never know with pop culture. I should find out if there is a seagull doll. I could ask people next time I'm in a bar or a coffee shop. Or I could do research at the library. I should get to the library soon, and catch up with my newspaper and magazine reading. There's a lot of disarming news I have to keep up with ... Not a very good joke. I tell better jokes at parties. After a couple of drinks.

I live overlooking Charlottetown Harbour because the water calms me better than Lithium or any other drug I've ever taken. I think Lithium was in one of the bottles the juggling psychiatrist was juggling that afternoon. There wasn't Prozac back then. Medication is referred to in *The Seagull*. Valerian drops. But the pharmacopoeia wasn't as enormous in those bygone days. Dr. Dorn does dispense valerian drops in *The Seagull*. For an asthma attack, if I recall correctly. A hundred years from now I wonder what people will be popping into their mouths. I've lived here five years now, the longest by far I've willingly stayed in one place. Finally settling down, I guess. When people ask me why I moved to the Island, and the question comes up without fail if I get into a long enough conversation, I don't have a definitive answer. Fresh start? To write? To escape? To get in touch with myself? I think that response might qualify as pop psychology, but I don't want to get into that. Before I moved to the Island, I did have a dream about living on a peaceful, serene, healing island, but that doesn't mean the dream was about Prince Edward Island, and I should get my wandering self over there posthaste. Vivid as it was, I didn't take that dream as a sign, no way. I also had a dream about Devil's Island, and I sure didn't swim off to there. But I did like the movie *Papillon*, which is set on Devil's Island. Must have been the escape scenes. Steve McQueen played Papillon. Steve McQueen also happened to be in the movies *The Great Escape* and *The Getaway*, among others. No use looking for any significant connections there. I never escaped from any prison. I tried to escape from my apartment once. I got so drunk that I went out on the porch and jumped off, landing on the first-floor roof. I must of thought I was going over the wall of all the prisons I was ever in. Or I thought I was the star of some prison-escape film. Then I jumped to the ground. All I did was hurt my knees. They only act up occasionally. It's not like a bad sports injury.

No one in my apartment building knows about my past or moods or the thick files that are scattered all over the country – and Germany, of course – attesting to my numerous defects. I always smile kindly as I pass my neighbours in the hallway or when I meet them by the whooshing and whirring machines in the laundry room, and, if necessary, I make up a heroic story about how I lost my arm on that fateful African safari. I did save our frightened guide from that lunging leopard ... or rushing tiger ... or enraged rhino ... I can leave the elderly ladies in the building smiling or in tears, being the company that they search for as they try to fill their empty widowhood with a little friendly talk. How gullible these old women are, fooled by my stump and politeness. But how can I fault them – I look so ordinary and unthreatening, like the grown sons who rarely visit.

I haven't left my apartment in a while. That's not healthy but lately I just don't want to face anyone, not even elderly ladies. It's not like someone has locked me in here and thrown away the key ... It would be nice if I could get some new posters of the Rockies. Ironically, I've never been to the Canadian Rockies, even though I've seen the Alps and Pyrenees and Appalachians. I told some of the German prostitutes I met that I grew up near the Rockies and my father – when I didn't have him as a rabbi – owned a fabulous Lake Louise resort where they could luxuriate at for free if they ever came to Canada. Why didn't I go to the Rockies? I don't know. Isn't that something, I have a tattoo of the Rockies emblazoned on my chest, but I've never been to the Rockies. The three sisters in Chekhov's play *Three Sisters* never make it to Moscow and it's their most fervent dream to go there.

Ann thought the way I live affected my moods. She thought I should redecorate, make a few changes, give the room a little different feel, but I don't want to lose the atmosphere of *The Seagull*. I told her she could decorate her place any way she wanted and I'd live the way I wanted. No *Star Trek* cardboard figures here. Most of the time we were together, it was at her apartment, hardly ever here. You know, I don't think we ever made love in this apartment. We sure did at her place. But that got to be less and less ... I simply like to live this way, with as few possessions as possible. Possessions make me feel confined and burdened, like being in jail, even though in jail I never went in for clutter like some of the other prisoners.

I'm going to have to score soon, for rent money. When I don't work at odd jobs, I shoplift, a pursuit I've become masterful at: food, clothes, trinkets, you name it, no problem. My real talent, however, is as a pickpocket. I've got the fingers of a magician, and having one arm gives me the advantage of being an unlikely and unsuspected Artful Dodger. When it's tourist season, the days long and leisurely, Anne of Green Gables cavorting on the main stage of the Confederation Centre, I live like a lord.

Tomorrow I hope to see a play. It's local theatre, another low-budget, off-season production, but I know the actors and enjoy their energy. Later today, if my mood gets better, I'll go to the Confederation Centre Art Gallery. I know I should go to my prosthesis-fitting, but if I'm going to leave this room, I'd rather go look at art. There's a new exhibit of paintings I want to see.

You shouldn't be surprised by anything I do or say. You know by now that I have a great many facets and interests. Art and theatre are merely two of my passions. I have told you I acted in *The Seagull*, that I was Trepliov, that I'm working on a play about Anton Chekhov in Charlottetown, but I've neglected to tell you that I've written three full-length plays, two of which have been put on by an Island theatre company to lots of controversy and little acclaim ... Maybe I have my reasons for not mentioning my finished plays before. Lately my confidence has been eroded. More than lately. But not everything is doom and gloom. Last year I even received an arts grant – how's that taxpayers, me still shoplifting and pickpocketing as the government tried to nurture my creativity and save my ex-con soul. Part of the grant money went to pay for the maquette. And my computer, which I got at a bargain-basement price and is now showing its contempt for me with the silent treatment. The argument on the phone earlier, that had to do with the play I'm working on. Have been working on and working on ...

The play is about Anton Chekhov and Charlottetown, even though Anton Chekhov was never in Charlottetown. Oscar Wilde, who was a contemporary of Chekhov's, did come to Charlottetown, and I thought of having both Chekhov and Wilde in the first act, maybe having the two great writers discussing which was a better play, *The Seagull*, performed first in 1896, or *The Importance of Being Earnest*, which saw its début in 1895, but that was cluttering things up with too many celebrities. It's not like having a battle of the bands. I've seen *The Importance of Being Earnest* a couple of times

3 4

on the Island, but not *The Seagull*. Whatever, Wilde only made it through one draft and he was excised from the play. His ego, kicking and fighting, didn't leave without a few acerbic, scandalously vitriolic remarks directed at the writer, me. Wilde did time but that doesn't mean we would bond if we met. If we did meet, I would tell him how much I like "The Ballad of Reading Goal." I never wrote poetry about when I was in the slammer. Can you image Wilde and Chekhov and Milton Acorn in the same scene. How about in a downtown Charlottetown coffee shop? A customer screaming at them, "Where were you when Henderson scored the goal in '72?" Wilde and Chekhov would probably think 1872, and who knows what Milton Acorn would have said.

35

The way my play works, Stanislavsky brings his renowned Moscow Art Theatre to Charlottetown. The first act takes place in 1902. Chekhov, despite his ill health, comes to visit Canada. The Moscow Art Theatre puts on a performance of *The Seagull* in Charlottetown, and Chekhov is in the audience. One of the Russian actors, the one who plays Trepliov, meets an Island woman, and they fall in love. She isn't interested in going to Moscow, and he decides to stay on the Island. They marry and start a family. Act Two is set in 1935, the Depression is going on, with their oldest son – they had four children – staging a new production of *The Seagull*. Act Three takes place around the time of the Sputnik launchings, fall of 1957. A granddaughter is directing and performing in a revival of *The Seagull*. And in the final act, it takes place in the present, there is a controversial new production of *The Seagull*. A playwright living in Charlottetown, who coincidentally happens to have only one arm, falls in love with the actress playing Nina. He is writing a play based on Stanislavsky's and Chekhov's 1902 visit to the Island. This visit never happened, but my play imagines that it did. And how the presence of this family started by a Russian actor and an Island woman has affected the Island ever since. When I told Ann without an *e* about the play, she said it would make a good episode of *Star Trek*. I want to finish my play, to see it performed, to make Chekhov come alive in Charlottetown ...

But I have written three plays. Each play came slower and slower to me. One play is about a German hooker who kills a young Ca-

nadian soldier, during the Cold War, when there was a Berlin Wall;
the second is about a daughter who returns home after seventeen
years away and blinds her incestuous father; and the third,
unproduced but still my favourite of the three, is about a series of
bungled suicide attempts with one hell of a detonated ending. But
I have loads of great lines and hilarious jokes in my plays despite
their dark themes. I just happen to see better in the dark, but that
doesn't mean I'm not funnier than the Devil after a few beers. Even
if I were a big-time successful playwright it wouldn't change a thing.
I'd still live the way I do. I'm fifty, feel like a hundred most of the
time, and have no desire to change. Anton Chekhov died when he
was only forty-four. He had all kinds of health problems, including tuberculosis. At the end, his heart gave out. But you know,
Chekhov had a glass of champagne before he broke free of the
earthly attachment, and died peacefully. Not that I'm comparing
myself to Chekhov in any way whatsoever. Absurd to put too much
store in connections and associations. You can twist just about anything into a suitable shape. Hell, Elvis Presley was born in January.
And Chekhov was born in January. And I was born in January. So
were millions and millions of other people through history. I'd estimate that roughly one-twelfth of the people on Earth were born
in January. Roughly, I'm saying. There must be certain statistically
more plentiful months for births. Elvis Presley might be the quin-
tessential pop icon, the King, the King of pop culture, during his
life *and* after. I should point out that Elvis starred in the movie
Jailhouse Rock, whatever that connection is worth. It's not like we
were all born on the same day in January. Elvis was born on January 8th, Anton on January 17th, and me at the very end of January.
Anton has nothing to do with pop culture, although you could
connect seagulls in a couple of ways, I have no doubt. Remember
the book *Jonathan Livingston Seagull?*

I'd put *The Seagull* on in Charlottetown, if I had my own theatre company. Chekhov was my big break. Not one of the most
memorable productions in theatre history, but I got to play Trepliov
in Toronto, and as the old song title goes, "They Can't Take That
Away from Me." They didn't want a one-armed Trepliov — it was
not Chekhov's intent to have such a deformity, the director said —

but I invoked the name of Stanislavsky and convinced everyone involved with the production that my one-armedness would get them publicity and put much coveted paying posteriors in the seats. That little theatre company, with the big ambitions of putting on a season of Chekhov plays, had been worrying about surviving the season financially. They didn't.

It depresses me that there are fewer boats in winter. The Coast Guard icebreakers open paths for the boats that do make it in and out of Charlottetown Harbour this time of year, like the glum and squat oil tankers which keep our little Island fuelled up. During the late spring the pleasure boats start to appear, and from my window I can watch their occupants dreaming of distant ports. But now the water is hidden under ice and snow, painted over by winter, even though the last few years the winters seem to be getting milder, with less ice. I look out my window and imagine spring, the water blue, blue as my moods, blue as my soul. Joni Mitchell's album *Blue*. In the days when albums were what people listened to. I had that album *Blue*. Actually, I gave it as a gift to that woman whose old man was killed on account of me. It had come out a few years earlier, but I was hoping it would give her some comfort. Ready for this connection? Joni Mitchell's first album was called *Song to a Seagull*. Ann had a Joni Mitchell CD playing one of the last times I was over. I had two arms when *Blue* came out as a record album.

God, the day is going by quickly. Even though there's no TV set or radio or clock in my apartment, I can estimate the time within thirty minutes or so any time of the night or day, quite a trick I tell you, unless I'm drunk, and then I'd be lucky to tell you the right month. I have no difficulty entertaining myself, thinking or writing, just like now. I did time easily, six years altogether, not counting the military and those delightful mental institutions, even if I always paced a groove down the centre of my cells. I don't pace as much any more. When I want, I go out and wander the downtown and close-by bars and coffee shops, being a sociable and amusing local celebrity, waving my stump, quoting from Acorn or Chekhov or Shakespeare or the Bible or from some novel or short story or poem I'd just read, depending on my mood and audience.

Talking at a bar with the struggling actors and actresses I know or with strangers is a great diversion for me. Especially with the actresses whom I promise magnificent roles. I'll make them all Hedda Gablers or Blanche DuBoises, I tell them. Or Ninas. Nina Mihailovna Zaryechaia, the young actress who my character Trepliov loves, in *The Seagull*. I like talking about *The Seagull*. I could identify somewhat with Trepliov. He is a perplexed, struggling writer, lacking confidence, his artistic footing less than firm. Konstantin Gavrilovich Trepliov. Kostia, to his actress mother, Irena Nikolayena Arkadina. I like to show off my ability to pronounce those Russian names from *The Seagull* ... Or I'll make them Gretchens, a role to challenge the most skilled actress, I tell them. Gretchen was the whore who was hugged by Hitler when she was a little girl.

I assume you've made some pretty uncomplimentary conclusions about me. You know I'm fifty, have lived on Prince Edward Island for five years, dusty-blond thinning hair, blue-eyed, red-nosed, a one-armed wonder, but what about my height and weight? Could you pick me out of a police lineup? Am I a little runt? Musclebound he-man? Grinning hunchback? A look-alike of Rudolph Valentino or of the Elephant Man? What about my intelligence? You already know that my soul is tormented. Would it be surprising if I told you I was a Jew? Relax, I'm not. Religion doesn't mean much to me, but all the foster homes I went through were more or less Christian. Since Germany I do think about the Jews, but not excessively. There's not many of them on the Island. I'd like to give Taoism or Buddhism a try, but I can't be bothered.

So, you have an image of me and I have an image of myself, and I'm sure we're both wrong. I sense in my heart of hearts you wouldn't like to see me near your loved ones. Relax again, I'm mellowing and rarely are any of my thoughts violent anymore. Seagulls. I think about seagulls a lot, almost to the point of preoccupation. I watch the seagulls from my window, and study them with an interest that never diminishes. I believe I can distinguish between individual gulls, and I give them literary names but I have my doubts if I really keep the birds apart. I imagine sometimes that I fly with them, making love with some exquisite soarer, perhaps

Lady Windermere or Desdemona or Medusa my love, without words, without motive, waiting for the inevitable helicopter blades. Medusa, now there was a bewildering woman. Can you imagine taking her in your arms – or arm, in my case – and giving her the most passionate, deep kiss, your eyes closed, of course, and when the kiss is over, you have to open your eyes? Then you would find out if the myth is true, or she's just some woman with a bad hair day you've met. There must have been a good reason why someone created that myth of the turn-you-to-stone Gorgons. And all the other myths. There are always reasons. But that doesn't mean we can figure them out accurately. Come to think of it, the snake-haired Gorgons were three sisters. But they have no connection with the three sisters in Chekhov's play. You know, I've never given my wooden seagull a name. Maybe I should. Strange. I've had it for as long as I've been missing my arm. Maybe I should name it after myself. Maybe that wouldn't be a bad idea.

39

Being truthful, I haven't been out of this apartment in nine days and need to leave soon. I'll shave, comb my hair, dress inconspicuously, and look like any other average guy out there. Except for my red nose and stump, I could appear like your brother or father, your boyfriend or hubby, or whatever else you call males. I wouldn't mind being a woman for a day or two, but I don't go in for dressing up like a lady. I've known my share of transvestites, in and out of prison; real sweethearts they were, screwed up from head to toe. Not that I'm the one to judge, but I realize it's just frail human nature always to be judging, busybodies conducting our petty hearings, wishing at heart we could preside over a grand inquisition.

Ah, the helicopter is getting ready to take off from the wharf, its blades starting to whirl. In my apartment I can hear the air outside being slashed. If I wish, I can furtively make my way to the wharf. The helicopter will be leaving soon. I've studied the helicopters just like I've studied the boats and seagulls.

I should go out now, but I'm afraid. There, I admitted it. Big shot that I am, ex-con, thief, three-play playwright, working on play number four, and I've become scared shitless even to take the garbage downstairs. It's either stick my hand into someone's pocket or stay locked in here until I suffocate. Maybe this is the price for a lifetime of turning the world upside down to suit my purposes. I should be working on my play. I should be talking to people in a bar or a coffee shop. I should be doing something. If the goddamn computer wasn't broken, I could be exchanging passionate messages with Mata Hari. Even before the damn thing conked out, she wouldn't answer me. Her passion for me might have been all gone. She could have fallen in love with another coded computer lover ...

I'll go outside and everything will be fine. I must go quickly, before the helicopter leaves. Maybe you and I will meet and become friends or fall in love. Maybe we'll marry and I'll be a good father, reading the right books to the kid, crawling on all fours – sorry, all threes – being a loveable prehistoric beast, growling away the world's unfairness and cruel tricks, finally comprehending the extinction of dinosaurs ... No, I must take control and face the truth. Fantasy is for suckers. So what if Anton Chekhov was never in Charlottetown. There still could have been an Anton Chekhov Theatre built right in the middle of the downtown.

I must get to the helicopter before it takes off or else I'll have to wait until tomorrow and that would be unbearable. Poor Trepliov at the end of *The Seagull*. Does himself in. You hear an offstage shot. A bang, not a whimper. A lot in life happens offstage. Bangs and whimpers, whimpers and bangs. Trepliov is fictitious. I may have created myself, but I am not fictitious. I would never shoot a seagull. For a laugh, I'll sneak up to the helicopter and embrace its whirling, shining, wonderful blades.

HER FEARFUL MEN

SHE SITS THERE NEARLY NAKED, IN a basement corner of the building where she works. Only a T-shirt. A gift from a former boyfriend. After she became pregnant, he fell in love with another woman. A month ago, she told him she was going to keep the baby and he was afraid, so afraid that she could see his emotions transform from arrogance to fearfulness like a strong sea suddenly storm-whipped into turbulence. I'll keep the baby and I'll keep the T-shirt, she had said, showing no anger. He told her it frightened him that she was taking everything calmly. I'm going to eat more now, she declared, because I'll be eating for two.

A man in freshly laundered work clothes is standing in the basement, looking at her. Without his glasses, he cannot read the lettering on her T-shirt: on the front, the name of a local art gallery and the dates of a group exhibition, *Daubing Paint on the Planet*, along with a stylized drawing of the Earth; on the back, the names of the six participating artists. A painting of her was in the show, as an emaciated Earth Mother. The first painting to sell, purchased by a couple in their early thirties who shared a dream of becoming wealthy art collectors.

She stares at a centipede moving across the cold cement floor. Oddity, she names the tiny creature. Whispers the name loud enough for the man to hear. When she was a child, her brother, whenever he was annoyed with her, would call her a pain-in-the-ass oddity. I'd rather be an oddity, she would defend herself, than a lost soul. Their father called himself a lost soul. She named a kitten Oddity that her parents brought home one Christmas. Before the winter was over, the kitten was found poisoned in the backyard. Her brother killed the kitten, she told her parents, even called the police on her own, but never had proof.

The man thinks of stepping on the centipede. He thinks of touching the woman. Her breasts. Her knees. Her mouth. Her lovely mouth. Rather, he takes off his belt and drops it to the floor, the metal buckle making a despairing sound. A sound that makes her think of being alone. Alone in a hospital room.

She looks up.

He has worked here for eighteen months. Does not want to lose his job. Not another job. Likes telling people that he works in custodial services, is the head of the custodial staff in the city's tallest building.

She asks him if he believes in an afterlife.

He hesitates. Sure, he mutters. God is in Heaven ... Remembers a Sunday-school teacher, a friend of the family, who gave him a ride home from school. Rubbed him with his right hand, circular strokes. Rubbed him as he sang a song about going to the seashore. Recalls how the Sunday-school teacher, years later, died in a car accident, a ten-year-old boy in the car, scarred terribly, survived. He, twenty-three then, went with his family to the Sunday-school teacher's funeral, but refused to be a pallbearer. His father had been one of the pallbearers. The man tries to think of the scarred boy's name.

"I'm considering quitting my job," the woman says. "But I don't know what else to do. Everything costs so much ..."

"Do you need any money?" the man says. He reaches into his pocket, but only has a couple dollars' worth of change. That's right, he had been at the track before coming to work. Pondering Tomorrow had come in a distant fourth. He had been so certain. It was his forty-ninth birthday. Lousy fucking luck even on his birthday. Tells the woman he was forty-six, had a big party with family and friends, more presents than he knew what to do with; she thinking he looks closer to his mid-fifties.

The woman hugs herself against the basement's coldness: "When she needed money, my mother would sell a book. My mother had a collection of first edition books, the only material things her father left her. My mother never married. Told me my father was a suicidal drunk who was killed before he could kill himself. We were poor except for the books."

"I never took to reading all that much," the man says, squinting to make out a few words on the woman's T-shirt. "I haven't had a drink in two-and-a-half years."

"My mother had an exquisite first edition of Darwin's *Voyage of the Beagle*. The price it brought. Paid for my second year at university. A copy of Virginia Woolf's *To the Lighthouse*, published in 1927, with a delightfully sweet inscription by the author, got me through most of my first year. I did not return for a third year. I went to university not far from here," the woman says, and removes her T-shirt suddenly, seeming to want to cast off something painful or burdensome. Her breasts are smaller than he had imagined.

"I hated school," the man says, and bends down to pick up the T-shirt. Holds the T-shirt up in front of him and reads, his lips moving. Touches the stylized Earth on the T-shirt, where he thinks the building they are in is located. "I was good at geography, though. I could find anything on a map," he adds, moving his finger to a different part of the country, where he had been born.

"You are like my father. In looks, even the same height. It would be like incest," she says.

The man quivers, as if an icy wind had hit him. He backs away, but only two steps.

"I'm not afraid of anything, not even incest," the woman says, and scrapes her fingernails up and down her thighs, drawing a chaotic red-lined map, mimicking an angry lover.

"Incest is not right at all," the man says, bunching up the T-shirt. He recalls the name of the scarred boy. And the argument, over a quarter of a century ago, with his father at the Sunday-school teacher's funeral. The man, fearing what the woman has said, the movement of her fingers, rushes from the basement, forgetting his belt on the cold concrete floor, but taking the T-shirt.

She sits huddled in the corner, awaiting the next man. A younger man, like a brother, but less fearful. It is the fearfulness that disgusts her. Both her father and her brother, for all their big talk and name-calling, were fearful men. Then she puts her hand in the path of the centipede and it crawls gently onto her arm.

44

THE BLUE JAYS
VERSUS
THE BLACK DOUGLASES

ALTHOUGH HE DISLIKED RISING early, for the fifth day in a row Matthew was awake before the others in the house. He wanted to be out of the house before his in-laws and his wife, Doreen, awoke; he wanted to walk alone as far as he could before dawn. In another week his Scottish vacation would be over and he needed to think about his future.

As he quietly dressed, Matthew noticed Doreen turn onto her side in bed. The scene of his pregnant twenty-nine-year-old wife, with the fidgety old border collie at her feet, evoked a smile from him despite his disapproval of dogs in bed. This trip to Castle Douglas had been good for their marriage, he thought. His wife hadn't tossed and turned in weeks. Back home in Toronto, ensconced in their twelfth-floor bedroom, she often kicked in her sleep, riding some nocturnal horse. They merely rationalized that her disturbed sleep was the product of nerves and tension. Unlike her husband, she had grown dissatisfied with teaching; yet she never quite had the courage to admit it to herself, let alone quit. A tranquillizer or sleeping pill and she coped. Now Matthew was pleased to see Doreen sleeping pill-less and placid. He considered the amazing change this trip had brought about in his wife and moved toward the huge wooden dresser in the corner of the room. Their first night in Scotland Doreen had pointed out with much pride that this immensity of woodwork was a sixth-generation heirloom in her family. Their apartment in Toronto was crammed with only modern furniture. Here, in the house she had grown up in, his wife worshipped the past, spoke incessantly about castles and legends and ancient, combative relatives.

"My family's clan had been most intimate associates with the Black Douglases," Doreen had boasted last week when they walked along the River Dee, waiting for the small boat to ferry them across the water to Threave Castle. She had vigorously rung the bell to summon the old man who ferried tourists and visitors to the island castle. A modest fee and the gates of history were swung open. Hardly Casa Loma, Matthew had joked as they approached the fourteenth-century fortress, but Doreen did not seem to hear. She began to recite a Robbie Burns poem for him. When they entered the castle she broke from her inspired recitation and claimed that Archibald the Grim, no lesser luminary than the Third Earl of Douglas, who had constructed the sombre edifice, had conducted more than one passionate love affair with a woman from her clan. "I might even have a few drops of Black Douglas blood in my veins," she bellowed, attempting to appear ferocious. The Black Douglases, which the town of Castle Douglas could thank for its name, had more than a minor reputation for pugnacity and skullduggery.

Matthew left the house without eating. It wasn't like him to skip breakfast, but his concerns upset his routine. This holiday would be over in a week and he could return to normal: full breakfasts, listening to the radio as he exercised on his stationary bicycle in the morning, reading about the Toronto Blue Jays in the sports pages. During the four weeks he had spent in the southwest of Scotland, Matthew had not met a single soul who had ever heard of one Toronto sports figure. The Blue Jays, the Raptors, the Argonauts, even the venerable old Maple Leafs, were only so much foreign gibberish to the rural folk he had encountered. Most simply wanted to know information about farming in Canada, which he couldn't provide, and a few of the younger ones eagerly asked about the political situation in Quebec. Still, Matthew felt a genuine affection for these rural people and this serene part of the world. He believed – or wanted to believe – they were without cunning or greed. In another week, he reflected, it would be as before. He assured himself that Toronto was not without its advantages, even with its cunning and greed.

Hungry and sleepy, Matthew left the one-hundred-and-ninety-year-old farmhouse and wondered if he could ever be happy here among the rugged, laconic men and sturdy, enduring women. When he saw the wavy greenness spread out before him under the moonlight his thoughts changed, moved hopefully away from uncertainty and artificial turf. He breathed in rapidly and deeply, as though running through an allotted quota of breaths that would be confiscated if not utilized at once. He gazed over his wife's family's farm, and thought that the sight was finer than a picture-postcard scene. He scolded himself for not yet sending the postcards home, making still another mental note to mail them before it was too late. He didn't want to omit one of his students. A postcard from the Lowlands of faraway Scotland would surely be a thrill for a city kid of seven or eight. He had told his students that he would be going to Scotland in the summer and their last art assignment before holidays was to draw what they imagined Scotland to be. Strangely, he had never seen so many variations on Toronto in his life.

Outside, a drizzle argued with the evaporating night. The morning was cold and damp, bone-invading, but Matthew hardly minded. Again the unexplainable transformation in him took place, as it had each morning he had escaped to his solitary explorations. He suddenly and illogically felt that he belonged here, should never leave, even though this trip was the first time in his thirty-eight years of complaining and worrying that he had ventured beyond Ontario's borders. The Kawarthas for him was the hinterland. He was thoroughly citified: a heart of pavement, a soul of concrete, he liked to joke.

He walked through the first old wooden gate, struggling to reclose it, and once again was overcome with the notion that here was the place to live and die, to raise children. So what if there was no SkyDome or Air Canada Place. A person could surely survive without traffic jams and shopping malls and cheering crowds. Matthew had trouble closing the long, ill-fitting gates on the farm, but Doreen's first warning to him during the initial tour of the farm was always to shut gates or else her farmer father would skin him alive. Another couple of splinters, a not overly extravagant curse,

47

and Matthew told himself that he wasn't too soft, that in time he would adapt. What could he expect anyway, he thought, after a lifetime of doors that neatly and easily locked, of elevators that guarded you from resourcefulness, of climate control that stunned the senses.

He walked gingerly toward the sheep on the hillside and forced a cough just in case the animals hadn't noticed him yet. As long as he kept his distance and didn't move too sharply they were good-natured creatures. Matthew counted the sheep and was forced to slow his pace to avoid miscounting. He needed to start over several times, but was determined to tally them correctly, as if an accurate count would draw him closer to Nature or make him some sort of quasi-farmer. It was easier to count cars, Matthew reflected; cars were orderly. As he counted, he wished that his students were with him. The nighttime intruder took a step too close and the startled sheep began to run, just as he finished his laboured count. Seventy-three irate sheep scampered for dear life and Matthew wondered what would happen if they stampeded in his direction. To be hit by an orderly car was one thing – but a rampaging sheep! For a second he had a grisly vision of himself mutilated, and then interred in dung, a victim of sheep wrath: Nature's poetic revenge for his pretensions. Matthew felt a sense of justice and proportion present on the farm that was absent from his apartment complex or the wilds of Yonge Street. In Toronto he associated justice with legalities and shrewd lawyers, here with the flow of life. But Doreen and her father had laughed when he asked – hypothetically, of course – if sheep ever attacked humans. How was he to know? He had seen stampeding buffaloes and cattle in old Westerns. Were sheep so different? After all, they ran fast and could become so agitated. You were safe on a street curb, but in the fields there were no out-of-bounds markers, no reassuring signs for pedestrians.

Soon there wasn't a single sheep in sight and Matthew's thoughts of ignoble mutilation and burial in sheep dung were replaced by calmness. Not one building over two stories; not one cranky, profane commuter; not one car-horn blast anywhere near. To Matthew it was another planet here in the Lowlands. After a lifetime of rushing and pressure, of waiting in lines and longing for weekends, a simple dichotomy materialized for Matthew: rural purity and city madness. He thought that if he had any sense he would stay here. But all Matthew knew was Toronto: the fierce, animating energy, the staccato sounds, the city's sensuality. He couldn't be like the farmer, quiet and secure and contented, deriving his sustenance and vitality from the land. His own job, his very existence, were in Toronto. Heaven knew that people were pleading for jobs and he had a good one. How could he possibly get a teaching job here? There were enough teachers who were part of the Lowlands; why in the world would they need him? But he would still inquire, out of curiosity, what his prospects would be of securing a teaching position in Castle Douglas or any of the nearby villages. Probably nil, he concluded, but he would find out, it couldn't hurt. Yet even if they were dying for Canadian teachers here, he couldn't take the job. *He had to return.* His bank accounts, his downtown apartment with the two-year lease, his students, were all in Toronto.

In a week he would return and resume his former way of life. A responsible, dedicated, reasonable adult doesn't just pack up and start anew without good reason. That was insanity. He wasn't Gauguin. He wasn't the Tin Man. After all, Tahiti was a disappointment. Hadn't Gauguin wound up with venereal disease in his elusive paradise? And the Wizard of Oz was a fraud anyway. Why take a chance on some little community that still thought a Blue Jay was purely ornithological and Maple Leafs grew on trees? How could he even consider exchanging Toronto for this rural community without good reason? But the good reasons were everywhere Matthew looked. He began to walk faster, to attempt to outdistance his turmoil and doubts. It is too remote here, he thought. There are limited cultural activities. He had no roots here. And if he really wanted the country, there was verdant and tranquil countryside without Brobdingnagian buildings and screechy cars just an hour's drive from his apartment. Two hours at the most.

His shoes were damp and he regretted not taking a pair of the farmer's Wellington boots. There were a dozen pairs at the rear entrance to the house but he never left that way. Everyone in Doreen's family had several pairs. Even Doreen's old Wellies were still there after five years, totems protecting the past, harbouring memories. How stupid to wear his city shoes. They were an insult to the

49

grass and a joke to the dung. But Matthew had made the same messy mistake five days in a row and each day the ground seemed muddier, more eager to swallow him up. He seemed to have an uncanny instinct for locating dung in the darkness. He'd have to buy a new pair of shoes before he left. When they were in town yesterday he had seen a pair he liked. Once again Matthew calculated what the price would be in Canadian dollars and immediately he began to worry about his savings, pension plan, and car payments.

For thirty measured paces he walked alongside tractor tracks, but was careful not to step in them. They were even muddier than the rest of the ground. *Machines here too.* Doreen and her father had tried to teach him to drive the tractor, but he just didn't have the knack. I'm a mental defective with mechanical things, he had joked after giving up on the tractor. I need automatic transmission even to have a fighting chance, Matthew said to cover up his embarrassment. The farmer had grunted patronizingly and Doreen looked disappointed. His father-in-law, shaking a walking stick, in his loudest and thickest Scottish accent informed Matthew that each of his four daughters was driving a tractor like a bloody pro by the time she was sixteen. Matthew remarked lightly that he hadn't learned to tie his shoelaces until he was close to sixteen, but he felt hurt and inadequate.

There must be some place on Earth, Matthew mused, without a single machine. He had the silly thought of Hell paved over like one enormous parking lot, congested with fuming cars and damned souls, all encased in machines, eternally rush hour. A Bay and Bloor of the lower depths; the CN Tower as the Devil's pitchfork. But Heaven, if there was indeed any justice, had to be barren of machines, a perpetual people's park.

Matthew began to walk back toward the farmhouse, confused as ever over his future plans. I'm getting older, that's all, he consoled himself; half my life gone, a few more grey hairs, and I'm thinking foolishness. He tried to blame the full moon. He searched desperately for fault, for reasons. Perhaps he would go crazy here and not have to return to Toronto. Maybe there was an excuse for staying. Tahiti and Oz, he mumbled to himself, Tahiti and Oz. He

heard a dog bark and wanted to bark back, to howl uncontrolla-
bly, but knew how preposterous that would be. Instead, he whis-
tled at the dog and the old border collie scurried toward him. The
night was fading; the drizzle subsiding. It was Doreen's favourite
dog on the farm, already ten tired years when she had left for
Canada; she didn't return to Scotland until she had a schoolteacher
husband and a baby on the way, five years later.

He knew Doreen would be close by. She had kept the dog near
her since their tearful reunion, even in bed against his protesta-
tions. In Toronto he won all their arguments. Then Matthew saw
Doreen running in his direction, so endearing in her Wellies and
father's oversized cardigan. In Toronto she dressed stylishly, never
exerted herself, was *too* mature. She was running and smiling as if
she had a joke to share. Matthew didn't alter his pace, still attempting
to think of excuses to remain in Scotland. Visions of Yonge and
Bloor infested with voracious shoppers, of the crowded subway, of
winter's dismal slush and endless grey, began to fill the negative
ledger. Here it was green and remote, removed from everything
that confined him. *Damn it all, he could start a new life.*

The dog reached Matthew first and began a morning serenade.
When Doreen reached him she threw her arms around her husband and whispered, "I want to have our baby here. Please, Matthew, let's stay."

The dog barked louder, Matthew could see some sheep wander back, and he felt Doreen's loving embrace. It was light now,
the grass glistening with dew and the morning awash with fresh-
ness. Even with his shoes caked in dung, his body chilled and damp,
painfully hungry and exhausted, Matthew could not recall the last
time he had felt so good. Yet after a few moments, a lifetime of
comprehensible memories holding him like the grip of the strongest
warder, he said without the slightest doubt in his voice, "Toronto
is our home. We belong there."

As he and his wife walked back to the one-hundred-and-ninety-
year-old farmhouse for breakfast, Matthew wondered if the Blue
Jays had won yesterday. Doreen had tears in her eyes, but began
another fanciful story about the Black Douglases.

DISFIGUREMENT OF THE SPIRIT

LIKE SOME TIRED SCAVENGER PICK-
ing over his spoils, Dr. Feinberg sat in his office and inspected the
photographs of the stooped woman with the pendulous breasts and
patterned abdominal stretch marks, turned his attention to the
burn-scarred factory worker, then to the genderless infant with the
cleft lip and palate, next to the frowning adolescent girl with pro-
truding eyes, flat forehead, and a nose that was far too close to her
eyes, and finally to the middle-aged banker whose face was a can-
vas of port-wine stains. Unable to concentrate on the photographs,
Dr. Feinberg thought of his family. He had difficulty talking with
his wife and his two youngest children, a boy and a girl. It was
only with his oldest child, Jared, that he could communicate, as if
they were brothers, not father and son. But since Jared had gone
away to university he had not seen his son as much as he wanted
the last three years. At times he ached to hold his son close. With
Jared so far away the doctor felt locked away from his son.

It was not difficult for Dr. Feinberg to feel trapped or impris-
oned, caught as he was in a life he was less than satisfied with. He
had married at forty, no longer able to withstand his mother's pleas
for grandchildren, to replenish what the family had lost during the
Second World War. That he had survived was an astounding story:
hidden as a boy by a Catholic Polish family, becoming their "son,"
reunited with his parents after the War.

He had considered getting married twice before, but neither
woman was Jewish, and he couldn't while his mother was alive.
Not that he feared his mother. What he feared was making worse
what she suffered, during the War and after. His father had left his

mother and their son in Canada, and went to live with a Gentile. She gave him the divorce, and it was heard, through relatives, that he had married the woman. The son couldn't make it worse. He was also afraid that by not having a family his life was incomplete; then he had three children in four years because fathering children was supposed to supply a continuity to existence. Three Jewish children. At least his mother had lived to see all three grandchildren. She died when the youngest was a month old. After the birth of his third child, he quickly got a vasectomy as if only that act could sustain his life. He still felt he was missing a great deal; his life seemed senseless and disordered. He didn't want to blame anyone or anything. At sixty-two, it was only young Jared's life that made sense to the doctor.

5 4

Dr. Feinberg glanced at the literary magazine containing Jared's first published short story, "Becoming Beautiful," and smiled to himself in recollection of the inspiration for the story. Jared, at twenty, already had three stories published and a detailed outline for the novel he was going to write as soon as he finished university. Dr. Feinberg had started novels countless times, the way some men repeatedly start exercising whenever they notice an admonishing anatomical bulge. All of the false literary starts were based on his medical practice, none of them getting further than a few pages of unimaginative descriptions about how unfair and ugly the world was. What wouldn't he trade for the ability to write; but at sixty-two, he did not have much with which to barter.

Dr. Feinberg had convinced Jared to spend his summer vacation with him this year, instead of travelling around the country as he had done in previous summers, the son a restless, inquisitive young man. In a week they would begin their summer excursion. He would take a full month off and they would go up North to the family's cottage and spend the time canoeing and exploring and talking, really talking. Talking about everything he and his wife never talked about. About madness and magic, about the capabilities and intricacies of the mind, about literature and its relation to life, about the creative process, about Nature with all its schemes and secrets. About being Jewish, not that he was any expert; he rarely went to synagogue, even during the High Holy Days. And when he had gone, it was to appease his mother. This summer, with Jared, Dr. Feinberg thought with anticipation, would be the most wonderful time of their lives together. He wanted to confess to Jared that he no longer loved his wife and thought his daughter and other son were self-centred and inconsiderate children. As soon as possible he wanted to tell Jared, and only Jared, that the lifetime of work that had made him wealthy and well-known had become little more than a chore, he might as well be on an assembly line for all the satisfaction he was receiving. He wanted to be more Jewish, but he didn't know where to start. With Hebrew? With Yiddish? Dr. Feinberg didn't want to go through the remainder of his life full of burdens and lies.

DR. FEINBERG REMOVED A SMALL FLASK from his office desk. He raised it to his lips and let the liquid drip to his mouth, counting the few drops in abject tally. *Empty, damn* ... A Jew doesn't drink too much, his mother used to say. To be *shikker* is not Jewish. He had sneaked into the house, drunk as a skunk, he remembered thinking. How do you say "Drunk as a skunk" in Yiddish, Mama? he had said to her, giggling, before he puked his guts out in the bathroom. He had managed not to drink for ten years. He had fought it. What kind of surgeon would he have been? Now he was starting again. Why? Couldn't he wait until after work? He wrote himself a note: Fill up the flask ... Buy Jared a present! The doctor daydreamed of leaving everything to Jared and envisaged a simple will: *All that is mine should be given to Jared Feinberg.* Then he licked the inside of the flask's spout. Very formally, as if before an exacting judge, he promised himself not to drink while Jared was home. He resolved to be optimistic and hopeful and not mention growing old once. Sixty-two was not the end of the world.

Reluctantly, with clumsy and irresolute steps, Dr. Feinberg walked into the reception room and there a timid-looking woman with a misshapen face was sitting quietly. Why couldn't she have missed her appointment, the doctor thought.

"Good to see you again," Dr. Feinberg said, with a fixed joviality he had perfected like a smooth golf swing.

"Hal-lo, d-d-doc-tor," the woman said slowly, sounding like someone intentionally parodying a person having difficulty speaking. She carefully replaced the magazine she had been reading in the same place she had found it. Dr. Feinberg stood unmoving as the woman stalled for time. Go home, he wanted to say, go home if you don't want to see me. At last she walked into the doctor's consulting office and attempted to conceal her fear by sitting in the chair across from the doctor's desk, and staring downwards, with her arms folded. Her posture revealed an eternity of Sisyphean drudgery. *Sisyphean drudgery* were the words Dr. Feinberg wrote several times on his prescription pad, waiting for his patient to speak.

Dr. Feinberg needed to get to know the woman better but found himself wanting to be anywhere else. She looked so pathetic, worse than last week when he had seen her briefly. So many of his patients were the picture of pathos, characters from the mind of some novelist who had given up hope and sketched hideous spectres just to keep busy. Once he saw himself as their saviour and thought they were special, chosen by a wise God who had good reasons for burdening them with deformities and disfigurements and sending them to him. Years ago he could look at his patients with genuine compassion and sympathy; years ago he could touch their damaged bodies without the least revulsion. Dr. Feinberg studied the note he had written to himself, then looked at his liver-spotted hands and wondered how much longer they would be of use to him; a few moments later, his expression controlled, he looked directly at the woman sitting across from him, as if attempting to initiate a high-stakes staring match. She raised her head and looked at the doctor. Why couldn't he get used to these faces? He preferred the deformed and scarred bodies, his imagination relieved to consider them headless. Heads made him uneasy and sad; heads were the very seat of what was pathetic. His partner, much younger than he and who was increasingly taking over more of his complicated surgery, could joke about his work, actually claimed that he got a kick out of looking at his patients. Just imagine you're strolling around side shows and freak shows, he would counsel with frightening joviality when Dr. Feinberg confessed his diminishing capacity to withstand the sight of his patients. Whenever Dr. Feinberg appeared to drift away into some retreat of self-pity or despair, the young doctor would ask if he could name all the actors who had played Quasimodo in the movies, or some other such question that made ironic light of deformities and imperfect Nature. At lunch the young doctor referred to his rhinoplasty patients as Pinocchios or Cyranos, his abdominoplasty patients as fatsos, and when a particularly well-endowed woman walked by, he lewdly cupped his hands and asked his sad partner how he would like to perform mammaplasty on that set of knockers. After over thirty years as a plastic surgeon, it was worse than ever for Dr. Feinberg.

57

"Half the battle, Mrs. Rindlow, is mental. There is a struggle inside which is just as demanding as the struggle outside," Dr. Feinberg said, pointing to his heart and then to his head, jabbing himself hard as if to hurt himself. "You must be prepared. I can't work miracles ..." The doctor felt he had said the same things to the woman last week, to a thousand other patients, but he couldn't be certain. His young partner said, joke with the poor bastards, kid around a little, life isn't all that serious, but to Dr. Feinberg life was only serious, more so at sixty-two. He felt like the lonely curator of a gallery of lost souls. It was only around Jared that he could even attempt to make jokes.

"Do what you c-c-can, d-d-doc-tor," the woman said.

"I would like to take some photographs right now, so I can study them." The doctor removed an instant camera from a desk drawer and placed it on his desk before the woman like a peace offering. "Before you leave have my receptionist set up appointments for x-rays with the medical photographer. Next time we meet I will have computer pictures to show you of what I will be attempting. I always like to take some shots myself beforehand, just to speed up the process," he said, unconsciously touching the camera.

"Of c-c-course, d-d-doc-tor."

"I won't be able to operate for another month. I'm going off with my son for a vacation."

"How n-n-nice ..."

Why was the flask empty? The consultation seemed interminable. Still, he could hear himself talking reassuringly to the woman as in his mind he could see himself and his son walking through the dense bush, careful not to get too lost. Maybe he should take his partner's advice and concentrate on teaching. He enjoyed teaching, and the classroom was not like retiring outright. Dr. Feinberg looked at his hands again and they appeared spoiled and worn, the liver spots dancing mockingly. With the woman's eyes burning through his head, the doctor wanted to chop off his hands. He gently turned the woman's head to profile and took the first photograph.

58

BY THE END OF THE WEEK Dr. Feinberg felt less depressed. He had spoken with Jared over the telephone the night before and his son had told him he had a new short story to read to him when he got home. And Dr. Feinberg had done more reading about Jewish history. It was too late for him, he felt, to learn Hebrew. He could remember Yiddish words and expressions, but when his mother died, there was no one else to hear them from. Just as he walked into the outer office, his receptionist said, "Dr. Hayes on the phone." Dr. Feinberg rushed into his consulting office and picked up the receiver, hoping he could speak with Jared once more.

"Good I got you early, Bernard," the voice said without any sense of hurry or crisis.

"Stepped in a second ago. What's the early-bird urgency?"

"You know that Rindlow woman I sent to you, the one with acute cranio-facial distortion?"

"I'm to see her this afternoon ..." Dr. Feinberg ran his index finger down his appointment schedule and found the woman's name. "She seems a rough one," he said, the woman's image multiplied a hundred times in his memory, her stuttering voice slapping his thoughts.

"She killed herself last night. Being her family physician, I was called in."

"Killed herself?" Dr. Feinberg said, going over the names in his appointment schedule again.

"I found her depressed, but not that depressed. How in the world can you predict suicide," the voice said with an unconvincing philosophical tone.

"I could have helped her ..." Dr. Feinberg's voice grew throaty and desperate, as if he were being choked. He looked at the computer pictures of the Mrs. Rindlow he had hoped to create. With a sharp-tipped pencil the doctor very carefully added a few more touches to the face.

"Something snapped, Bernard," the voice said. "I was sure the plans for corrective surgery encouraged her."

"It would have taken time. Why couldn't she have waited?" Dr. Feinberg said, and darkened the eyes and extended the chin a bit more on one of the computer pictures. He thought about reconstructing the mouth further.

"I'll tell you, Bernard, she was messy about it. Jumped in front of a subway train."

"I didn't have a chance. I only saw her twice ..."

Which subway station was it? he heard himself ask, but didn't hear the other doctor's response.

After the telephone call, Dr. Feinberg opened Mrs. Rindlow's thin file folder and gazed at the five photographs he had taken of her. His eyes journeyed along the outline of the woman's face as if he were an explorer studying a map that he didn't trust as authentic. He could have given her a new life. She should have come to him years ago, when she was younger. Dr. Feinberg felt a wave of sadness overwhelm him; there would never be "after" photographs for Mrs. Rindlow. She seemed to have cheated him by her suicide and suddenly the sadness was replaced by resentment. He did not know what to do with the incomplete file. He had had patients who had backed out at the last minute or refused additional operations, but Mrs. Rindlow seemed to have outwitted him by some devious plan. This time Dr. Feinberg was denied even a chance. He wanted to blame someone, to register a complaint, to receive a proper explanation. Nothing. He would tell Jared about Mrs. Rindlow. Jared would make sense out of the whole crazy thing. Then the doctor recalled Mr. Lefkovitz. Why hadn't he thought of him before? Mr. Lefkovitz swelled into a huge memory creature and stumbled into his office, scolding the doctor for his forgetfulness. He had removed by dermabrasion Mr. Lefkovitz's concentration camp number and then a week later the man killed himself. Pills, neatly, leaving a note with only a few words of Yiddish ad-

59

dressed to a world that didn't read Yiddish. When he had first started his practice, he had offered to remove his mother's concentration camp number, and she had struck her son, the only time she had ever hit him. Dr. Feinberg had refused to remove another person's concentration camp tattoo after Mr. Lefkovitz, as if it had been his fault that he couldn't stand the sight of his numberless forearm. That was twenty years ago, the year Jared was born. Now so many young people were having tattoos put on. His son would never do that. A little earring was as bold as his son got with ornamentation. He had had an argument with his wife over Jared's earring. It's what kids are doing, he argued. Why don't you wear a ring in your nose? she had said angrily to her son. I went out with a woman with a ring in her nose, Jared told his mother, and she thought he was being cheeky. But only twice, he said. She smoked too much for me. Smoking for her was a political act. Dr. Feinberg had laughed at Jared's remark, and his wife had accused him of being blind to what was happening in the boy's life. He was considering quitting school. But he hadn't quit, had he?

Dr. Feinberg took out his recently refilled flask and began to drink. He drank for Mrs. Rindlow and for Mr. Lefkovitz. Would he really have removed his mother's concentration camp number had she wanted? He began to talk to Jared as if his son were in the office. If they could only have a conversation in Yiddish. The doctor thought about the wilderness and a two-person canoe gliding through a lake no other humans had ever seen before. The lake was immeasurably deep in secrets. His mother would never have approved of such a trip.

The receptionist announced that the first patient of the day had arrived, a teenage girl with a large, crooked nose. Dr. Feinberg almost began to cry when she came in with her mother, the girl looking shy and embarrassed and trembling with life. He put away his flask and removed the instant camera. The girl smiled at the doctor and her nose looked even larger, more crooked.

DR. FEINBERG WEPT FREELY when he embraced Jared at the airport and then spent five minutes apologizing for being too emotional.

Two earrings. They look good, he told his son. But your mother ...
Before they had reached the car, Dr. Feinberg had told his son about
Mrs. Rindlow and Mr. Lefkovitz. And the story about his own
mother, the boy's dear grandmother, hitting him. What was the
number? Jared asked, and the father admitted he couldn't recall a
single numeral. While they had been driving back from the airport, the son had read his latest short story to his father. Dr. Feinberg
wanted to drive straight to the cottage but he had so many things
to get in order before they abandoned the city world. The reunion was still affecting him two days after his son had returned home.
Jared acted like he had never been away.

After a fitful night of anticipation over the trip and doubts about
the value of his work, Dr. Feinberg awoke early the morning he
and his son planned to leave, and went to his study still dressed in
his pajamas. He looked solemn as he sat at his desk, a single small
lamp illuminating him at work. Jared, getting out of bed a few
minutes after his father, stood silently and unnoticed at the room's
threshold, observing the figure of his pensive father. Several framed
photographs of Jared decorated the wood-panelled walls while a
single photograph of his wife and two other children occupied a
corner of the desk. His wife had several photographs in their bedroom of all three children, but this was his study. To Jared his father appeared like a hunched-over prophet from another age. A
prophet with wire-rimmed glasses, old pajamas, and his perpetual
crew cut, grey and neat.

"Got any time for me?" Jared finally asked.

"For who else, son?" Dr. Feinberg said and enthusiastically waved
his son into the study. "All packed?"

Jared came to the desk and kneeled next to it, as though in am-
biguous worship, and said, "With all our gear we may never have
to come back."

The doctor smiled in approval and then started to describe what
he was doing, seeming to have been caught in the act of something underhanded that required a plausible explanation.

"Putting in some recent photos. I want everything in order before we leave. In case we do come back. What do you think?" he

said, turning the open photo album toward his son and watching the young man's eyes for a reaction.

Jared looked thoughtfully at the ten photographs, five on the left album page, five on the right album page. In the five left ones the woman's chin protruded and her ears winged out, making her look like a sad pelican in various poses of grief; in the other five she was almost beautiful, the chin shaped into inconspicuousness and the ears aesthetically flattened.

"It always amazes me, Dad," Jared said with childish awe, "how you can reconstruct a person, bone structure and all."

"This woman was a real mental cripple. Now I hope she can begin to live. This is my best, Jared, don't you think?" The doctor leaned back in his chair and regarded the photographs with the cautious pride of an artist who had laboured long and hard over an elusive creation yet still remained uneasy about the achievement – unsure what was missing.

"I thought mother was your best," Jared teased, placing a hand on his father's shoulder.

Dr. Feinberg saying nothing to his son's statement, turned back to the beginning of the album, and then said by way of a formal announcement, "You haven't seen these pictures either. I prefer it much better when they come to me young."

"You made a glamour queen out of her," Jared said as his father adjusted the desk lamp so that it shone directly on the two album pages. This album was thick and filled with photographs. Dr. Feinberg had thirty-one other albums, one for each year of his practice, all arranged consecutively on a long, sturdy shelf above his desk. From the start of his own medical practice, Dr. Feinberg had taken "before" photographs and then, after the plastic surgery, photographs capturing the results for his private collection. He purchased his first instant camera thirty-two years ago, on the very day he moved into his office. At the top of each album page was a single circled letter, either "C," "E," or "R," corresponding to "Cosmetic," "Emergency," or "Reconstructive." At the bottom of each page he had a sentence or two about his own life at the time. There were many more pictures for his diagnosis and planning of work, taken by a specially trained medical photographer, but they remained at his office, along with the computer pictures that he had started using several years ago. These thirty-two albums were his, proof that his life was not merely insignificant tinkering. A night or early morning did not go by without Dr. Feinberg looking through one of the albums, becoming absorbed with its stories and memories, telling himself he could write a great novel about the malformed or injured. He was more pleased than a compulsive philatelist when he could add photographs to his private collection.

"Glamour queen, my foot. It's enough they can walk down the street without feeling they want to hide," Dr. Feinberg said.

"Let me see mother again," Jared said eagerly, nearly ordering his father.

Dr. Feinberg removed the twenty-two-year-old album and turned to his wife's pages without comment. He did not look at the photographs and sat with a strained expression.

"You can tell it's the same person. With some of them you can't," Jared said, leaning forward to get a closer view.

"It was nothing more than fixing her nose. Another 'C'," the doctor said, tapping his finger at the circled letter. From the bottom of the page Jared read aloud: "There is no more invigorating, captivating, magical emotion than love. It is the bleakness of winter, a blizzard rages outside, yet I feel the exhilaration of the brightest summer day."

"Uneventful and perfunctory rhinoplasty," the doctor added with a harshness that better belonged to profanity.

"You don't like doing nose jobs, do you, Dad?"

"Most of them not. Some of them do correct breathing abnormalities but too often the case is vanity and not rooted in mental anguish." The doctor spoke with the hollow authority of a participant at an enforced séance.

"Can you always tell?" Jared asked, watching his mother transform before his eyes. She was young then, only five years older than Jared was now. Her expression in the "after" photographs seemed mischievous and appealing to Jared. "Someone with a wrong-shaped nose," the son said to his father, "might be suffering excruciating mental anguish. You could call it a disfigurement of the spirit."

"Disfigurement of the spirit," Dr. Feinberg repeated in melodious echo. "No denying that, son, but more often than not they just don't meet their own standards of beauty. Or the illusions that magazines and TV and movies have given them."

"Was it that way with Mother?"

"She needed to change herself at the time. It helped her through her divorce. A symbolic change more than anything else. Like a new hairdo …"

64

Rachel Feinberg, at the end of her unhappy two-year marriage, had been a patient of Dr. Feinberg's. She told him of her mixed marriage, of going against her parents' wishes and marrying a Gentile. I'm not Jewish enough, Dr. Feinberg told her, and she said he was every Jewish mother's dream. *A doctor*, she said. I'm a forty-year-old doctor who has never been married, to a Jew or to a Gentile. If you ever want to try a nice Jewish *maidleh*, she had joked. She no longer mentioned her nose job and took great pride that her daughter and both her sons had what she considered *perfect* noses. The doctor and his patient fell in love and were married less than a year after the masterful operation. A Jewish wedding.

Dr. Feinberg turned to a squint-eyed, tiny-mouthed, prognathous gargoyle he had transformed into merely a homely person, tolerable, two dark eyes staring appreciatively into space in the "after" photographs, the mouth enlarged, and a deformed lower face that had acquired more human dimensions.

"So many operations on this one. I could never do enough. Can you imagine going through life looking like that?" Dr. Feinberg shuddered at the memory of the woman, not at the photographs. "Usually the car accidents or burns are the worst, present the greatest reconstructive challenges, but nothing could compare to *her*."

"Just think how she would have been regarded in the sixteenth or seventeenth century, Dad. Superstition would have gotten her stoned to death or burned at the stake."

"Our times are infinitely crueller," Dr. Feinberg said sadly.

"Let's look at another year, Dad," Jared responded cheerfully, attempting to counter the moist, self-pitying quality in his father's voice.

"The year you were born," Dr. Feinberg said with a quick uplift in mood, and pulled another album off the shelf. "The happiest year of my life."

As Dr. Feinberg opened the album, Jared said with a disturbing seriousness, "I'd like my face changed. Then I could be a completely different person."

"What an odd thing to say, son. You're a handsome young man." Except for the small nose, Dr. Feinberg thought how much Jared resembled his mother, but kept the thought to himself.

"Only jesting," Jared said, contorting his face and affectionately shaking his father's shoulder. "Don't be so down, Dad."

Dr. Feinberg began to turn the pages of the twenty-year-old album, slowly wandering through a procession of cleft lips and palates, of too large and too small breasts, of prognathous and opisthognathous faces, of lop ears and minuscule ears, of webbed toes and webbed fingers, the scared, mutilated, misshapen in orderly pictorial array, the doctor effortlessly recalling each patient and the story behind his or her transformation. He narrated with much excitement and more than a hint of joyous nostalgia as he was pulled into the worlds the photographs evoked for him. When Dr. Feinberg came to Mr. Lefkovitz's pages, Jared pressed his fingers to the album to prevent his father from proceeding.

"You never discussed this one with me, Dad. *The number.*"

"He was in the same concentration camp as your grandmother."

"Why did some people have it taken off and others not? Look, you don't have a letter here."

For the first time Dr. Feinberg realized that he hadn't labelled Mr. Lefkovitz's page "C," "E," or "R."

"What about your other patients who had numbers?" Jared asked, his expression puzzled.

"I didn't have that many," Dr. Feinberg said and removed an earlier album, finding three other concentration camp survivors he had treated. None of them had labels either.

65

"That's strange," the doctor said, as though accidently discovering an enormous break in the Earth and peering down into the suddenly inescapable chasm.

"Would you have a number removed, Dad, if you had one?" Jared asked, touching his father's left forearm.

"I really don't know, son."

"I wouldn't," Jared said quickly, tracing a number on his left forearm, starting to fashion a new story in his mind. "I'm going to call my next story 'Disfigurement of the Spirit'," the young man said, standing up and putting his arms lovingly around his father. "How's that sound for a title, Dad?"

Dr. Feinberg, staring at his hands as though they belonged to someone else, did not respond. After a few silent seconds, he pulled another album from the shelf above his desk, and opened to the first page.

66

MEMORY-CONVULSIONS

CRAIG COULD NOT REMEMBER EVER hating anyone as much as he hated the man in the apartment next to his. He had tried to be reasonable, waiting until eleven or twelve each night to ask his neighbour to turn down his stereo. During each visit the man told Craig to go to Hell and then turned the music up louder. On the fourth night that Craig had asked him to turn his music down, the man shouted at him that if he complained to the landlord or called the police, he would cut off Craig's balls and throw them from the balcony. Craig thought of moving to another apartment, but he was sick of moving, of doing what other people told him, whether it was his parents or the doctors who had treated him over the years or the belligerent man next door on the ninth floor of his downtown apartment building. That was what was missing from his life – control, Craig concluded, control over his everyday life. When he was younger and had attempted to exert control, he wound up being treated for one mental problem after another. Control, he firmly believed, was the one ingredient that would keep him from his damn feelings of helplessness, would make him well on his own terms. That was why Craig was visiting his parents' house after not seeing them for three months: he needed to get a gun to try to gain control over his life.

The spring night was clear, full of crisp sounds, and cold after an unseasonably mild afternoon. It had been nearly warm enough, Craig had told his parents less than a minute after coming into their house, to take off all his clothes and run through the old neighbourhood. Both his father and mother cringed at the memory of their son, as a teenager, doing his periodic late-night runs through the tree-lined streets. But that was years ago and Craig was well, had lived on his own for over two years without any serious problems. Craig had known exactly what he was saying – he was still capable of hurting his parents with a few well-delivered words. Even the generous monthly cheques that his father sent him could not turn Craig into a forgiving, dutiful son.

Craig, with one of his father's small handguns hidden in his jacket pocket, left his parents' house after another apology for bringing up the past. He could have taken any of his father's numerous guns, but wanted the smallest one, not one of the heavier, more powerful guns that his father had in his large, valuable collection. Craig hated guns, even the hunting rifles his father had taught him to use as a boy. You have a gift, a genuine gift for marksmanship, his father used to say during each hunting trip. The son hated that he had spent years trying to please his father. Craig had memory-convulsions about the animals he had killed, their eyes aflame with his father's eyes in nightmares.

Craig always associated guns with what his gun-collecting father called "action" movies. Action movies were the Westerns, war movies, and cops-and-robbers movies that his father used to take his son to. Whenever a gun appeared on the screen, the father would whisper its identity to his son, a game the father enjoyed. There never seemed to be a gun he couldn't identity, but Craig didn't know if his father was always correct. The first action movie – a Western – that Craig's father had taken him to was twenty years ago, when the boy was seven. There were more action movies, his father's cinematic passion, the guns identified during the movie and discussed afterward, until Craig was old enough to resist going. Now he needed a gun, one of his father's guns.

Across from his parents' house, under the arch of two hardwood trees that Craig used to stare at from his second-floor bedroom window and think about running away from home, the taxicab was waiting. It had taken only fifteen minutes for the son to pay his courteous visit and steal the gun – the driver trying to catch forty winks in the front seat. Craig woke the driver up with a fierce rap to the roof of the taxicab, the man jerking awake and saying, as if under cross-examination, that he must have forgotten where he was, you know how it is, old pal, two jobs just to make ends meet, work like a dog. I'm a remittance man, Craig said, but the driver did not understand his passenger's self-mockery.

The awakened driver, starting his car, began to tell Craig the details of a vivid dream he had had the night before about mountain-climbing, asking his passenger what he thought the dream meant.

"Does it have to mean anything?" Craig said, displeased that the cabdriver had taken him for a trusted confidant. On the ride over Craig had refused to say anything other than the address he wanted. But now he had a gun.

"Ah sure, everything means something. That includes things in the external, concrete world and in the internal world of thought," the cabdriver said, rapidly releasing his words with a cocky, streetwise erudition, eager to get into a deep discussion, especially after having been thwarted during the ride over. His three favourite topics were dreams, psychoanalysis, and professional hockey. He wrote down all his dreams – and any dreams he could elicit from passengers – in a large notebook, and carried the treasured dream register with him in his taxicab, reading from it between fares. His goal was to write a screenplay based on the dreams and sell it to a big filmmaker. A successful screenplay was his only way out of his taxicab prison, as he called it. The cabdriver figured that he had a better chance with a successful screenplay than with the lotteries, which he felt guilty about playing so often.

"Some things mean more than other things. See that diseased, leafless tree," Craig said as the taxicab stopped at an intersection. "Chop it down and so what?" The feel of the gun in his jacket pocket made talking seem of little consequence to Craig.

"Believe me, old pal, that tree is important ... *essential* ... *absolutely essential*," the cabdriver argued as he drove on, pressing his body against the seat to reinforce the seriousness of his words. "That tree contributes to the order of everything. It's a necessary part of the whole. Take this cab, for instance. It's also essential, even if there are hundreds of them in the city. Who's to say what this world can do without and what it can't do without. Everything has meaning. It's all part of an incredible, interconnected plan. They say if

69

you throw a single pebble into the ocean, it changes everything, all future history. Try that theory on for size, old pal ..."

Craig farted softly and wondered if the cabdriver thought his passenger had just changed the course of human events. Becoming increasingly annoyed with the cabdriver's comments, Craig said, "Life has meaning only because people give it meaning. It makes as much sense to say things don't have meaning. People twist things all around to suit their own purposes."

The next fart was loud but the cabdriver ignored it. Perhaps if he had farted into the ocean, Craig thought, the cabdriver would have been impressed. The sour odour filled the taxicab and Craig inhaled it. He smiled at a random thought of Aristotle farting in front of his students at the Lyceum. A philosophy professor at university had told the class the story, in the only course Craig had received an A during his eight years of pursuing higher education part-time, between treatments and hospital stays.

Annoyed by his passenger's cynicism, the cabdriver continued to talk, with even more conviction and vigour, the dedicated missionary denied and therefore pushed to greater effort to win over the unbeliever, but Craig drifted away, only partially listening. He was experiencing everything differently from the silent ride over to his parents' house. The passenger looked out the window through new eyes, his thoughts weightier, even his body seeming altered and charged through.

Craig's hand became fused to the gun, in a combination of fear and dread and imagined strength. Control, that would be his salvation. He would regain control over his life, and confronting his bullying neighbour would be the first important step. The gun seemed to have a rapid pulse and the pulse coincided with Craig's.

If he pulled the gun out now he could make the jabbering cabdriver go anywhere, do anything, Craig thought. The hell with pebbles thrown into indifferent oceans, the gun would affect the cabdriver's history in no uncertain terms. Maybe he would take the gun out merely to see the cabdriver's reaction. Could he prate on so foolishly with a gun to the back of his head? But Craig kept the gun hidden, afraid that the weapon, once out in the open, would begin firing on its own. No, this gun was for one purpose: next time his neighbour threatened him with emasculation or anything else, he would pull out the gun and gain control.

The cabdriver, acquiring energy from his trip through the city, began a lecture on Freud, a lecture he tried to give to those he sensed would appreciate his knowledge. The cabdriver had "discovered" Freud a year ago, but was unconcerned with any current opinion on him. Having read several old books on Freud – and having seen the sombre movie biography one night on television and videotaping it so he could watch it often – the cabdriver considered himself an authority on Freud, and related facts, theories, and obscure anecdotes about the famed neurologist, spouting Freud's ideas as an enthusiastic cook might share pet recipes with a friendly neighbour. Infantile sexuality, Oedipus complex, sexual suppression ... the concepts jumped from the cabdriver's mouth without pattern or elaboration. In his mind the cabdriver saw the immortal Sigmund Freud as Montgomery Clift, the actor. As his mind showed the movie again, the cabdriver felt her knew Freud personally.

7 1

"He was a Jew. Did you know that?" the cabdriver said to his passenger as if revealing a particularly risqué piece of information.

"What?" Craig mumbled, having heard only the words *Jew* and *that*.

"Freud was a Viennese middle-class Jew. The Jews contribute to the world of ideas all out of proportion to their numbers. How do you account for that, old pal?"

"They're good pebble throwers," Craig said, alert again.

"Huh?"

"They stand by the ocean and toss pebbles in all the time," Craig told the cabdriver. He instructed the talkative man to drive around the downtown area for a while before dropping him off at his apartment building. Craig wanted to plan out exactly how he was going to deal with his noisy, obnoxious neighbour, to determine if it would be necessary to put a bullet hole in the man's wall. The downtown lights soothed Craig, made him feel he was in some dazzling foreign city.

After a few seconds the cabdriver burst out, "Oh, I get it. That's good ... Freud had a sense of humour too, old pal. He told great jokes. If you're interested, you should read Freud's *Jokes and Their Relationship to the Unconscious* ..."

The night, to Craig, seemed to be getting brighter and colder. The rows of streetlamps were like spotlights illuminating the downtowners. He could point the gun at pedestrians and make them do anything he commanded. Anything but undo the past; anything but start over. It wasn't the first time he had been told what to do by another person. The neighbour was only louder, nastier. His parents, doctors ... Maybe he *should* move to another apartment and avoid the stupid confrontation. Craig's thoughts wavered from pointing the gun at everyone in sight to discarding it, but the gun stayed fused to his hand. He was going to scare the hell out of his damn neighbour and gain control over his life once and for all. Then his father could have the gun back, his collection complete again.

"You going to the playoff game tomorrow?" the cabdriver said excitedly, his hands leaving the steering wheel in worshipful gesticulation.

"Wasn't planning on it," Craig answered.

The cabdriver removed six hockey tickets from the car visor and fanned them apart. "I got some extra ones. Can let you have them for cost and a twenty-buck handling charge per ticket. Try getting tickets for tomorrow's game."

"I dislike crowds and screaming," Craig said with very little emotion. His father used to take him to professional hockey games regularly and all Craig could remember of the games was his father cheering at the top of his lungs after a home-team goal, claiming that hockey wasn't all that different from the business world: only the most aggressive and toughest triumph. On occasion they would see a hockey game *and* an action movie in the same week. Craig had shown much ability in various boys' hockey leagues, leading his team in scoring one season, then at fourteen decided never to put skates on again. His father took him to a psychologist, but even after months of sessions the boy refused to play hockey anywhere.

"Some of the stars you see today will be tomorrow's legends. You can tell your grandchildren about seeing today's stars in their primes," the cabdriver said.

"Not many Jews in professional hockey. How do you account for that?" Craig said, unable to smother a self-satisfied smirk.

The cabdriver shook his head in puzzlement, returning the hockey tickets to the visor. He would have no trouble selling them later tonight or tomorrow, he thought.

"If hockey were played with pebbles instead of pucks, perhaps the Jews would star," Craig said before the cabdriver could come up with a plausible theory of his own.

"You got yourself a quick wit, old pal."

"Keeps me sane." Craig did not like the word *sane*. Certain words he could not use without being stung by painful memories: *sane, gun, hunting, action movie, crazy … sane crazy sane crazy sane crazy …*

73

"My writing keeps me sane," the cabdriver said, tapping hard at his large notebook. "I have a younger brother who's not quite right in the head," the cabdriver added, tapping his head as hard as he had tapped his notebook.

Craig could tell the cabdriver about madness, about licking meals off the floor and head-banging symphonies, but he was tired of telling strangers about his sicknesses and cures. He had had his refusal to skate, his naked romps, his descents into personal darkness. Now he wanted real control.

"The other night I dreamed about every hockey team going the entire season without scoring a goal, over eighty games a team and not a blink of the old red light," the cabdriver said to his passenger. "What do you think that weird dream means, old pal?"

"That you slipped on Freud on the ice in your last life," Craig said.

"I get it, old pal … *Freudian slip*," the cabdriver exclaimed and accelerated the car so he wouldn't get caught at another downtown traffic light. A late-evening stroller, oblivious to the taxicab and Freud and hockey, tried to make it across the street and the cabdriver slammed on his brakes, skidding past the intersection and barely missing a parked car. In the confusion and horn-honking the cabdriver hadn't heard the sharp noise directly behind him. The angered driver swore at the pedestrian as the man, unperturbed and unscathed, finished crossing the street. When the cabdriver turned around to see how his passenger had withstood the abrupt stop, he saw blood coming through Craig's pant leg.

"My finger squeezed accidently ... accidently," was all Craig groaned as he closed his eyes in pain. Slumped down in the back seat of the taxicab, he thought about the action movies he used to see with his father, a world of guns going off without cessation.

74

THE SECOND ACT OF
THE DISILLUSIONED ILLUSIONIST

Home from university for a weekend visit in early November, nineteen-year-old Millicent, the oldest of the four children at the kitchen table, stood up, and announced that she was quitting school to pursue an acting career. She wanted to share with the family the exciting news that she had a small role in a musical — *it's a start* — and that she was going on the road — *a national tour, can you believe it?* Her disclosure turned into a dramatic performance as she revealed that she was also writing her own play, had been working on it all summer and since September, not bothering to attend many of her classes, and that she would not be going back to university.

There was a silence at the table, broken by thirteen-year-old Laurel, who said with wide-eyed awe that she had never known anyone who had written a real play, although she had a dream recently in which she acted in a school play with a teenage movie star who wore a mask and wouldn't give his name. She had improvised all her lines and had kissed the mysterious movie star on the lips. Then she reprised her dream kiss, complete with sound effects and dreamy-eyed swoon. Sixteen-year-old Tiffany, touching her recently inserted lip ring, told her younger sister that it wasn't healthy to dream about masked movie stars.

As Laurel and Tiffany argued over dreams and movie stars and disguises, and Millicent provided more details about her fledgling acting/writing career, their mother, uttering a low moan of despair, slapped her oldest child. The son, Tyler, fifteen but the smallest one in the family, jumped up, and tried to move between his mother and older sister. The father grabbed the son, thinking he was going to attack the enraged woman.

"You are the first one in our family to go to university," the mother said, shaking her hand as if she were attempting to cool it off after dipping it into hot water.

"I don't want to be a student, I want to be an actor. I want to be completely immersed in theatre," the daughter said, smiling, gently touching the skin where her mother had slapped her. In the play she would have the daughter slap her mother back. But she wasn't concerned with physical gestures, not at this stage. Plot, characterization ...

"You have a full scholarship," the father stated in his most authoritative fatherly voice.

"First one to quit university in our family," Laurel said, as if working on a comedy routine, her thin eyebrows arching mischievously up and down like Groucho Marx's thick eyebrows, though the young girl had never seen Groucho in movies or on television, and the father raised a hand to her, but did not strike. "A snake poised to strike," Millicent whispered, said it twice. "I'm going to include this scene in the play," Millicent declared. "In the second act."

"Include what?" the father demanded to know.

"*Everything*," Millicent said, the one word full of pride and reverence and hopefulness.

The mother hugged her son, as if that might rectify all their family's disagreements. The father hugged Laurel, as if attempting to out-hug his wife.

"I have to write this down now, or I'll lose it," Millicent said, standing from the table and starting to go toward her old room, with its walls covered with pictures of the greatest playwrights and stage actors of the last fifty years.

"What's your play about?" Tiffany asked, and her older sister stopped and looked back at the table.

"About giving up," the mother said, before her daughter could describe her work.

"I'm not giving up on anything," Millicent stated defiantly. "My play is about a famous illusionist who becomes totally disillusioned with magic."

The father, cracking his knuckles loudly, more loudly than anyone in the family had ever heard, cupped his hand over Laurel's ear and then pulled a small white mouse with a long grey tail from behind his youngest daughter's ear.

"When did you become a magician?" Laurel said, reaching for the mouse her father was holding, the well-behaved creature climbing unafraid onto her extended arm.

"He was a magician before we married," the mother explained, her eyes deflected to the floor, as if revealing some deep, dark, perhaps incriminating secret.

"You never told me, Dad," the aspiring actor/playwright daughter said.

"I could never make a living as a magician. I had a family to help raise," the father said. "I didn't have a full scholarship," he added angrily, and reached for the mouse but it would not leave Laurel's arm.

The son, cracking his knuckles in a meagre imitation of his father, pulled a quarter from his younger sister's other ear.

"I didn't know anyone in our family could do magic," Millicent said. "But an illusionist and a magician are two different things, even though there is overlap between the two types of entertainers. When I was doing research for my play ..."

The mother waved her hands over the table, preparing to do a magic trick.

"You going to make the table disappear, Mom?" the son asked.

"This table is bad luck," the mother said, pounding first her left fist, then her right fist, then both fists at once on the table, a drummer angry at an instrument. She looked disappointed that nothing had appeared on the table.

"This table has been in the family since the early 1800s," Laurel said, repeating what her mother had said many times before, in both good humour and in bad humour.

Same table at which the mother had told her husband she was pregnant with each of her four children, or so the family story goes. Same table where a great-aunt, who, after returning from a third trip around the world, and could sing glorious arias from Bizet's *Carmen*, so much like an operatic soprano that if you closed your eyes you'd think you were in a great opera hall, had died of a rare tropical disease, putting her head down on the table and dying peacefully. That, supposedly, was a fact.

"Are you going back to school or not, Millicent?" the father asked. He cracked his knuckles again, but not as loud as before.

"I've quit. I'm going to act and I'm going to write *The Disillusioned Illusionist*. I've written one act and I'm starting the second."

Cracking his knuckles still another time, as loud as the first time, the father said, "You better tell your mother you're going back to university or ..."

"Or what?"

"Or I'll make you disappear, young lady."

Millicent grinned, a grin that the father interpreted as contempt and the mother as loathing. "I wonder if I can work that into the play," she said, her grin changing into a thoughtful frown. She wasn't averse to including a little fantasy in her play, but basically her vision was realistic, of a difficult and sometimes harsh world.

"He can do it," the mother said, shaking her head knowingly.

"Sure hope Dad doesn't make Millicent's CDs disappear too," Tyler said, and only Laurel laughed, her eyebrows bouncing in adolescent delight.

Millicent took several more determined steps toward her old room. The father started saying words in a language that no one in the room understood. Saying words and waving his hands perfectly parallel over the table.

Before she reached her old room, Millicent was gone, not a trace of her anywhere in the house.

"I was never disillusioned," the father said. "I had a family to raise and it was damn hard. Harder than doing any illusion ..."

SWEATY WOOL ARMADILLOS

NOT COUNTING THE LAST SIX months on Prince Edward Island, I've lived in Toronto all my life. People like my accent here on the Island. I've been maintaining this Southern accent – not southern Ontario, but Deep South U.S. – my only connection with my father, except for going to university in the province where I was conceived. Dad, who was originally from New England – born in Vermont, brought up in Maine, went to university in Massachusetts – wanted to be the next Tennessee Williams. He spoke with a Southern drawl. I picked up the drawl, and out-drawled him. My nickname at school is "Y'all." I actually like the nickname, in a self-deprecating, contrary way. Use it all the time at school, even on my essays and exams. My real first name is Orpheus, which I do not like to use. The play that changed my father's life, he claimed, was *Orpheus Descending*, the first play by Tennessee Williams my father saw. At least I can be thankful my sentimental dad didn't name me after the main character of *Orpheus Descending*, Val Xavier, *Valentine*, who, at play's end, happens to get murdered in a most gruesome manner by some of the town's angry menfolk.

My father spent a great deal of time talking about Tennessee Williams and his characters. His life, he told me more times than I can remember, could have been a play by Tennessee Williams, not a thought a maturing child could really get his head around. He said his life, like the lives of many of the characters in Tennessee Williams' plays, was complicated by sexual peccadillos. My father first tried to explain the rift between him and my mother, when I was four or five, by saying it was because of his sexual peccadillos.

What does a kid that young know of sexual peccadillos or a father's euphemisms? I called *sexual peccadillos*, a phrase I associated with the smell of alcohol, *sweaty wool armadillos*, made up a story about the sweaty wool armadillos, a story I have added to and revised over the years, a kind of world-in-microcosm personal fairy tale. I've read very little of Tennessee Williams' work, seen only two plays of his, both before I was ten, and those because my father took me, somehow convincing the ushers that a kid so young would appreciate Tennessee Williams, but I feel I've lived through them all, the way my father used to talk about Williams' work. However, life isn't a play, and my life is not on the smoothest course currently. Maybe if I stop using my Southern accent on campus, I can start to get my messed-up life together. Or maybe the mess is just too messy. I'm no quitter, so I have to get my head clear and straight, finish my first year, and have a better second year. I'm planning on staying on the Island for the summer. Everyone tells me the summers here are the best. And the beaches. God, don't I know about the Island beaches, at least one beach in particular.

8 O

But summer is a few months away, and I have to get through my first year. I haven't received any personal mail in several weeks. I've written to people since I started school here, and no one writes back. I thought that maybe the post office got my address screwed up, but no, the clerk, leaning against the counter separating us, said the post office was aware of my existence and my correct mailing address. But in a helpful, compassionate way, not threatening, even though a paranoid person might interpret the clerk's look and tone of voice as threatening. Not a single letter. You expecting letters from your parents? the concerned clerk asked, and I explained that those are two people who won't be writing to me. My father won't write anyone, even if his life depended on it. He hasn't personally written me since his last catastrophic play failure, fourth in a row. With that letter he sent me photocopies of the reviews. He won't write anything anymore, he's made a religious vow, not plays, letters, graffiti on a bathroom wall, even a little postcard, nothing, not a word. My father sent an impersonal printed card, like an invitation to a big wedding, to everyone he knew, announcing that from this day henceforth he would refrain from using the written word.

That was two years ago, and as far as I know, he has been true to his vow. If anything, Dad is bullheaded. Last I heard, he lives in a real poor section of New Orleans, with a woman my age – the information was bitterly passed on to me by my mom – not that nineteen isn't a great age. I also understand my mother blotting me out as far as letters are concerned – and hanging up on me when I phone. She's still angry at me for going to university here. She yelled out a tirade and a half when I told her I'd applied and been accepted to UPEI. I could barely get out of my mouth my reasons for selecting the Island as the place to equip myself for the world. "No, no," she screamed, "anywhere but *there*." You'd think I was going off for my university education to the most dangerous part of the world. She met my father on Prince Edward Island, in a touristy place called Cavendish, and the marriage lasted twelve years, of which, she claims, eleven were in virtual silence. They weren't peccadillos or armadillos to her. Yet it hadn't started in silence and animosity. Dad had been visiting here, recovering from something like his hundredth drinking bout and a wrecked marriage, and working on a play, a Tennessee Williams-like play, as usual, dealing with the fact that he was forty and not famous, that's his description; Mom was taking her annual librarian's vacation, picking a different Canadian location or European country each year, no real desire to marry, at thirty-six fairly set in her ways – and they fell head over heels in love, that's her description. But there was me, she smiled, and I smiled back, and neither one of us could read the other's enigmatic smile. My mother calls her smiles enigmatic, and I take after her in that regard. The Island is not for you, she proclaimed. Was I conceived at Cavendish? I asked, asking the question directly for the first time. Right on the beach we made love, like that famous sultry love scene in *From Here to Eternity*. I rented the movie that night, and waited for the scene, and there were Burt Lancaster and Deborah Kerr, and they were my mother and father, in the sand, creating me, so to speak.

I haven't received any mail since I went to a party in downtown Charlottetown, half-polluted already, and met the cutest girl I'd ever seen. We talked for a few minutes, mainly about the meaninglessness and randomness of existence, which I thought was exciting, because she was so passionate about it, and then we went out on the back porch, and it was a cool evening, and we made out for about five minutes before we were making love, she hotter than anything in *From Here to Eternity*. I thought what got her to like me was my story of the sweaty wool armadillos. I didn't use a condom, and I worried for weeks. I realize I still worry but what can I do? I'll go to the doctor and then I'll sleep peacefully, I hope. I assume she'll find me if I got her pregnant. Wouldn't that be something. My parents meet on the Island nearly twenty years ago and I get conceived, and I meet the girl of my dreams, and maybe I get a disease or maybe I get her pregnant or maybe none of the above. I've never done anything like that, ever. When I went to tell her my name, she put a finger on my lips and shook her head hard, and I told her anyway: "Y'all." She didn't ask me where I was from, or what I was studying in school; she didn't even comment on my Southern accent or that people were calling me "Y'all." She didn't ask me anything. I asked her name, and she shook her head even harder. Then she went inside, I assumed to go to the bathroom, and I stood out on the back porch, shivering, but hoping we might repeat our love scene when she returned, thinking that my father could turn this into a Tennessee Williams-style scene in one of his plays, if he was still writing plays, which I'm pretty sure he isn't. But she didn't come back out to the porch, and when I went to look for her, she was gone. I asked people, everyone at the party, and those who had seen her said she left – a few people told me she had tried to sell them dope earlier in the evening – no one knowing who she was.

My doctor's appointment is tomorrow. I have a paper that's due in two days on alienation imagery in contemporary Canadian poetry, and I'm nowhere near done. I know I'm going to flunk out, unless I transform my life significantly. My mother thought I was crazy to go to university on Prince Edward Island. "Going to P.E.I. was unfortunate for me, and I don't want you to go," Mom told me after I announced my decision, and tearfully added, "I should have visited Whitehorse or Yellowknife on my vacation."

Maybe Mom was right. But heck, had she visited Whitehorse or Yellowknife, I wouldn't have been conceived. And I could have had first-year academic problems anywhere. I would have really gone down the tubes at a large university, in a big city. But I'm not going to deceive myself about my problems here. No one writes me. My one sexual experience in six months, and it's a complete disaster, despite the girl being so cute. I have to see the doctor, just to confirm that nothing is wrong with me. I'm flunking out. If I can just get through my first year, I'll be all right. No more drinking. No more going to parties. No more using my Southern accent, even though I'm so used to talking that way that I'll have to really work at losing it. I'll just think ahead to the summer – a procession of adorable sweaty wool armadillos on a romantic beach, me there to cheer them on – and I'll get through my first year.

INFLATABLE DOLLS

I DON'T KNOW IF MY LAW PARTNER telling me about his peculiar dream triggered it or not, but I had my old dream last night, the one I started having in my third year at university, when I had been working on a history essay on Hitler. My law partner's dream, which I found incredibly humorous and he found painfully distressing, was in the same genre as my recurring dream, if dreams can be put into genres. He sat across from me at lunch, having his second beer, and told me that in his dream the Law Society of Upper Canada forced him to defend a neo-Nazi, *pro bono* yet. The trial was being televised all over the world, his whole family was there, even relatives he didn't know he had, and in the middle of the trial his wife, sexily dressed, walks up to him and starts to massage his shoulders, saying he is too tense, tries to seduce him in public. I chuckled at his description, and he became angry, said it wasn't funny. He asked me if I would defend a neo-Nazi, and I said no without hesitation. I didn't say the neo-Nazi shouldn't have legal representation, just that it would be a little too insulting for a Toronto Jew whose mother had been in Auschwitz to be the one. He ordered a third beer, and asked if I thought the dream indicated there was something wrong with him, psychologically that is. I told him it was a fascinating dream, and convinced him that his subconscious was entertaining him. I started to tell him about my recurring dream, but I stopped.

Sprinkled periodically through the past three decades, my subconscious would treat me to the dream, or variations of it, a few times a year. Like a rented movie I keep forgetting to return and that manages to restart itself on the mental VCR. I hadn't had the dream in months, but it was so vivid the other night. I've always intended to write down the dream, maybe write it out as a story or something, but I never get around to it. I don't know if it would be a comedy skit or a surreal tragedy. What I do know is that it will occur again, that's not the mystery. I can't predict when or what will bring it forth. I'm always twenty in the dream.

Yes, the dream, my thirty years of nocturnal reruns. I am in the back seat of a stretch limo. Super-stretch limo. Maybe they were just called limousines thirty years ago, but I can't remember exactly. A dream anachronism or two won't hurt. Being in the stretch limo, that in itself is no big deal. In fact, I almost didn't get in when it pulled alongside of me, not liking ostentation or confinement, both of which that excessively long limo seemed to embody. But there I was, in the back seat and sitting with the fast-talking deal-maker. And there was Hitler. To be precise, four Hitlers. Inflated. Staring at me. I stared back, unable to close my eyes or move my head. I was listening to the deal-maker's business pitch and staring at the four inflated Hitlers. I looked for a sharp object, but everything, at the time, seemed to be blunt, including my thoughts.

Financial figures were being thrown at me. The deal-maker thought I would be perfect for the job, a well-read, historically-minded, intelligent university student, and someone had given me the highest recommendation. Who? I asked. Someone at the university was the most he would reveal. My history professor? Another student in my class? Who? I knew my Hitler, he said, and I told him that I had been doing research on Hitler and Nazi Germany only since the beginning of the semester, and using secondary sources, nothing primary or original – what kind of expert could I be? The deal-maker discounted my modesty and said my knowledge of Hitler was great, the envy of the most experienced historians. When I first had the dream, I was nearly finished with the history essay on the Führer. It was a very difficult essay for me to write, the only time I had to ask for an extension. I was a twenty-year-old middle-class kid trying to comprehend historical evil, and sincerely wanting my essay not to be just another undergraduate essay.

I waited for the four Hitlers in the back seat of the stretch limo to start speaking. I assumed it would be in German, but hell, it could have been any language. Hitler had halitosis, I said to the deal-maker. I must have read that while I was doing my research – but it became important to me in the dream. Halitosis Hitler the megalomaniac, I said to the deal-maker over and over, trying to enunciate clearly, and he told me that the inflatable dolls weren't going to have scented breath, as if I was being lewd or preposterous. He started throwing more figures at me: cost per unit, potential sales, world-wide distribution. Hitler, the deal-maker revealed pompously, would be the first in a successful line of inflatable dolls. Other big historical figures. There was no end to the business possibilities. "Combine an excellent product with aggressive marketing, and success follows," he said. I wasn't impressed and told the deal-maker his idea was more suitable for trite wax-museum stuff. Or warped tabloid stories. Not inflatable dolls. He was insulted. He offered me one of the inflated Hitlers, as a sample, a token of his appreciation for my knowledge about the Führer, and I told him I had no place in my room to put an inflated – or a deflated – Hitler.

Finally I was able to take my eyes off the deal-maker and the inflated Hitlers and I saw the back of the driver's head. His uniformed back. I imagined it was you know who, but I knew that was impossible. Even in my dream I knew that my subconscious was being influenced by the books I had been reading and the essay I had been trying to write. But I was in the back seat of a stretch limo with a fast-talking deal-maker and four inflated Hitlers that were the exact size of the genuine article, in the deal-maker's enthusiastic description. "Good my mother and father can't see me," I mumbled.

"You want to cut your parents in on the deal?" the deal-maker said, and I told him he should peddle his deal in Hell, but added that they might have higher standards than those in the nether regions. I've never undergone psychoanalysis, but if I ever do, I'd get right to my dream.

"Stop this vehicle," I said. "I have a class to go to, an essay to get done." The deal-maker told me he wasn't finished with his business proposal and I said I was finished listening to his idiotic nonsense. "Tell your driver to stop," I said, and the deal-maker told him to speed up. I tried the door but it was locked. Ostentation and confinement. This was a trap, I was thinking, I'll never be able to get out of the limo. The deal-maker didn't seem strong or large – smaller than the inflated Hitlers – but he was seated and it was difficult to tell. But I wasn't someone who resorted to fighting or violence, wouldn't allow myself to resort to violence, even in my dream.

"Where are you taking me?" I demanded to know.

"Don't you want to be one of my executives?" the deal-maker said.

"I'm not going to peddle inflatable dolls," I said emphatically.

The deal-maker offered me a very high starting salary. Rubbing his hands together in an obnoxious kind of gleefulness, he said, "A clever, educated, ambitious Jewish lad like you as one of my executives will get us international publicity, will catapult sales."

I felt in my pocket, and there were my keys. Were they sharp enough? I wondered. The deal-maker told me about my good grades – in the dream, he knew every school grade I had ever received and rattles them off – about my background, my parents' background, and I was fingering the keys – to my dorm room, to my parents' house, my bicycle lock – finding the sharpest one. I'm having great difficulty getting the keys out of my pocket, becoming frustrated and anxious. Afraid he's going to catch on to my intention, I say, "Well, I know you aren't going to drive to Germany."

The deal-maker began to laugh, real boisterous, belly-shaking laughter. "You're an amusing lad," he said, ending his laughter. "Be an executive in my company. I'll make you rich. I'll make you a household word, famous, admired, revered."

"I'm a university student. I just want to get my degree, go to law school, and then spend my life defending people," I explained.

"Such tiny aspirations," the deal-maker said. "Reach higher, reach for the moon, reach for the stars, higher, higher," he encouraged, pounding at the ceiling of the limo. Just when I thought he was going to punch a hole through the roof of the limo, he reverted to his former imperturbable demeanour and asked in a subdued tone, "How much do you want, lad?"

I told him he could go fuck himself. I rarely swear, outside of
the occasional *damn* or *hell*, considering swearing a lazy form of
expression. But in that dream I swear my head off. I told the fucking
ugly stupid prick to go fuck himself and skip the candlelight and
foreplay. He smiled and said that everyone has their price, not indicating in the least that I had been bad-mouthing him, and the
imperturbable asshole leaned forward to pinch the cheeks of all
the inflated Hitlers. Real affectionate pinches. A few seconds later
he flicked a switch on the side of one of the Hitlers and it started
to speak. From actual Third Reich speeches, the deal-maker informed me with unconcealed smugness. Then he flicked a switch
on another Hitler. And on the third Hitler. Quickly the fourth.
There I was, cursing up a storm, in the back seat of a super-stretch
limo with four inflated Führers who were giving four different
speeches. *Auf deutsch.* It was Hitler's voice, or how I remembered
Hitler's voice from old documentaries and recordings.

The deal-maker was telling me to think it over, extolling the
limitless business potential of his proposal, the financial rewards, asking me why I needed to be a lawyer, claiming that he was giving
me the opportunity of a lifetime. I finally got the keys out, took
the bicycle-lock key − it was the sharpest one, I decided − and
lunged at the Hitler directly before me. What a glorious bursting!
The deal-maker screamed. I mean, he lost his imperturbability. I
went after Hitler number two. The deal-maker caught hold of my
hand and tried to get my keys away. "These dolls are the prototypes, the result of years of work," he stated in a booming, angry
voice. I got number two before the bastard got my keys.

"May I have the keys back, please?" I said courteously, even
though I wasn't feeling courteous toward the fast-talking deal-
maker.

"You have caused a great deal of damage," the deal-maker told
me, no longer enraged.

"Only half of your prototypes," I said, wishing I still had the
keys, or real long nails. Long nails might have done the trick.

"I should sue you for everything you have," he said.

"Sue to your heart's content," I said. "It would be a great trial,
a cause célèbre. I'll defend myself. Bring the evidence. Tape them

up and inflate them yourself, you hot-air bullshit con artist. Turn your fucking self into a line of inflatable dolls."

"You're rude," the deal-maker said. "I thought I would like you, but your behaviour negates any possibility of friendship."

"We all miscalculate occasionally," I told him. When I reached for my keys, he moved the hand holding the keys behind his back and said, "You won't harm the other two prototypes, will you?"

"My keys," I requested assertively. I was acting as if I had control, some bargaining power, although I was the one locked in the deal-maker's stretch limo. We were moving fast and I didn't recognize any of the scenery that was zooming by, didn't know where in the world I was. I asked the driver to slow down, and the limo picked up more speed. I told myself that if the driver turned around, and he was trying to look like Hitler, I'd pull his fucking little moustache right off.

"Here," the deal-maker said, and handed me the keys. "However, if you harm the other dolls, I will have you sent to –"

He didn't finish his threat. The two unpunctured Hitlers were continuing with their speeches. Resorting to courteousness again, I said, "May I return to my life now? I'm supposed to be at university. I want to do the footnotes for my essay on Hitler." I still had to come up with a title. It was critical I think of a good title for my essay, I told the deal-maker.

In German, the deal-maker ordered the driver to open the back doors, and the driver obediently pressed a button and I saw the little door locks rise.

"Such an amazing electronic mechanism," I said with as much disgust as I could spit out in a dream. The car stopped. "Where am I?" I asked.

"You will find your way home eventually," the deal-maker said. "You must pay a small price – a long walk – for your destructive actions. You are not in Germany, as is obvious." He laughed, not as boisterously as before, but an ugly, irritating laugh all the same, and moved himself between the two Hitlers that remained inflated, putting an arm around each one.

"Everyone has their price," the deal-maker said. "I couldn't find yours today." Before he could say anything else, I punctured one more of the inflated Hitlers and was pushed out of the limo, and it sped away before I got number four. I fell to the pavement, and it seemed like from a greater height than out of an automobile. I thought I had been terribly injured, but all I could find were scraped knees and bruised hands.

That's the dream, the way it slithered through my sleep last night. I'm always twenty, but some of the other details change. I've never punctured all four Hitlers but I intend to one of these dreams. I always yell after the limo, "Hey Hitler, you want to read the essay I'm writing?" I completed the essay in the middle of December. It had been due at the end of November. Initially, I was quite pleased with my effort. I worked hard on that essay, but I sure didn't get one of my best grades on it. C minus. Never told my parents about that essay's grade. I probably would have received a better grade if I had written about my dream. A much better grade.

ENDANGERED

TRYING TO IMPROVE THE WORLD
has led to the end of the world, at least the end of my world in
this beautiful rural community. I find this thinking both humorous and sad. Unfortunately, it's the sadness that persists. Twelve years,
a third of my life, was spent as a teacher in this place.

I don't want to cry, not here at the bus station, not with *them*
watching. I should be thankful there are only seven demonstrators
now. How did they know I would be taking this bus? I wouldn't
be surprised if they had a sympathizer in the ticket office.

In my suitcase I have a dozen of the books I'm taking with me
to show strangers in distant places. I'll talk about the need to help
the environment, and how frightening people can become when
their world is threatened not by pollution or the greenhouse effect
or pesticides but by ideas. I'd like to take out one of the books
now and wave it at the demonstrators, books printed on 100 percent recycled paper, but I'm certain they'd miss the irony of that,
and I don't need any more trouble.

I have to hand it to them, they are quiet now and well-behaved.
But I'll never forget their anger over *the issue*. What was the real
issue, anyway? The environment, the book, the welfare of children,
or was it me? Thinking back, the environment seems to have been
last on the list. Maybe I should have just kept my mouth shut, but
it made so much sense to confront the issues. It still does. But things
got out of control.

I'm not going to look into the eyes of the demonstrators; let
them stare at my back. I'm more concerned with how my students will remember this whole wretched mess in ten or twenty

years, when they have children of their own. *Ten or twenty years ...*
Ozone depletion, greenhouse effect, global warming, species extinction, overpopulation. I had stressed the urgency of the problems, the need to confront the problems now.

That I'm finally going to travel and write is some consolation,
a counterweight to the sadness I feel. If only I could get Kimberly
and my other students out of my thoughts; if I didn't love the town
so much.

At first, I had wanted to spare them. Childhood should be a
time for learning and laughing and growing. But my students were
being barraged by talk about environmental hazards and disasters,
temperature changes and rising water levels, rain forest deforesta-
tion and overpopulation. No matter how much I thought about
the threats to the environment, I still questioned how anyone could
comprehend environmental disaster on a large scale. Certainly not
the parents of my students. But the vision of the children, I learned,
was clearer than their parents'.

It was going to be just another weekly writing assignment. I
believed in the educational importance of the weekly writing exercises for my eleven- and twelve-year-old students. And it was the
students who were the ones who brought up the subject of the
environment during the Friday-afternoon current-events discussion.

I remember how one little boy kept saying, "stick the garbage
in your mouth," to a little girl sitting in front of him during our
first discussion about the environment. I had written, "Recycle!
Reduce! Reuse!" on the blackboard, and students were offering
ways to meet those goals. I interrupted the discussion with an attempt to explain what was wrong with that type of insensitive, rude
behaviour. Then the discussion about the threat of environmental
disasters intensified, despite my efforts to ease the anxiety of the
students. I decided that the best way the students could deal with
their fears was to confront them directly. Like looking a bully in
the eye, one of the students said, and another added that there were
lots of bullies threatening the environment. A third student said that
was a figure of speech, a "toxic" figure of speech. We discussed
recycling and reducing and reusing; listed alternatives and possible

94

solutions. After a little thought, I wrote on the blackboard: "What should be done to reduce the world's garbage?" Before the class ended I heard another "stick the garbage in your mouth" insult. Strange, that little boy's first essay was on the beneficial uses of compost. He became quite the little proponent of organic gardening.

I was amazed at the quality of most of the essays. These essays were better – or at least written with more feeling – than their earlier essays on exotic lands, or farm animals, or the advantages and disadvantages to living in rural regions.

During the next week's current-events discussion there were more questions and comments about the threats to the environment, more revelations of nightmares and fears about the world the students would be inheriting. To my surprise, the quietest student in the class stood up and revealed, "In some of my dreams, there are skin-cancer mutants so ugly you have to close your eyes." I'm no psychologist, but it seemed some of the children were deeply, perhaps dangerously, affected by the threats to the environment. So we started to compile a list of the "evils" that contributed to environmental danger, which included cars, overconsumption, overpackaging, greed, fossil-fuel overuse, pesticides, food additives, genetically modified foods, industrial pollutants, hazardous waste – I was amazed at how aware the children were of the threats. One student chimed out the slogan, "Drive Less, Walk More," and was soon joined in an enthusiastic chorus by the rest of the class. The first suggestion of an anti-car campaign was made and discussed. The next essay assignment was "If you could have your own television special, what would you say to people about automobiles?" I was even more impressed with these essays.

After the third essay assignment the idea of a compilation of the essays – for the students, for their parents, for the community – began to form in my mind. Another week, another essay assignment, and the idea grew. I discussed my idea with a local publisher, and in her words, the project sounded "hopeful and sensible and sane." She gave me a reasonable estimate on cost and suggested avenues for funding.

The idea of a book would not leave me alone. I actually began having fantasies about the book: national distribution with a wide readership; a statement to the future from those whose futures were most in jeopardy. And the wildest, most far-fetched fantasy of all: the book being read by politicians and corporate executives and business leaders, and somehow slowing down environmental degradation.

For the next essay assignment the students suggested the topic themselves: "Describe the world you imagine after the greenhouse effect has increased." As I read those essays, I began to appreciate the extent of the students' fears and our classroom reflected their concerns. During the first month of discussions, the current-events bulletin board was expanded into an entire wall, dubbed their Environmental Wall, covered with newspaper and magazine articles, along with drawings and posters by the students. Nearly a quarter of the wall consisted of a skull-and-crossbones mural, and underneath, the students plastered newspaper and magazine photographs of environmental problems and disasters.

As the weeks passed, I would get an occasional call from a parent, asking why I was giving the assignments. Parents told me they were being lectured by their children for all sorts of "environmental evils." More than one parent thought that the "Drive Less, Walk More" campaign was excessive. Another told me her little boy had told his father that he wished a famous environmentalist was his dad, which set off quite a family argument. A few parents congratulated me on what I was doing, but cautioned me to be mindful that these were children I was dealing with and changing the world was certainly a tall order. I still had not disclosed my plans for a book, not to the students or their parents.

After the fifth essay assignment, I told my idea to the students. My disclosure stirred a great deal of classroom excitement. The students' enthusiasm further encouraged me, and I became more confident about the project.

It took three more essay assignments before I finally made the decision to do the book, even if the money had to come out of my own pocket. Joyfully, I spent my evenings editing the essays, choosing illustrations done by the students, preparing everything for publication. I selected what I thought were the best six essays for each of the first eight topics, and wrote a short introduction to each section. I asked the students to suggest a title for the book, *their book*. It became the liveliest class discussion yet. The class narrowed down the choice to three titles, and Kimberly's suggestion, *Warnings from Our Voices*, won in a close vote over *Each of Us Is Responsible* and *Be Kind to Nature*.

I invited speakers about the environment to come to our Friday-afternoon class and they were all impressed by the students' questions and comments. I began to feel rejuvenated as a teacher. But my rejuvenation was not lacking its worrisome shadows. I was starting to get more phone calls from parents telling me that I was making their children's fears worse. I tried to be tactful and asked the parents to wait until the book was published before they made any judgements.

Four months after our first discussion, the book arrived on schedule – a miracle, the publisher joked – an ambitious print run of a thousand copies, to be sold at ten dollars each, the proceeds donated to an environmental organization. The students had earlier formed their own Protect Our Planet Club, and proudly wore "green" buttons to school every day. It wasn't long before I received a fresh barrage of phone calls from parents. With a great deal of patience I explained the aims of the environmental organization the students intended to donate to, trying to calm fears that I had created a classroom of wild-eyed eco-freaks. "My kid is so obsessed with the Green Movement that he blends in with the grass," a father said to me at the local Farmers' Market one Saturday morning.

At the well-publicized book launch, I sat with the students at the front of the school's library, a copy of the book on every student's lap, a TV camera and a tape recorder capturing the event. Pesticide-free apples and pure fruit juice were served; the students' art work decorated the library. The cooperatively written "Walk More, Drive Less" song was sung to the audience, much to the delight of the TV and radio reporters. I had never felt such pride.

97

Then, one by one, the less bashful students read their essays. I couldn't believe the size of the crowd. Or the emotions of the parents.

"Why don't you move to the Amazon if you're so concerned with the rain forest ..."

"Teachers shouldn't be instigators ..."

"No way you're going to change anything ..."

"That essay on overpopulation and family planning is not for my child ..."

"You've brainwashed the kids about cars ..."

Some parents removed their children before the book launch was over. One parent grabbed my arm and said, "This environment stuff is all the children talk and think about now. You've made my child obsessed."

I told the apprehensive parents that I only wanted the children to understand the world around them, to overcome their fears, and have hope. I pointed out that many of the essays emphasized the need to change wasteful habits, to be wiser consumers, to be more sensible about the way we conduct our lives, and the parents needed to set good examples. With an interviewer's microphone in front of her, one mother asked, "Am I supposed to be happy that my daughter can rattle off the names of a hundred carcinogens, and then tell me that's only the tip of the cancerous iceberg?"

As I grew more uneasy, another parent opened the book to one of his child's essays and read: "I'm so afraid I'll never have a chance to be a father. Extinct species and loss of arable land are terrible. There will be nothing left on our planet unless people come to their senses soon ..." This, the parent yelled, was unsuitable for an eleven-year-old to concern himself with. Another parent, whose daughter had written an essay about the dangers of overpopulation, told me that his child had suggested he get a vasectomy, for the good of the world.

I told the parents that their children had expressed their thoughts eloquently, but the father annoyed with his daughter's birth-control recommendation shouted in my face, "It's damn scary." The mother asked why there were so many skull-and-crossbones on the classroom wall and in the book. "If you believed in all this ecological doom-and-gloom," a parent said, "you'd be afraid to leave your house." All the time the TV camera and the tape recorder were going.

Long after the book launch was over, I sat alone in the school library and held back my tears. I couldn't understand why I hadn't foreseen what had happened.

Evening meetings over the book were held. Psychologists, clergy, and educators spoke to the parents. There were debates, accusations, furious arguments, letters to the editor, phone calls to radio talk shows. One meeting was so raucous and full of venom that I began to tremble and was unable to express myself adequately.

When Kimberly, whose moodiness was well-known, fell into long silent periods at home, spending her time drawing blank landscapes and gas-masked people, her parents withdrew her from school and publicly accused me and the book of bringing on their daughter's condition.

The controversy over the 150-page book would not subside. I stopped listening to the phone-in shows, I stopped reading the letters to the editor, and I made excuses to avoid the meetings and media interviews.

It became harder and harder for me to teach as my effectiveness was questioned, not just by anxious parents, but also by my colleagues and the principal of the school. It was as if I were personally attacking the town — and the locals were being blamed for the world's ills. It was as if I were the one who was ready to contaminate the supply of air, pollute the water ... I was told that if people stopped driving cars, the economy would fall apart. I was asked why my marriage had fallen apart and my wife had left the town four years ago. Details of the divorce were made public. We simply didn't love each other any longer, I tried to say.

I became nervous and irritable, even cried at times when I was alone in my apartment, and began to fear that I might be heading for an emotional breakdown. Just remaining cheerful in front of my class took more energy than I thought I possessed. I found it devastatingly ironic that I had been able to deal with the frightening statistics and horrid environmental scenarios without anywhere near the emotional turmoil I was experiencing now.

99

I began to have nightmares. Not about the threats to the environment, but about my job, my life. I still loved the town and the children, and I tried to think of reasons to stay and fight. I found myself avoiding discussion of the environment, even when the students initiated the topic. After the spring school break I started calling in sick, missing at least a day of school every week, and avoiding people altogether after school hours. For the first time in my life, I took tranquillizers.

With less than a month left in the school year, I informed the principal that I would not return to teach in September. He said that he wasn't surprised, and accepted my resignation without objection. I told him I was going to see the world – I already had a flight booked to England. Airplanes, he mentioned, used a great deal of fossil fuel.

My last three weeks of teaching were as tense and close to hell as I ever want to get. I was unable to explain the truth to the students for my leaving, that I was trying to save myself. By the time I was ready to leave, nearly 900 copies of *Warnings from Our Voices* had been sold and a second printing was planned.

AS I WAIT TO BOARD MY BUS TO THE CITY, I can no longer keep from crying. I'm going to miss my students more than I can describe. I do intend to return one day, and talk to them when they are adults and have children of their own. I'll talk to them about the town and the world and the environment. Maybe then I'll find out if me being a teacher made a difference.

THE ART OF DRINKING

SEBASTIAN – THE NAME HE HAD
been using the last month – stepped out from the downtown pub
shaking his head, sad and perplexed, appearing as if he were reas-
sessing his life. Need to head home now, he thought. I'll find a
new drinking establishment tomorrow. Important not to go to the
same place too often. When am I going to learn?

Earlier, he'd been in the pub ten minutes, had already finished
his first beer and done two impressive performances, when the bartender pointed to the plaque over the bar – BRENDAN BEHAN DRANK
HERE, 1961 – and claimed that his father, as a young bartender, had
personally served Behan when the famous Irish writer had visited
Toronto. The bartender had said the same thing during each of Sebastian's three previous visits.

Then success: A patron standing nearby said, "I don't know
Brendan Behan from Adam, but I think you should have a plaque
put up for this fellow. Give him another beer. On me."

Sebastian expressed his appreciation, and the patron said, "Worth
it to hear you do your imitations."

A patron at the far end of the bar requested that Sebastian do
Charles Laughton and the bartender grumbled, "We heard it last
week." The classic-film enthusiast came to Sebastian's defence and
told everyone in the pub that he does an incredible Charles
Laughton.

Sebastian put his drink down on the bar counter, contorted his
face into a sinister expression and, a picture in his mind of Charles
Laughton as Captain Bligh in the 1935 version of *Mutiny on the*

Bounty, improvised a humorous speech about whether it is prefer-
able to drink beer or wine with spaghetti dinners.

"His Richard Burton is great," someone called out, and a few
other patrons who had seen Sebastian on other nights declared their
favourites: Humphrey Bogart in *The Maltese Falcon*, Gary Cooper
in *High Noon*, Spencer Tracy in *Boys' Town*, Al Jolson singing a song
in the very first talkie, *The Jazz Singer* ... The man to Sebastian's
left requested Lorne Greene, as Pa Cartwright, adding with gin-
and-tonic nostalgia, "I used to love *Bonanza* when I was a kid."

A more nationalistic patron, shaking his beer bottle above his
head, accused Sebastian of not doing Canadians, and Sebastian
pointed out that Lorne Greene was Canadian. "You telling me Pa
Cartwright was played by a Canuck?" the man said, surprised by
what Sebastian thought was an obvious fact. The artist in him responded, "I don't really worry where the people I imitate came
from."

A smiling, attractive tourist from England remarked that she had
an uncle who would do Winston Churchill at every family gathering, whether anyone wanted to hear him or not, then asked if
Sebastian could imitate women, and he immediately imitated Mae
West in *I'm No Angel*, followed by Canadian-born Marie Dressler
in *The Vagabond Lover*. After that he did a little of Mary Pickford's
role in *Coquette*, revealing afterward that "America's Sweetheart"
was born a short cab ride from the pub.

"Why don't you go on stage? With your talent you'd make a
fortune," an admiring fan said, motioning for the bartender to give
Sebastian another beer, and Sebastian had to admit that he couldn't
do any kind of performing professionally, profusely thanking the
admirer for his generosity. Unless he was in a drinking establishment, he could barely carry on a conversation, he was that nervous around people. In drinking establishments he was a convivial
soul. "You should see a shrink about your condition," the bartender
told him, and Sebastian countered with a masterful Montgomery
Clift as Sigmund Freud, even though his Montgomery Clift in *The
Misfits* or in *The Heiress* is stronger.

"Is there anyone you can't do?" the most drunk of the patrons
asked, and Sebastian gave his standard explanation: "After I've seen

someone on film or TV, with a little work I can get close to the voice and mannerisms. Not perfect, but fairly close. The person has to be dead, I've never figured out why. I'm inept at imitating anyone living."

In the middle of imitating Laurence Olivier as Hamlet, a powerful performance that had most of the pub patrons captivated, an extremely tall man walked to the bar, read the BRENDAN BEHAN DRANK HERE, 1961 plaque, and silently waited for the bartender to serve him. In a matter of seconds, this man was the subject of all the pub's conversations.

Moving near to Sebastian and looking up at the gigantic patron, a fairly tall woman, about six-foot-one, Sebastian estimated, cooed with affectionate curiosity, "My friend and I were wondering about your height," and the giant disclosed with almost religious fervour, "Seven feet, four-and-a-half inches."

The towering man was asked if he played basketball and he replied that he was too uncoordinated for sports. Then the magnificent words were uttered, but for the giant, not for Sebastian: "Let me buy you a drink."

The giant said, "Sure my lucky night," and Sebastian thought he heard an echo of words he had said many times before.

Sebastian started another imitation, but not a single person in the pub was paying attention to him. He ordered another drink, and even the bartender did not comment on his imitation of an about-to-be executed Sydney Carton, played by Ronald Colman, uttering the final lines of *A Tale of Two Cities* – "The original 1935 film version, based on the Dickens novel, my second 1935 film of the night," Sebastian said to an unreceptive audience. When he left the pub there was no applause or farewells for him.

He considered going back in for one last drink, but scolded himself that he should learn to heed his own advice and not go to the same drinking establishment too often. He would be better off at home, anyway, he decided. Earlier in the day he had rented a stack of old videos. He would watch one or two films before going to sleep. Already he was thinking about selecting a new name. As he started to walk away from the pub, he wondered if Brendan Behan had ever really drank in that pub.

MAKE-BELIEVE

SHE WAS SITTING ON THE CUSH-
ioned window seat, at the corner of the built-in bookcase that occupied an entire living-room wall, squeezed to one side by the two
people on her right: a large-shouldered woman and a narrow-faced
man. Donald saw her immediately when he entered the living room,
the way a stranger's face you mistake for a long unseen friend's face
captures you, startles the senses, then you realize it is, after all, a
stranger's face. Donald hadn't wanted to come to this party – too
many people who would be there knew him and his ex-wife as a
couple – but he changed his mind at the last minute, shutting off
the movie he had on his VCR halfway through. He had never rented
a movie like that before. The picture on the video-cassette box had
three outlandishly buxom women lavishing their attention on a
bald, bespectacled, heavyset man. He should have returned the awful
movie before he came to the party.

"Glad you got yourself out of that tomb of an apartment of
yours," said the host, Max, patting Donald on the back, and then
forcefully pulling off his overcoat. "Two full years living in sin, do
you believe it?" Max said – did he ever stop telling people he and
Jennifer weren't married; my mother, bless her eighty-year-old heart,
still calls it living in sin, and heck, I love that description – and
inspected him, as if attempting to determine what was different,
when it was the same old Donald.

"Go in there and have a good time," Jennifer, the woman Max
lived in sin with, said. Donald had gone out with her years ago,
while he was still married, and he wondered if she had ever told
Max. Their affair ran its course in a month, a lustful, furtive, im-

moderate month – he had never had sex in a car when he was young, and they used her car as if it were a compulsory motel room. Andrea, his wife, knew, but said nothing. His marriage lasted another three years. Andrea's story, when she bothers with a matrimonial post-mortem, is that they had outgrown each other. Married too young, and simply outgrown each other. Donald always thought of pants that were too short when Andrea said that. He hadn't seen or talked to his ex-wife in weeks – it wasn't that they weren't still on speaking terms, on the contrary, she was friendlier after the split up than he could ever recall; yet every word he said to her felt excessive and painful – but a friend had called him that morning and said he had driven her and her friend to the airport, a well-deserved vacation, wouldn't I love to be going to Paris this time of year. It was from the same informative friend that Donald had first heard that his ex-wife was seeing someone new, a man young enough to be her son. He found out that the man was only nine years younger than she. Their son was seventeen and their daughter was fifteen, both away at private school. The divorced couple was dividing the cost of their children's education in half; Andrea offered to pay more than half, she did earn more than he did, but Donald insisted on fifty-fifty. Young enough to be her son, indeed.

Jennifer led Donald to the kitchen and poured him a glass of white wine, without asking what he wanted, or if he even wanted a drink. She poured herself a glass of wine, and clinked glasses with him: "My dreamboat is having a difficult time being dreamy," she said, and drank all the glass. "He can't get an erection to save his life …" She was about to reveal more, when Max walked into the kitchen with another guest. "Get out of your shell," Jennifer said, and gently pushed Donald toward the living room. "We'll talk later."

All the faces in the living room were familiar, from work, from other social functions, except hers. And her hair; he could easily pick out four colours, and there were two or three more blended in. He couldn't recall the last time he had been so curious about a person, felt such a fascination. If either of his two children, when they were still a family, brought home a young friend with hair like hers, he would have questioned her influence on them.

Donald went to the large-shouldered woman, and asked her how she was, and the woman's face seemed to lengthen, snarling at him. That's right, one of his wife's closest friends. What confidences did they share? Maybe, in private, it was more than they had outgrown each other. He wanted to defend himself, but he didn't know from what charges or accusations. The narrow-faced man remarked that he hadn't seen Donald in six months, and the large-shouldered woman said that Andrea had blossomed incredibly the last half year. She left on vacation this morning. I know, Donald said, grappling with a smile that he wanted to be relaxed and untroubled, feeling himself trying out several unsuccessful smiles. "Can you imagine Andrea strolling down the Champs Élysées?" he heard a woman standing near the window say. Her husband added, "Paris will get the amorous juices flowing again." Had they been discussing him and his ex-wife even before he had entered the room? They must have seen him coming in the front door, Max ripping away his coat, Jennifer dragging him into the kitchen. The large-shouldered woman, he decided, looked like one of the three women featured in the video he had been watching, and he wanted to throw this observation at her. He would have walked away – wasn't he expert at fleeing indelicate situations, extricating himself – but he feared that if he stepped too far from the window the unusual woman would disappear. He estimated that she might be twenty-five years younger than he, and certainly the youngest person he had seen at the party. He did pick out a fifth and a sixth colour in her hair. But she didn't have any makeup otherwise, a fresh, most pleasant face.

The narrow-faced man said he was going to get himself another brewski – Donald recalled how Andrea, after a party, years ago, had gone on about how she hated when men said *brewski*, and he had argued that women used that expression also, and they wound up arguing over the term and its use, as if it were a theological debate. A nice, cold brewski, the narrow-faced man repeated, and asked the two women on the window seat if they wanted

107

anything. The large-shouldered woman said red wine, and the other woman shook her head no. How did her voice sound? When the narrow-faced man stood, Donald wanted to plunge into his seat, but remained standing. He thought of asking his ex-wife's friend to leave, to offer her a bribe, but the woman seemed welded to her seat.

"Your divorce finalized yet?" the large-shouldered woman asked. His ex-wife had been the one with the quick reply, able to handle herself verbally. He always thought of what to say too late.

"All final and official," Donald said. "Etched into the eternal void ..."

"What a poetic description," the large-shouldered woman said. She called to a divorced friend across the room, and asked if she ever considered her divorce etched into the eternal void.

"I was married once," the other woman said. He smiled at her assistance; he found her voice lovely. "For less than a month. We had it annulled."

"I was married for nineteen years," Donald said, seeming to make a sullen confession.

"I remember your fifteenth-anniversary party," the large-shouldered woman said, an ah-ha, gotcha recollection. "Subdued was the predominant mood, I recall ..."

"I'd prefer an intense, brief embrace rather than protracted unhappiness," the unusual woman said to the large-shouldered woman, who responded, "Whatever turns your romantic crank."

The woman stood up, and she was taller than Donald had thought. As tall as he was, not that he was tall. Average, he liked to think of himself as of average height. "We're virtually the same height," he said, and wished he hadn't made that remark.

She ran her hand across the top of his head to the top of her head, back and forth several times. "Pretty much exact," she said. "I have a brother who's a giant. The only one in our family over six feet and he's just under seven feet."

"I bet he can easily slam dunk."

"My brother is totally klutzy," she said, and walked over to the end of the large bookcase.

"You're not leaving?" Donald said, moving in her direction.

"I need to stretch."

He stood next to her, smiling and looking at her through his glass.

"I had the window seat to myself, till those two invaded my space," the woman said.

"Space invaders," Donald said, and wasn't displeased with this remark, especially when she laughed, however slightly.

"They remind me of my parents, only they dress better. My parents are the worst dressers in the world."

The man looked down at what he was wearing.

She touched his sports jacket and told him he looked fine, some-   109
where between debonair and casually enchanting.

"Where do you know Max and Jennifer from?" Donald asked, running a finger across the spines of some books.

"I'm doing volunteer work at the food bank. Jennifer's been very nice to me. I don't really know anyone else around here."

He wanted to ask her personal questions, know her age, but he didn't want to reciprocate. He should have worn a nicer sports jacket, Donald thought, not this ragged old thing. "Was it difficult getting the annulment?" he asked.

"I get depressed thinking of that."

"Marriage isn't my favourite topic either."

"I'm never getting married again."

"I doubt if I'll ever give it another try."

"You're not sounding definite."

He raised his right hand and said, "I swear to all these books that I will never enter holy wedlock ever again."

"Therefore we cannot be married together," she said, and kissed him on the mouth. He pulled away, and turned to see who was watching him in the living room. He held out his glass, as if to say, See, I didn't spill any.

"Did I embarrass you?"

He wanted to kiss her back, to argue that he had been less in-hibited when he was younger — how much younger? He wanted to say he felt like a kid inside, that growing older was only an imposed calendar calculation. Andrea had said that. "No, I'm not embarrassed. Overjoyed. Overjoyed is what I am."

She kissed him again, and he closed his eyes, didn't pull away. He knew they was being watched. Everyone in the living room was watching them. The man was probably back with his brewski, and was probably nearly finished with it. The large-shouldered woman was probably taking notes, preparing to give a report to his ex-wife, to the world. My God, I'm not married, I'm single, Donald reminded himself. He thought he heard Max's and Jennifer's voices. He didn't know if the woman he was kissing had her eyes open or not, but he didn't want to open his. Donald told himself he would allow the woman to end the kiss. Had he ever kissed anyone this long? Her tongue danced in his mouth. He imagined himself in poorly fitting pants, pants he had outgrown, and with an erection. He wanted to put his glass down, but couldn't reach the bookcase. He didn't know her name. But he knew she had an annulment. Not when. Not from whom. Not why. As she kissed him, that question latched onto his thoughts: Why had she gotten an annulment?

The kiss ended. Whistles, hoots, clapping. Donald opened his eyes but he didn't want to look into the living room. He was facing the bookcase, not seeing the titles. Had Max and Jennifer told the woman to do this? He never appreciated their earthy sense of humour, but they wouldn't go this far. He was only semi-erect. He glanced down and saw that it wasn't noticeable. He felt the woman take his hand. They were holding hands in the living room. He wanted to act drunk, giddy, irresponsible, but he didn't even know how to do that properly.

Donald looked out into the room. Only a few pairs of eyes met his. He turned to the woman and said, "I hope I'm not too old for kissing a too young woman at a party."

"I wouldn't call thirty-one too young," she said, and Donald felt both relieved and disappointed.

"You look more like twenty-one," he said.

"My mother is in her late fifties and looks about forty. My father, on the other hand, looks seventy-five, when he's not much older than my mother …"

"Thirty-one is actually a very good age. At least I'm much younger than your parents. I'm forty-eight," Donald said. He wished he were wearing a hat or a cap now. Andrea said he looked younger with a hat on, that his thinning hair added a few years to his appearance. Seventeen years older than the woman, he thought ... almost like Andrea and her young lover ... Except that Andrea was forty-three, and the man was thirty-four.

"Is that ordinary, usual behaviour?" he asked, pointing to his lips, not daring to touch them as though a touch could erase the extraordinary sensations the woman had given him.

"Would it matter to you?"

"Trying to make small talk. I'm terrible at small talk."

"This isn't a job interview or an audition. That's when I get nervous."

"You an actress?"

"Yes. No. In and out of that incarnation ..."

"Were you acting before? When you kissed me."

"You know why I kissed you?"

He shrugged his shoulders, looked sheepish, confused.

She moved closer to him, stared at his face for a few seconds before she spoke: "Because a couple of months ago I almost died, and I didn't die, and I refuse to be afraid ..."

Did he want to know anymore? His son had almost died when he was seven, hit by a car, but he recovered, and you would have to observe him closely to detect that his walk wasn't quite right.

Donald went to touch her hand, and she withdrew it.

"What's wrong?"

"You want protracted happiness?"

"I want ... I want to sit somewhere quiet with you, and talk."

"I have to leave."

"I'll get my coat."

"I can't see you."

He pointed to his lips again, was going to say something about the kiss.

"That was our intense, brief embrace."

She began to walk away from him and he grabbed her arm. The woman looked at Donald, but made no attempt to pull her arm away. "You capturing me?"

"Sorry," he said, releasing her arm. "I didn't hurt you, did I?"

She held her arm toward him: "You could kiss it better, if you don't get intense about it. A medicinal kiss ..."

He wanted to kiss her arm the passionate way she had kissed his mouth, but he kissed it gently, the way he would kiss a bruise or injury of his daughter or son when they hurt themselves as children. Still holding her arm, he said, "If you're hungry, we could go out to eat." When she didn't answer right away, he sweetened the offer: "Any restaurant in the city. Any type of food."

"I'm going home. To be by myself."

"How do I contact you?"

"Not a good idea."

"That's not fair," he said, reaching into his back pocket for his wallet.

"I hope you're not going to give me a business card."

He was, he was going to give her his card. With his former home telephone number stroked out and the telephone number of his apartment substituted. "I was going to give you the key to my heart," he said, and finished his wine, wanting to spit his stupid, idiotic words into the empty glass ... *the key to my heart*.

Jennifer came by and asked the woman if she was enjoying herself; she called her Phoebe. Then she tried to lead Donald away, saying she had to confer with her dear friend. Later, he said, and when Jennifer persisted, he told her that he and Phoebe were having an important conversation. "I thought you didn't like men, Phoebe," Jennifer said as she walked away.

Donald stood silently, his expression pleading for an explanation.

"Jennifer tried to fix me up with her brother and that's the way I dealt with it."

"Her brother is a nice man."

"I didn't want to go out with him."

"You don't want to go out with me, either."

"Intimacy gives me problems."

"We wouldn't have to be intimate," he said, realizing he still had an empty glass in his hand.

"You should get yourself another drink," she suggested.

"I could get you one, Phoebe?"

"Phoebe isn't my real name. It's the name I gave myself after I got out of the hospital."

"How long were you in the hospital?" he asked.

"Could we talk about another topic?"

"Of course ... certainly."

"Suppose I told you I killed my boyfriend ... that we were never really married ... there wasn't an annulment –"

"Killed as in murdered?" he asked.

"Killed as in murdered," she said, and smiled, started and stopped a laugh. She put on her coat, told him that she would meet him for a coffee later that night, at eleven-thirty, mentioned a down- 113 town coffee shop she liked, and left the party.

Donald didn't meet her at the coffee shop. He stayed at the party and listened to Jennifer pour out her unhappiness and frustrations to him. That night he thought about the young-looking thirty-one-year old woman with the multi-coloured hair, decided he had made a prudent decision in not meeting her, and dreamed that they met by chance in Paris, and his ex-wife saw them kissing, and shouted at him that he was an adulterer; he turned to his ex-wife and told her they weren't married any longer, and when he turned back to the woman, she was gone. But a week later he had another dream that he was in Paris, except that the woman was with him throughout the dream, and kissed him as intensely as she had at the party. And when he awoke in the morning, he considered it one of the most marvellous dreams he had ever had.

A SECLUDED ABODE
OF SENSEFULNESS

Rosalind stood outside the door to what used to be her sewing room and tried to imagine what her daughter and her daughter's boyfriend were doing. For a little over three years Rosalind had not gone into the room; she had removed her sewing machine and furniture, put them into the spare bedroom, and that became her sewing room. The old sewing room was the one her daughter had wanted – wanted as her own secluded abode of sensefulness, those were the words her daughter as a seventeen-year-old had spoken, crying, frighteningly thin, scars she refused to explain on her face and arms and legs. The old sewing room was at the rear of the house and led to the back porch, which in turn led to the tree-filled backyard. That would be her room exclusively, no one would be allowed to set foot in it without her permission. An iron-clad, I-swear-to-God bargain Rosalind had made with her seventeen-year-old daughter. And her daughter promised she wouldn't run away again, wouldn't live on the street. The mother sewed the dark, thick curtains that her daughter requested for the former sewing room's three windows, and paid for the lock to one door and the daughter paid for the lock to the door leading to the back porch. What happens if I need to get in? Rosalind asked her daughter after the locks were installed, sturdy, expensive locks, and the daughter said, I need to have all the keys, Mom. If it were a real emergency, the fire department could break the door down. They're trained to do things like that. But one little key could save so much trouble and expense. The only way I'll come home to live, Mom, is if I have that room. The best memories I have are in the backyard. When Dad used to live with us. That was so long ago, my child. The mother remembered that her husband first told her in the backyard that he didn't love her anymore.

It was quieter than usual, but Rosalind could still hear the Gregorian chants. The most common music to emanate from the room, but the range was wide: jazz, blues, country, classical, reggae, gospel, old rock, new rock, hip-hop, opera, show tunes ... The volume varied, from barely audible to sounds so loud that the mother could not comprehend how two people could do anything in that loudness unless they were wearing earplugs. What she did know was that they were in the room, preparing themselves. Her daughter and her daughter's boyfriend. They wanted to look as much alike as possible. They had a resemblance to begin with. Facially, not their bodies. Her daughter was thin and he was heavy. They were the same height, though. Now, unless you are very close to them, close enough to touch, it was difficult to tell them apart. She had to gain forty pounds and he had to lose forty pounds. Thank God her daughter didn't decide to gain eighty pounds, Rosalind thought. Her daughter's boyfriend could have lost eighty pounds and Rosalind wouldn't have cared. He could have died and she might have had to hold her hand against her mouth to keep from screaming with joy. From the first evening her daughter had brought her new acquaintance home to meet her mother – Mom, let's have a really sumptuous dinner, he's precious to me – Rosalind had disliked the young man; she was already uneasy with him when during the middle of dinner, he said: I would like to show you my penis, as I show you my face or my smile, but we live in a world where such an act would be deemed as bad, and I would be condemned. In a different, more enlightened society ... If only she could blame him. Late at night, her sleep disrupted, she sometimes thinks of killing him. But she knows her daughter would find another boyfriend, another partner for her art. Her daughter had the idea in the first place, Rosalind knew, even though she told her mother, when she talked about her project, that they had the idea – revelation – at the same time. When you see our art, Mom, it will all be worth it.

Rosalind's ex-husband, who lives far away, on another continent – she thanks her lucky stars for that – explained Rosalind's concern away with the words *adolescents* and *hormones* during one of their rare telephone conversations. They split apart when their daughter was fourteen, but Rosalind thinks they should have called it quits long before that. Rosalind reminded him that they were both twenty. He still thought his daughter was a teenager. He has a new baby, maybe that strains his memory, Rosalind thinks. We're even planning to get married, he said, but why rush things. She was thinking that they had rushed things – he wanted to be a father, almost from the moment they had met. Rosalind, already thirty-eight then, had thought she would never marry, was uncertain if she ever wanted to be a mother. When her daughter was born, however, she wondered how she could have waited so long.

The man she has been dating, he's seventy, looks sixty, runs, swims, bicycles, says they should break into the room, get in through one of the windows, volunteers to climb in. Claims the art performance is a cover for something else, something sinister. They have an arts grant, Rosalind told him, the second one they have received for the project. Papier-mâché sculptures, music, video, dance, a multimedia presentation. Anything can be called art, he said. They've turned themselves into art, she said. A year they have been working on the project. A full year, not missing a day. They both have their jobs, earn their way, then come home and spend every spare minute on their project. They have taken the same name: Frolic-Dada-Some. Dada was an old art movement, but they want to make it new; it touches their souls and psyches. S-and-P art, they call it. They wear similar clothing. The way they speak, walk. I think they want to become the same person during their performance. They don't mean that for real, Rosalind's fiancé tells her. I think they do, she tells him. Then you'll have one artsy-fartsy mouth to feed. You shouldn't have let him move in there. What do his parents think? His parents aren't alive. Have you confirmed that? A child wouldn't lie about that. People can lie about anything. She asked me to sew their costumes. What an honour, Rosalind. Did you get an arts grant to sew their costumes? Why are they so secretive about their art? It's evolving, taking shape. She doesn't want other consciousnesses to alter it until they're ready to perform their art. Performance art. They're performance artists. You are being fooled, Rosalind's finacé said, and she responded, I don't question that I love you, don't ask for confirmation. Love and art are two different things, he said. Not for my daughter and her boyfriend. Even if it is art, who cares? Two twenty-year-old kids who spend most of their time locked in a room, dark, thick curtains always drawn. She doesn't go into the backyard. Yes, she does. Late at night. You know what they do out there? Preparatory exercises for their art. They're fooling themselves, fooling you. She's my only child. Maybe you should have left her on the street, at least she was performing a tangible service. Rosalind broke off their engagement when he said that, but he pleaded for forgiveness and promised to go to the performance, to keep an open mind. Rosalind wished her daughter weren't so involved in the performance-art project, but she knew she couldn't change her daughter's mind.

Frolic-Dada-Some female and male refused to perform any of their show for Rosalind and her fiancé, even after the man offered them money for a sneak preview, starting at twenty-five dollars and working up to a thousand. The male Frolic-Dada-Some was almost willing to take the money, but the female Frolic-Dada-Some said her art was incorruptible. You got arts grants, didn't you? Rosalind's fiancé said with a nastiness that made the female Frolic-Dada-Some say that she wouldn't let him touch her ass for a thousand dollars, and that they had received their grants for artistic merit. She did describe Skit One of their performance to her mother and the man. Skit One – their performance was divided into twenty-one skits – was "Mrs. and Mr. Oxymoron Fuck Their Brains Out on Stage, In Stages: Comedic Crying, Sad Laughter." It will be simulated, won't it? Rosalind asked pleadingly, and her daughter answered, We serve our art. What about the law ... the laws of decency? Rosalind's reinstated fiancé asked, What about them? Later, when he and Rosalind were alone, the reinstated fiancé said, When I was twenty I had urges and desires, but I had both of my feet planted firmly on the ground, in this world, and he banged one

foot after the other, several times, on the floor, like a horse trained
to count.

Frolic-Dada-Some female and male had rented a vacant store
downtown, sent out hand-drawn invitations, placed newspaper ads,
stapled and pasted posters around the downtown area, and gave an
interview on a mainstream radio station and another interview on
an alternative radio station, the tapes of which they intended to
use in their performance piece.

The premiere of the performance piece was scheduled for her
twenty-first birthday, eleven days before his twenty-first birthday.
They had constructed a temporary stage that occupied a quarter
of the rented store's floor space. Over a hundred papier-mâché
sculptures of anonymous, unsmiling people were situated around
the stage. Gregorian chants came from four speakers. Every single
one of the seventy-five folding metal chairs was filled, and two
dozen people sat at the foot of the constructed stage. Rumours
there would be live sex. Rumours there would be celebrities attending. Excitement in the air. A young person – male or female,
no one was sure – wearing a purple mask and entirely dressed in
bright orange, who refused to utter a word or change expression,
handed out professionally done programs, as good in quality as you
might get at a large commercial theatre. A beautifully designed silk
banner proclaiming the title of the performance piece, A SECLUDED
ABODE OF SENSEFULNESS, covered the large front windows of the
store; several other identical banners were hanging on the walls of
the store. The performance was scheduled to begin at 8:00 p.m.
Rosalind and her reinstated fiancé were there. They almost hadn't
come. They had heard the rumours, and Rosalind didn't want to
see her daughter do that, whether she was serving her art or not.
They compromised on the last row, and would leave if necessary.
Rosalind's reinstated fiancé, looking at the audience and impatiently
waiting for the performance to begin, said to her, who needs to
find life on other planets when we have these people? They're artistic, counterculture, Rosalind defended those in attendance. Most
of them are very interesting, creative people. The place, the mood,
everything is in perfect balance, a young man sitting in front of

them said to his friends, then one of his friends said, I hope they use condoms. There was no sign of the performers. The more past 8:00 p.m. it became, the more talking took place in the audience. Two police officers arrived, a woman and a man. You here for the live sex show? one of the counterculture people said loud enough for everyone in the audience to hear. The Gregorian chants ended. The conversations became louder. The police officers left. Good this is free, Rosalind's reinstated fiancé said, or I'd demand my money back. By 9:00 p.m. only a few people were left. Rosalind was worried that something might have happened to her daughter.

120   Frolic-Dada-Some female and male were in bed in their room, holding each other, congratulating themselves on what they were fairly certain was a successful performance. Tomorrow they would go to the store, which they had rented for two full days, and take the videos from the three cameras hidden in the room. They were already planning their next performance piece, incorporating the videos from this performance. In the grip of his excitement, Frolic-Dada-Some male asked Frolic-Dada-Some female to marry him, and she said she was married to her art. She disentangled herself from him, got out of bed, and opened the dark, thick curtains. It would be a commitment to our love and to our art, he said. From now on, she said, I want to keep the curtains open all the time.

EXECUTIONS AND
THE MEMORY OF EXECUTIONS

"HE USED TO BE A JUNKIE," I
hear one of the three male voices in the room say, but I keep my
eyes shut and don't move. It is a soft voice. The smoke in the room
is coming from his chain-smoking. I don't want them – the three
voices standing around me – to know I'm listening. I'm alert, hearing their every word, feeling their presence the way a deep-sea diver
feels the water at the deepest level. I'm only pretending to be asleep
or dead or numb; my actor's imitative skills can simulate any of
the three postures.

"How does a body survive that kind of life?" a high-pitched
voice says, little curiosity in his voice. He is standing the closest to
me of the three; as he speaks he is also eating something. Before
and after his words, biting and hard chewing. Nuts or crackers,
something solid, but I don't want to open my eyes to find out. Vile,
despicable torturers, I think, with loathing but not even a nudge
of fear. Nothing in this commonplace confinement distresses me.

Before being brought to this room, I was riding a bicycle, an
expensive racing bicycle of the lightest modern alloy. Riding fast,
breathing in unison with the wind. It was near a cliff along the
sea, the dark analgesic water inches away, but I did not fear a fall
into the sea. Death by drowning used to be one of my boyhood
fears, the frequent landscape of my nightmares. I used to be covered with fears: fears of death, of losing control, of being tortured
by pitiless adults. As I grew older and matured I passed from fearing death to imagining ways of dying, and eventually to an
indifference to death, my death, the deaths of others – strangers,
friends, lovers, I ceased to make distinctions. I remember what my

first supervisor showed me when I originally came to work under his jurisdiction, something he had written as a young man and was still most proud of as he approached retirement: "I have stood in front of countless firing squads; I have felt around my neck a hundred slip-nooses tied by a hundred hands; I have bitten into capsules containing the strongest poisons ..." It took me years to understand what he had meant, the feelings behind the words, his complete lack of cynicism or unease with life.

"The ways to kill a person are innumerable; the ways to die are all the same." I wrote that five years ago, during one of my imprisonments – an imprisonment of deprivation and total isolation on the other side of the world.

"I knew a woman who slept with him," the animal voice in the room says – a voice suffused by a peculiar, difficult breathing. A sickly man, perhaps with a heart condition. He lights a cigarette, takes an audible drag, and coughs. The smoke in the room increases, but I've been confined in rooms with a thousand times as much smoke.

I will not open my eyes. I trust my senses more when my eyes are closed. Pretending to be asleep. Or dead. Or numb. Sometimes I really am numb. I have come upon corpses and thought about nothing out of the ordinary; observed lifelessness with the detachment of a tired battlefield surgeon or a jaded artist painting cadavers. Corpses, the stench of stale decay and even staler mystery, but my thoughts were unrippled, protected. I even stopped staring at the corpses, stopped wondering about their deaths, about their last thoughts before lifelessness. It was the image I was concerned with, nothing but the surface image. A corpse, I came to realize, has no history, no artistry, no compelling mystery.

A finger touches me lightly on the left buttock. Without any shock I suddenly realize that I'm naked. I don't feel cold or unclothed, but I am naked. Naked and lying face down on a large table covered by a coarse cloth, perhaps an old woollen blanket once used for picnics in the countryside. The finger moves over my left buttock, making a careful design, an outline of a distant star not yet discovered by powerful telescopes, and then the finger goes down the back of my left leg to stop at the top of my heel;

next a hand slaps the heel as if to discipline someone unruly, maybe a soldier who refuses to obey. I do not stir; my self-control is strong. I have endured torture before and uttered nothing. I have a life-time of training to withstand pain. I have never revealed secrets to any enemy.

"His file states he has a birthmark here," the animal voice says and pinches the skin on the back of my right calf. From bicycling I have well-developed, muscular calves.

"It was surgically removed," the soft voice confidently tells the animal voice.

"His face has been modified many times. Look at the photographs and medical reports in his file," the high-pitched voice, continuing to bite and chew and swallow, adds like a schoolboy answering a simple question in class.

"He still has the scars around his knees," the soft voice says in a raised tone.

"Of course it is him," the high-pitched voice shouts.

Do they know I'm conscious? Are they pretending not to know? I'm shrewd enough not to be tricked or deceived. The finger returns to touching my left buttock, new designs, a circle of distant stars. Let the finger do more, let it transform into a hypodermic needle, I will not move a fraction of an inch, will breathe only enough to remain alive; I know the science of breathing. Now there is the smell of pipe smoke. The soft voice has switched from his foul cigarettes to a sickly smelling pipe tobacco.

"The woman said he would take hallucinogenic drugs, then start to make love immediately," the animal voice says in a lewd way. The voice's lewdness becomes stronger: "This one could go on indefinitely. She stayed with him three days. The report is interesting, charmingly obscene, but she wasn't reliable."

"You sleep with her too?" the soft voice asks, also lewdly.

"That would be unprofessional, against regulations," the animal voice answers, and laughs wildly, as if being ordered to laugh. The finger touches my upper leg, a light scratching seeming to want to relieve an itch; without warning the finger is withdrawn.

"I personally know half-a-dozen men who have enjoyed her. No hallucinogenic drugs were taken by them to perform. It's in

I 2 3

her file, all the names, the places, transcripts of everything that went on," the soft voice says, his lewdness becoming an antiseptic officialism. "She was infected with ideas we could not tolerate."

I don't know who they're talking about. I don't recall taking hallucinogenic drugs ... or recent lovemaking. A finger presses hard into the small of my back. I am certain it is not the same finger as before. More of a claw than a finger.

"His skin feels hard, pebbly. Maybe they did something chemically to strengthen the skin," the soft voice says.

"A knife will still go through," the high-pitched voice declares. It is a cold statement, yet without threat. He is no longer eating.

"You'd have to push down hard," the animal voice says; his words are an emotionless challenge.

"So I would push down hard," the high-pitched voice whispers solemnly, and claps his hands twice for emphasis.

After the second clap, the animal voice orders, "Roll him over."

I feel a powerful set of hands turn me onto my back, but I give no indication that I sense anything. My darkness has been changed through my eyelids; probably a strong overhead light. Yet it is still darkness for me. How long have my eyes been shut? I closed them while I was riding my bicycle along the sea, expecting the crash, anticipating the explosion of skin and concrete. But how did these three find me? Going near the sea is unlike their usual behaviour. They took my cyanide capsule along with my clothes. Better to act dead than to be dead. I would kill myself in an instant if I believed in an afterlife the way they believe. Then without end I could ponder the consequences of my act. Commit suicide again and again, like jumping rope. Jump death jump death jump death ...

More smoke in the room. All three are smoking now. One a pipe and the other two cigarettes. I used to be able to distinguish different brands of cigarettes by their smells. My senses have lost a portion of their acuity. At parties, in those days when I still cared to socialize, I could impress people, draw them around me. I'd close my eyes and ask someone at the party to blow smoke in my face. Hardly a second of thought and I'd recognize the brand. People couldn't resist trying the test – those who didn't smoke would borrow cigarettes from others – and I'd get it correct nearly every attempt. I could entertain at parties with my amusing talent.

The three voices keep smoking. Smoke is everywhere, tiny clouds, I can visualize foul stinging storm clouds over the sea. Maybe I'll cough, as I did at parties while I was correctly guessing the brands of cigarettes. One of the voices coughs particularly hard, not the animal voice this time though; the soft, pipe-smoking voice. Coughing as language, linguistically impure, fierce, an animal in pain, but not too much pain. An image of a slaughterhouse strikes me; laughter and coughing coming from the slaughterhouse. Expensive foreign paintings hanging along the walls, both the paintings and the walls spattered with blood. Inside the slaughterhouse, the bespattered walls are art too.

In my youthful exuberance, when I first started making my reputation, I could withstand any type of pain, what would be unbearable to others. What a prodigy I was then. I reached the highest classification in my unit earlier than any person had before me. The faultless sense of smell. The imitative skills. The endurance. The ability to concentrate under all conditions, pure concentration; the three fools around me would call it mystic or spiritual, but it was an intense, total effort of the mind over the body. I used to look forward to being apprehended and interrogated, even though I never admitted this to my superiors – who in their right mind would? You would be considered a danger, a liability worse than the enemy, and summarily tossed into the sea.

"Kill him now," the high-pitched voice says, stabbing me in the chest with his finger.

I'm not frightened. I know that the high-pitched voice said what he did only to scare me. They won't kill me, not these three, not right now. They do not have the voices of executioners. During my life, I have heard the voices of executioners. Once you hear such a voice you never forget it. Corpses you can forget or grow hardened to, but not the voice of an executioner.

I've dreamed of these three, years ago. The most vivid of dreams. I know exactly how they look without seeing them: the soft voice, the high-pitched voice, the animal voice with his difficult breathing. I know how they dress and move and act, their smallest mannerisms, their least consequential gestures. If I painted them, I could include the tiniest details: a thread dangling on a uniform; a sleeve too long, food stained; shoes tied tight and polished to the colour of the night sky. All three are uniformed, I know this indisputably. The uniform of the enemy.

My mind puts me back on the bicycle – my favourite physical activity. Fast as I can pedal. Exertion, yet never fast enough, never close enough to the sea. I remember crashing my small bicycle when I was a boy: horrid scraping of both my knees, complications, the stay in hospital, operations, the anaesthetic-scented dreams of recovery. I lived abroad when that happened. What was done with my racing bicycle? Its light weight is a marvel of technology.

I was never a junkie, why do they keep repeating that? Now three sets of hands are touching me, my face, my body, twisting, poking, scratching. What do they think they're doing, performing an autopsy? They are minor officials: dirty uniforms, languid expressions, ugly as file cabinets.

I almost feel pain. I am almost ready to scream. But I won't. Rub my face in silk, rub my face in silk, that's what I'll think, that's what will keep me in control, block out the pain. I should chant the words out loud and confuse the three voices. There was a time when, as I was being tortured, I would think of cradlesongs and reading the skywriting of artful gods and picnicking on coarse woollen blankets under a sky of brilliant colour, that did the trick. It will be time to speak soon. To baffle them. They'll assume I am mad or delirious, or maybe they'll think I am cunningly feigning madness, trained to behave this way. They think they know all the pertinent facts of my life – my lives. "Rub my face in silk ..."

"We don't want you to say anything yet, friend," the animal voice says.

"We're not ready," the soft voice quickly adds.

"When we want you to speak, we will tell you," the high-pitched voice shouts directly into my ear.

Why do they say "we" – all three voices? *We.* A three-headed, ugly, file-cabinet monstrosity. I need to keep speaking.

"... Rub my face in silk ..."

"That's what he was saying when we found him," one of the voices says.

But I don't remember saying that before, not around these three voices. Perhaps in dreams, years ago. Once I had the most wonderful ability to recall my dreams.

"Shut up!" the animal voice commands.

"Speak later!" the high-pitched voice says with equal force.

Pain ... That's not a finger. A lighted cigarette being pressed down like a finger into my face. I must concentrate on being silent again. Silence is the real weapon against them.

I've seen others tortured, tortured into corpses, identity-less forms left far from the sea. I've choked on the smoke from fires set by the enemy. I've known secrets. I know secrets. I've never talked under torture or under pleasure. Cradlesongs, skywriting, picnicking ...

"He has a fever," the animal voice says.

The high-pitched voice laughingly shrieks, "Junkie's fever."

I hear a briefcase being clicked open. My senses are still receptive, even if they have lost past sharpness. Another cigarette being lit. A piece of paper being ripped.

"Why are we keeping him alive so long?" the soft voice asks, the breath from the voice pushing against my closed eyelids, not as a lover, but as a curious animal finding another animal in the undergrowth.

"He may know something," the high-pitched voice says.

"The woman he slept with claimed in her report that he didn't shut his eyes for three days. He paced around her bed when they weren't making love, still aroused. She watched for hours."

"Why the hell did she watch?"

"She wanted to see when his ardour would go away."

"How heartwarming, he appealed to her scientific inquisitiveness."

"Was she with us?"

"For a few months at the start."

"Where is she now?"

"She has fled the country because of what he has done – fled for her life."

127

That can't be true. Who are these three voices talking about? I can no longer differentiate who's speaking, one voice turning into another. The smoke has replaced all the air in the room.

I hear a door being pushed open. It is a big heavy door, like the door of a slaughterhouse. A fourth voice enters. Another cigarette. I know this brand. A woman I loved years ago smoked the same brand, in a room on another continent, a room that felt as confining as a diving bell in the deepest sea.

I sense the fear in the other three. The executioner is here. At last the executioner. If there is an afterlife, I can watch the execution over again. This execution will be better than the previous one. Strange how one gets used to being executed. When I was young and the sight of a corpse still made me tremble, and I feared death by drowning more than anything else, I never thought I would get used to being executed.

DISPUTES

I'M BACK IN MY PARENTS' HOME, NOT for our family's once-a-month Sunday gathering, but for my mother's funeral, and someone offered me a *kichel*, have a cookie, Jules, she lived over seventy years, had a good, full life, who's to understand why God took her now and not later. Then I heard someone else ask my oldest brother how he was going to vote in the referendum. *Kichelach* and referendums, the two have become connected in my mind. My mother died two weeks before the 1995 referendum, the latest one. It's the 1980 one that is just as vivid in my memory. In 1980 I was a university student, going to school in the States, much to my mother's consternation. I like to think those were better times, but I don't know. I hadn't started working my way up the corporate ladder then, didn't have a mortgage, wasn't married, and couldn't even conceive of myself as a father. My sister is playing with my son and my daughter, asking them if they like music. She's going to try to convince them to take up the flute, I know. Everyone is here, except my mother, who was in the house then, in 1980 ...

LEAH WAS STANDING RIGID NEAR THE CORNER LAMP in the living room and playing her flute for the family. Only her husband, Hal, was listening closely, seeming to conduct his wife with his forefingers in an imaginary orchestra. My two older brothers, Daniel and Murray, were sitting on each side of our father on a colonial-style couch — there's a different couch now — and arguing with him over René Lévesque and the referendum, but mainly René. My father claimed in a deep, authoritative voice that Lévesque was going to take the province to ruin; his two bearded sons – I was always clean shaven – repeatedly countered that Lévesque was the saviour of French Canada, the first real Canadian political hero since Louis Riel. The argument grew particularly heated when my father proclaimed that Lévesque and his gang of Péquiste fanatics were a threat to the Jews in Quebec – all nationalist fanatics were, he shouted, and his head-shaking sons retaliated with their own emotional arguments into each of his ears. My father recalled Quebec in the 1930s and told his sons about Adrien Arcand and his fascist thugs and the hatred for Jews in the air back then. Daniel, a teacher at a French CEGEP, and Murray, a producer for *Radio-Canada* who dreamed of being an influential Quebec writer, told him he was embedded in the past, that Lévesque was the future. When my father became frustrated with his sons' arguments he folded his arms over his chest and declared: "The heck with Lévesque!" He had already uttered the slogan twenty times.

Aunt Lillian and Uncle Herschel sat in thick armchairs opposite each other and were facing the colonial-style couch / combat zone. They shook their heads at what the three debating men were saying, but from their expressions it was impossible to determine who they were supporting. I was visiting for the weekend from Yale, sitting in a rocking chair, an electronic chess game on my lap. My perturbed expression indicated that the device was more than a worthy opponent. I was the only one of the group who didn't regularly attend the dinners on the first Sunday of each month at our family's house in Westmount.

My mother, a short, thin woman, entered the room with a trayful of freshly baked cookies, or *kichelach* as she liked to call them. The activity in the large living room, her living room, went on like a three-ring circus as she stood, waiting to be acknowledged. She surveyed the activity in the room and felt a wave of sadness. She liked it better in the old days, when her two oldest sons were still married and her grandchildren scurried around the house; both her ex-daughters-in-law, kids in tow, had moved out of Montreal. The family seemed to be shrinking, not growing as it should. She had already given me a lecture on choosing a companion carefully, that marriage was for life, that I should learn from the errors of my brothers' less than satisfactory matrimonial ways. She stepped toward me and held the tray under my chin. "Eat a *kichel*," she said with the authority of a mellowed but once tough drill instructor.

"The diabolical thing cheats. It's programmed to cheat," I said, looking at my electronic chess game, not at my mother.

"It's only a toy," my mother said sympathetically, nearly shoving the tray into my face.

"I'm not hungry."

"I made the *kichelach* specially to celebrate your visit. It won't kill you to have one tiny *kichel*."

I took a cookie and made a chess move at the same time, not looking up at my mother. "I'm playing at the highest level, grandmaster four," I announced to the gathering, explaining my loss. I held the unbroken cookie in my mouth as I spoke and I must have sounded like a comic imitating a drunk. I began to rearrange the miniature chess pieces for another game.

Uncle Herschel and Aunt Lillian each took a cookie before my mother could order them to eat. They bit into the cookies and declared together that Freda's cookies were delicious, their faces luminous with satisfaction.

On the couch, the three men were becoming more agitated, three sets of arms moving madly in the air like fighter planes engaged in a dogfight. Figures in Quebec history were praised or condemned indiscriminately. Chronology and good sense fell by the wayside. Montcalm, Papineau, Abbé Groulx, Taschereau, Duplessis, Lesage, Henri Bourassa, Robert Bourassa, Lévesque, the Roses, Robert Charlebois were praised or condemned as if they were sitting in the prisoner's dock in the living room and listening to the verdicts. 1759 and 1837 and 1937 and 1970 fused into the same charged moment.

"Eat, don't argue like *meshuggeners*. You have to argue on Sunday, one day a month the family is together?" my mother said to her two oldest sons and husband, giving me a condemnatory glance for not attending all the gatherings.

"The Jews don't have a single goddamn thing to fear from the
PQ," Daniel said angrily, amazed at his father's unrelenting para-
noia. "There's no secret society of anti-Semites hiding in the
Laurentians waiting for the word to attack."

"Quebec had anti-Semites in the thirties," my father said, pointing a trembling fist at a large picture window that seemed to have
a delegation of Jew-haters peering sinisterly through it.

"Look at the calendar in the kitchen, Papa. 1980 it says. You
threw away all the old calendars from the 1930s a long time ago,"
Daniel said, straightening the wrinkles in our father's suit coat with
gentle pats, trying to mollify his intensifying rage.

"It's the same! Fascism has one face but lots and lots of disguises."

"Eat, don't talk. You want to have a stroke on a Sunday?" our
mother said to her husband.

Each of the three seated men took a cookie with a fierce, combative gesture. They bit into the cookies as if biting off the pins on
grenades.

When my mother turned in the direction of her flute-playing
daughter, her son-in-law already had his arm extended like a young
boy eagerly motioning gimme, gimme. With a single scooping motion he grabbed six cookies, three for himself and three for his wife,
and said "These *kichelach* look *geshmak* and *zaftig*." Hal made a great
effort to speak Yiddish during these family gatherings, more so than
anyone else in the room. He was the only Gentile in the family
and worked diligently to act Jewish, not to be the outsider that he
was. My mother wasn't enamoured of him, to put it mildly, and
confided to more than a few friends that her smiling son-in-law
was hard on her nerves. She didn't care if he liked her cookies or
not. My father thought he was a fine young man, after all he was
already making $30,000 a year, had an office on St. James Street,
and he was barely thirty, but that was no reason to marry his daughter. He looked like a strong German athlete, my mother once commented, even though his family came to Canada from Norway at
the beginning of the twentieth century.

The tray still held another three dozen cookies as my mother,
clearing her throat, returned to the centre of the living room. She

always baked or cooked too much food, as if she were expecting a famished army. Again she cleared her throat.

"I've forgotten to ask you something very important," she announced loudly, straining to fill the large room with her presence. "And now that we're all together, I must ask."

Leah increased the loudness of her flute-playing to compensate for our mother's intrusion. The debate on the couch was threatening to turn volcanic yet no one was really worried. Once a month, without deviation, there would be an equally animated discussion, about one topic or another. I had seen arguments as I grew up and I had no reason to believe my father and brothers' discussions had turned docile in my absence.

"About what, Freda?" Uncle Herschel inquired, a piece of delicious cookie still in his mouth. He stood up and took two more cookies from the tray, then sat back down.

"Everyone should sit down. It won't take very long ..." Except for my mother, only Leah was standing and she kneeled next to her husband's chair, still playing her flute. He patted her on the head in encouragement.

"What's wrong?" my father asked his wife, turning from his disputatious sons, happy to have a momentary breather.

"What has to be wrong? I just have something important to ask while we're all together."

"Are you all right, Freda?" my mother's sister, Lillian, asked, leaning forward with concern. Lillian was the older sister by a year but Freda appeared at least ten years her senior. Lillian had been brought to Canada from Germany in 1938 as a teenager while Freda was not able to immigrate until 1947, already a weary woman of twenty-three who had seen too much. A year later she had her first child, determined to have as large a family as possible.

"Couldn't be better," she said and handed the tray to her seated sister, then brushed some crumbs off the front of her dress. She disappeared into a bedroom as casual speculation began about what "something very important" might be. In a few minutes my mother, having changed into slacks and a sweater, returned with a handful of brochures and a single silver pen that she was waving nervously.

"Listen to me before you say yes or no," my mother said as she reoccupied her strategic place in the centre of the room. She moved like a veteran stage actress in perfect control of her movements, using her body to convey subtle and not so subtle emotions.

"What's the question?" my father asked as his sons argued on, each lighting a cigarette and smoking like Lévesque.

"Please listen. At first people get upset. You should hear the excuses and see the faces." My mother made a distorted face that was a composite of all the unreceptive people she had encountered in the last week of canvassing.

"You feeling ill, Freda?" her son-in-law asked. He stood and extended his arms as if offering assistance to someone about to collapse.

"Sit! Sit!" my mother said to Hal; I never heard her call him by his first name. After her son-in-law sat down, she said to her daughter, "Leah, darling, could you play a little later? I don't need the competition."

Leah stopped playing with a shrill note, not finishing her song. "No one asks Kathryn Moses to stop playing," she said, pouting exaggeratedly.

"Moses plays the flute?" my mother said in confusion.

"Not as well as Abraham or Isaac," I said, still involved in my chess game, my expression now more hopeful.

"I'd say she's among the two or three best flautists in the country, Mama."

"Is she Jewish?" my mother asked earnestly.

"Who cares, Mama? She's an artist."

"*Who cares?*" my mother said, her hurt unconcealed. "A Jew cares." She glanced at her son-in-law with a forgiving smile, as if he had a disease that had pocked his Gentile face.

"The Jews are prominent in the entertainment field," the son-in-law said so ardently that his body quivered, then nodded approvingly at his wife. He was an expert at naming Jews who had made a contribution to society. One Sunday, when I was home for spring break, during a discussion of Jewish writers, he rattled off the names of forty Jewish writers non-stop, amazing everyone in the room; even my mother had been impressed. The next month, he gave each member of the family an Irving Layton book, *autographed*. When Daniel received his copy, he said the names Bjørnstjerne Bjørnson, Knut Hamsun, and Sigrid Undset, telling Hal that they were famous Norwegian writers, Nobel Prize winners for literature, 1903, 1920, and 1928, respectively. Daniel must have looked up the names the week before, just waiting to pounce on Hal.

"Not in hockey though," Murray said with a sarcastic twist of his nose, leaning back on the couch for the first time. "Name one Jew who's scored a hat trick recently."

"I don't know about recently, but Alex Levinsky did have a successful career in the NHL," Hal said.

"Don't bicker. Listen to me," my mother said, coughing until all eyes in the room were on her, and then saying, her face contracted by an apprehension that would make one think she was facing a group of irate and hostile strangers: "There is an organ-donor program this month and I believe in its value with all my heart and soul. Don't say no before you hear the facts," she said to the various expressions confronting her. Daniel looked like his internal organs were being removed on the spot; Leah thrust her flute into the air; I offered a booming protest about my body as shrine and squeezed my nose for emphasis. I wasn't quite as mature in those days.

My mother distributed a brochure to each person in the room as one might in a kindergarten class, still holding ten after the distribution. She fanned herself with the brochures and breathed deeply for a silent half minute. Then she dramatically read the contents of a brochure in her best teacher's voice. When she read she had less of a Yiddish accent than when she spoke casually. The brochure was in the form of questions and answers, and anticipated all the doubts and reservations the squeamish could have. Omitted, however, were any questions and answers concerned with Jewish burial customs.

"Jews should be buried with all their internal organs in place," I said, not being in the least religious or observant, but I had had a Bar Mitzvah, like my brothers – Leah had refused to have a Bas

135

Mitzvah, and I think my mother somehow tied this in with her eventually marrying Hal – and I had done a fair amount of reading on Jewish history and traditions.

"Jews also believe that saving a life is the most important thing. There is no higher *mitzvah*," my mother argued confidently.

"I think how the body is regarded after death depends if you're Orthodox or not," Hal added.

Murray read the bilingual brochure aloud in French, keeping the debate over Jewish burial customs from becoming too heated. "French organs are just as important as Anglo organs," he said after completing the reading, looking directly at our father.

"*Trés bien*," my mother said, uncertain whether her oldest son was serious or not. She could never understand her sons' senses of humour. Fortunately, Leah never displayed much of a flair for the comedic, at least not in her mother's old-world, European eyes.

"All you have to do is fill out the organ-donor card and keep it in your wallet at all times. Isn't that simple as can be?"

The organ-donor card was attached to the brochure, but the perforation along its border made it easy to remove. I detached my card from the brochure and said, "Never gave it a thought before. I once considered donating my ears to science."

"My body's unconditional, money-back warranty isn't up yet," Daniel quickly added, looking at me and Murray as if challenging us to come up with a better one-liner.

"Be serious," my mother scolded her sons.

"I'll sign, Freda," her son-in-law said and reached for the pen my mother was then holding in her mouth like a drinking straw. Leah tapped her husband's extended hand with her flute. "I want you with all your parts," she said, our mother certain it was not a joke, not from serious Leah.

"It's after he's dead, darling," our mother explained.

"Mother, really, I don't want to be morbid. Hal is so healthy."

"Let's not rush," Murray said, holding up an open palm like a traffic cop trying to stop an oncoming truck. Then to the tune of "I've Grown Accustomed to Your Face," he sang: "I've grown accustomed to my internal organs ..."

"Are my sons comedians night and day? Tell me, Sy, why can't they be serious for five minutes?"

"Humour is good," my father said to his wife. "How else do Jews survive?"

"In Israel, with jet fighters and bloody fast tanks," Daniel exclaimed, jabbing a victorious fist into the air, sneering at Murray.

"Please, it's not a joke. Nothing can be more serious, my darlings," my mother told her sons.

"It sounds most worthwhile," my father said, despite knowing he did not want his organs removed – the thought appalled him. He was afraid his wife would get upset, and when she got upset she cried.

"Sign, it's a *mitzvah*," my mother said. Her son-in-law smiled; he always smiled at the sound of Yiddish or Hebrew words. Pavlov's dog could not have been more reliable.

"I thought Jewish people can't have autopsies," I said, acting like I had said something intelligent in class.

"It's not an *autopsy*," my mother shrieked, making *autopsy* sound like the most obscene word in the English language.

"Pretty close. It's desecration of the body in my book," I told her.

"You learn that kind of talk in Connecticut?"

"Got to stay sharp to survive in the States, Mom."

"You could have gone to McGill and then you wouldn't talk this way."

"I used to swear horribly, in English *and* French, before I was intellectually rehabilitated in New Haven."

"*Gottenyu!* How much can a person take?" my mother said and pressed the temples of her head. "Just sign, everyone, before I have a nervous breakdown from all the jokes." She read aloud again the portion of the brochure stating that if potential donors no longer wanted to give up their organs, all those persons had to do was destroy their cards. She tried to placate her jittery family with the sensible proviso.

"It can be all or any organs you want to bequest. Write what is your preference on the card, there's a special space. But once your eyes are closed by death, they never open again."

"Did Aristotle or Plato say that first?" I asked, starting a new chess game after my most recent defeat.

"See, he should have gone to McGill like Daniel and Murray," my mother said, looking at the ceiling, finding yet another opportunity to reproach me for going to Yale.

"It was Spinoza," Daniel shouted, "as he was getting booted out of the fold, his Jewish organ-donor card taken away."

"Bull, any kid knows it was Descartes. I think therefore I've got internal organs to bequest," Murray said, reaching for a cookie after finishing his joke.

"That *kichel* looks a little bit like a heart ... a human heart," Daniel said, pointing to the cookie our brother was about to bite into.

"You know, these cookies are heart-shaped, more or less," I said.

"As if you know the shape of a heart," Daniel told me.

"You are giving me an awful heartache," Leah said, not pulling off her disgusted expression very well.

"I don't think I'll ever see anything as lovely as an awful heartache," Daniel responded in falsetto.

"You know that Joyce Kilmer was a man," I said.

"Who's Joyce Kilmer?" my mother said, in exasperation.

"The poet who wrote the poem that Daniel the McGill man maliciously mangled," I said, getting a little too carried away with my alliteration.

"Sign, and take the card back to Yale with you."

"What about the prohibition on autopsies?" I repeated, wishing I had a reference book on Judaism with me to show my mother.

"That's only for Orthodox Jews, I'm fairly certain," the son-in-law pointed out once more. His wife blew two random notes, a salute to her husband's erudition.

"I'm going to scream if my own family doesn't act serious like normal people. The thought, while you're alive and thinking, that you will be helping someone after you're gone is gratifying."

"The snake, in the Garden of Eden, that's who it was. *Once your eyes are closed by death, they never open again* ... such mellifluous poetry," I said, with a triumphant smile as I defeated my electronic chess game. "Checkmate, you creepy contraption."

"You could wind up in a tabloid writer who writes better than you," Daniel said to Murray, zestily punching him on each arm.

"Over my dead body! A tabloid writer does not get one of my internal organs. Can I note that exclusion on the card, Mom?" Murray said.

"*Gottenyu! Gottenyu! Gottenyu!*" my mother yelled at the top of her voice, but she couldn't stop the living-room banter.

"It's an unselfish act," the son-in-law commented, taking the pen from his mother-in-law and signing the card with a great flourish. Then he handed the pen to his wife. She acted as if the pen were boiling hot or contaminated. After a few seconds of thought, she quickly signed her name and gave the pen to her Uncle Herschel.

"You might wind up in a PQ body," my father said to his brother-in-law, pleased with his remark.

"There are worse places, Sy. Why can't you give Lévesque a chance? You forget so soon what you thought about Bourassa and his cohorts?"

"A conspiracy, you and my *indépendantiste* sons."

Uncle Herschel signed the card and gave the pen to his wife, who signed without comment and then returned the pen to her husband. He immediately tossed the pen onto the couch and it fell between Daniel and our father.

"See how simple and painless? How about my husband and sons?" my mother said.

"What's the point of giving one or two organs? I might as well throw in the whole kit and caboodle," Daniel said as he picked up the pen and signed. "I could outfit all of Lévesque's cabinet."

"As long as you sign, I'll even laugh at your jokes," my mother said, watching the couch intently, prepared to push anyone back down who might try to escape.

"You're a real humanitarian, Mom," Daniel said as he shoved the pen into our brother's stomach.

"That's how Cain killed Abel," Murray said, pulling the pen from Daniel and intentionally twisting his brother's wrist in the process. He signed and emitted a woeful sigh, sounding like he had just given away all his worldly goods to a charity that still wanted

139

more. "Pop, here you go. The burden falls on you to carry on our family's lofty tradition of uncomplaining generosity. We'll all wind up ensconced in nice warm *goyish* bodies."

"I'd rather have a screaming dybbuk in me for eternity," my father groaned. He hesitated, the pen against his chin, tapping a warning message to himself. My mother took two menacing steps in her husband's direction, stopping a foot away and saying, "Sy, you'll be helping both science and humanity. People complain there's nothing they can do, that the world's too big, but there are small, important things they can do, and filling out an organ-donor card is one of them."

"You've convinced me, I'll enlist," my father said and signed the card. Murray took the pen back from our father and signed the French side of the card.

"That's not necessary. You already signed one side," my mother said, cringing as if her oldest son had done something sacrilegious.

"Where have you been the last few years, my wife? Our son is paying homage to Bill 101 and the wisdom of the State. Besides, *chas vesholem*, what happens if the attending doctor can read only French or refuses to trouble his mind with English?" my father said, making no attempt to hide his contempt or anger.

"I hope that's not another joke. All this joking and I feel I'm listening to a *tsedrayt* comedy show."

"It makes good sense to me to sign both the sides. I feel subversive talking English here all the time. We should speak French once in a while. We don't want to be the enemy," Murray said.

"Yiddish would be fun, too," the son-in-law chimed in enthusiastically. "An entire Sunday of Yiddish."

"You should take the next boat back to a *shtetl*, Hal," Uncle Herschel said, Aunt Lillian laughing for the first time during the evening.

"Remember to keep the card in your wallet at all times or else it is of no use," my mother said, seeming to gain her second wind. She took the pen from Murray and slapped it into my hand.

I placed the electronic chess game on the floor and inspected the pen, looking for flaws.

"Only our genius who goes to Yale hasn't signed," my mother said, and it did not sound like a compliment.

"I'm still having difficulty accepting that it's permissible for a Jew to have an autopsy," I said and held the pen over my head in defiance.

"Jules, darling, everyone in this living room, all good Jews," my mother said, then paused as she looked at her son-in-law, who smiled at her as if he were just made an honorary Jew, "has signed. You'll be helping the world by signing the organ-donor card."

"You sound like I'm going to die before the clock strikes midnight. Let me think it over for a few years, Mom."

"Of course you will live to be a ripe, ripe old age, that's not the point. People have wills, don't they?"

"So why do I have to sign when I'm only twenty-one? I'll sign at thirty-two, like Murray."

"I've got ninety-nine signatures so far, darling. Please, you'll be number one hundred even. Make me happy for a change."

"That's it, a quota!" I exclaimed with the enthusiasm of Archimedes as I sprang up, shaking the pen furiously. "I'm not signing this card on principle."

"See, he goes to Yale, he's too good for McGill," my mother said, describing me as if I were a notorious criminal.

"Let the boy do what he wants," my father defended me.

"He's got a good mind of his own," Aunt Lillian offered in support of her nephew. "He was on the dean's list last year. You told us how many times, Freda?"

Leah resumed playing her flute. My brothers and my father continued their argument about the nature of fascism and anti-Semitism in 1930s Quebec; they seemed to resume the debate at the exact place they had stopped a half-hour before. Uncle Herschel and Aunt Lillian stood up and went to the front closet to get their coats, wanting to flee my mother's growing irritation and determination. The son-in-law started to whistle in accompaniment with his wife, who was now playing "Secondhand Rose." She could play all the songs from *Funny Girl* and intended to do so before the evening was over.

"Okay, okay, don't sign the card, Jules, my youngest," my mother said sadly and in exhaustion, unconsciously pressing her breasts in a theatrical martyr's gesture.

"Is it my fault I'm the baby of the family?"

"I wish I could have had more, then you wouldn't be the baby. Four children, nevertheless, shows Hitler."

"Ah no, don't bring up Hitler again, Mom. Hitler has nothing to do with organ donations and going to Yale ..." Making an angry face, I said without a trace of humour, "Did Mengele do any experiments with hearts?"

"How can a Jew talk like that?" my mother said, biting hard into a finger and turning away from me. She allowed the brochures she had been holding to fall to the floor. Hal was quick to pick them up but my mother was not interested in taking them back.

"Easily, Mom. I move my lips as my brain tries to make some sense of history."

"Please, Jules," my father warned.

My mother began to cry, at first delicate little sobs, then bursting into a body-convulsing torrent. Everyone in the room except me went to console her. Members of the family turned from time to time to give me an angry or berating look. My mother's crying increased. Leah jabbed the flute into my side, and I had to do everything to hold back from grabbing it from her. Whenever my mother wanted me to do something I was against doing, she made reference to Hitler, that me being alive and doing well was the way we kept defeating the hideous, odious Führer.

"All right, I'll sign, every damn organ I have," I declared gruffly, giving in to my mother's persistence.

My mother turned and said, "Such a good Jewish boy."

"Now you have a hundred donors, Mom," I said in resignation.

"My goal is five hundred," my mother said, her expression illuminated into a woman's overcome by the prospect of prosperity, walking to the tray to get one of her delicious heart-shaped kichelach for herself.

MY THOUGHTS RETURNING TO MY MOTHER'S FUNERAL, I asked my brothers, sister, brother-in-law, and father, one by one, if they still had their organ-donor cards. And I could hardly believe it, they all still did. When my two children get older, I might consider asking them if they want to sign organ-donor cards. I should also try to convince my wife, for my mother's memory. For now, I'll have another *kichel*, but these can't compare to the ones my mother used to make.

143

YOUNGER THAN THE RUSTING,
RATTLING 1975 CAR HE WAS DRIVING

As SETH DROVE ALONE IN THE RAINY
April night in the banged-up old clunker, listening to a baseball
game on the car radio, he kept reminding himself that he was back
home, that Toronto wasn't another foreign city. After living in other
cities, after playing minor-league baseball in so many temporary
places, Seth had thought that life would be different if he returned
to Toronto, four years older and wiser. Now he felt he had awoken
in an unfamiliar city. Seth, twenty-three years old and more depressed than he could ever remember feeling, might as well be arm-
less and chained for all the confidence he had that he could do
anything with his life. I never cried on the mound, I never did, he
thought, and angrily shut off the radio, as if the play-by-play com-
mentator had just described him weeping on the mound and then
shoving his manager away when the man came to remove him from
the game. Suddenly he realized that he was younger than the rust-
ing, rattling 1975 car he was driving, and the absurdity of that
thought jumbled his thinking. There were seven twenty-game winners in the majors in 1975, five in the American League and two
in the National League, he whispered, somehow wanting the information to push the sputtering car along. Seth knew his baseball
history and statistics. He had planned on winning twenty games
by his third or fourth year in the majors. A lifetime of baseball fantasies, now all of them as rusted as the car he was driving.

Earlier in the night, he had driven past SkyDome. Once he had
been able to imagine himself pitching inside any major-league sta-
dium; he no longer had any desire even to see a game. Years ago,
when he was one of the city's best amateur athletes, Seth used to

think that it was he who brought the city alive; now he knew the stupidity of that notion. Everything was going on despite him. With a stale persistence it all went on. It did not matter if he screamed or remained silent, rushed around waving his arms wildly or stayed hidden. If he died at that instant the city would go on without a moment of mourning. Seth felt severed from the city, amputated like a useless limb from its enormous body. He was driving in the city but failed to feel part of the city.

Seth searched for attachment, to graft his self to the city, to gain confidence and reviving breath. He was determined to fight his depression. To his thinking there was no one left but a prostitute as companion, the connection to the city. Around a small section of downtown he drove searching for a woman to be near – *the woman*. Even for a short time the companion couldn't be just any-one. Too many nights had gone bad and disagreeable for him. She had to be young and beautiful and not too touched by her profes-sion. Seth drove around and inspected streetwalkers, their umbrel-las raised against the rain. *Parasols*, he preferred to think. Parasols raised against the brilliant sun. Lovely parasols, lovely ladies. Seth desired romance, someone soft, someone who would appreciate him despite his inability to succeed as a professional baseball player. So what if money was exchanged – people everywhere dealt in money everyday; economics was an undeniable fact of life but he would not allow it to ruin his night. The dampness made him feel even lonelier, more apart.

The car's windshield wipers moved up and down in condem-nation, monotonous warning. *Fool, fool, fool,* bent down the garru-lous wipers. *No, no, no,* went up the wipers. *Fool, fool, fool, no, no, no ... fool, fool, fool, no, no, no ...* Seth drove on and received another smile, another inviting look. The invitations were varied, the ren-dezvous mysterious, the moment exciting. His body wanted a woman; his loneliness demanded abatement.

Seth, in a dark, recently dry-cleaned suit, was dressed as if he were going to an important social function. He had intended to visit his parents tonight, had started to drive in the direction of their house, but couldn't face them yet. He hadn't even told them that he was back in Toronto. First he wanted to find a job, to show them that his life wasn't falling apart because he had stopped playing baseball. That he had always wanted to be a great pitcher – not merely an athlete or a baseball player, but a great pitcher – seemed such a joke to him now. The last two weeks he had been staying with a friend – a friend who remembered how difficult it had been to hit Seth's pitches, and who had lent him the old car to visit his parents – to face them. God, he had said, this car is older than me. It's a collector's item, vintage, valuable, his friend had said. Had he made the majors, Seth thought, the first thing he would have bought with his big contract was a fancy sports car.

At a stoplight the depressed driver looked into his rearview mirror: his hair was neatly combed, his beard trimmed, and his tie straight. The windshield wipers continued with their unwanted entertainment. A car horn sounded to inform him that the light had changed. He would have realized it eventually – couldn't they wait? The honking was rude and rasping: *move, you idiot.*

Seth returned to the block with several women adorning it, others staring out from a restaurant's streaked window, not eager to exhibit their wares in the rain. Slowly he circled the block. The choice had to be more than impulsive. He could explain why his contract had not been renewed and his baseball career ended. He could explain about the injuries and subsequent operations. The car heater was hissing frantically and the borrowed car was warm.

A slender woman leaning against the restaurant's façade was the one Seth decided upon. He went around the block to think, to make his decision definite. Maybe he should visit his parents, he thought, or go back to his friend's apartment. Slowly he drove down a dim one-way street and headed for the block's east corner. The car couldn't go slowly enough.

At last Seth pulled over to the curb and turned his face to the selected woman's direction. In his effort to communicate Seth felt the breath escape from his lungs and he nearly choked with fear. What was there to fear, what? He breathed deeply, concentrated on the situation. Her face appeared pale and sickly, but beautiful, a damaged heroine.

The woman walked two steps toward the car and Seth rolled down the driver-side window as if the woman's limited movements had commanded the act. His thoughts became more disordered.

"You want a date?" the woman asked in a voice that sounded girlish to Seth. Her face looked even paler with the car window down. Such a fragile woman. So nice to hold in his arms, to kiss gently. She was dressed in a long grey raincoat that had the bottom three buttons open to expose taupe-stockinged legs and a blue, silky slip. It took Seth a few seconds to realize that the woman was not wearing a dress under her coat.

"I wouldn't mind having a date ..." The rain was entering the car and getting Seth wet. He squeezed the steering wheel and moved his head more toward the opened window. "I do want a date." The second statement was to compensate for the timidity of the first. He hadn't wanted the first utterance to sound shaky but it had left his mouth that way – damn traitor! The second statement was firm.

"Go round the block and I'll meet you a little ways up the street," the woman said and pointed to the one-way street Seth had just driven down.

"You can come into the car. It's raining." He genuinely didn't want the woman to get any wetter. She might catch cold. She looked fragile and pale enough.

"No. Do like I say if you want a date ..."

Seth couldn't understand why the woman wouldn't get into the car but he did as he was instructed, as if the woman had been an umpire during a baseball game. When he was on the pitcher's mound during a game in which he had been doing poorly, and that was hardly rare the last season, Seth had a recurring fantasy about breaking his left arm and being put into a hospital where he would be cared for by a beautiful, compassionate nurse. The nurse would soon fall in love with him and he would heal quickly. Then they would leave the hospital together, he able to throw harder than ever, never losing another game. The nurse would be exquisite in her white uniform. Kind and exquisite and completely in love with him.

An umpire's booming voice or the fans booing or his own teammates complaining would end the fantasy but Seth would fall into it at another futile time. As he drove around the block the fantasy returned to Seth and the woman in the long grey raincoat was the nurse.

When Seth stopped next to where the woman was standing, she deftly closed her umbrella and slid into the car, a look of relief on her pale face.

"April showers bring May flowers," the woman said without looking at the driver.

If he could be certain a beautiful, compassionate nurse would care for him, Seth wouldn't mind breaking his pitching arm ...

"Make a right at the light and go straight after that," the woman instructed the driver. "The hotel I use is on the left side of the street before the next light."

"We can go to my friend's apartment. He has a great music collection and he's not home tonight," Seth said enthusiastically, as if trying to impress a young woman on a first date.

"Sorry, but we have to go to my hotel or nothing. That's the way I always work."

The woman was acting jittery and Seth did not know what to say. The windshield wipers continued with their warnings and condemnations.

"Do you want a date or not?" the woman said after a brief silence. She looked at Seth and he lost all fear. He inhaled her perfume as if it were the most potent spring fragrance. With a dainty movement she reached her hand across the seat and lightly touched Seth's cheek: "I like your beard." Then she brushed her hand against his lips and he kissed her fingers. "You're gonna have a nice date," the woman said, and smiled at Seth. Without much discussion, they agreed on a price for a simple date.

As they turned onto the next street, Seth looked expectantly toward his passenger's legs, but the bottom three buttons of her raincoat were now fastened. Her closed umbrella was between them lengthwise like a wall through which no words could pass.

The silence in the car upset Seth, and he said, "This car isn't mine. My friend is sentimental about junky cars," forcing the words through the wall.

"I'd prefer a newer, classier car, but what can you do?" the woman said, looking out the passenger-side window, gazing into the night. To Seth, she was acting as if meeting an ex-minor-league left-handed fastball pitcher was a daily occurrence for her.

Maybe this was her first time working the streets, Seth thought hopefully. Maybe that's why she was acting oddly. Her behaviour was bordering on rudeness. Wasn't she supposed to be friendly to him? After all, he was her – Seth didn't want to think of himself as a customer, not this time. He wanted to announce to the woman that he was a major-league pitcher with a blazing fastball and sharp-breaking curveball, the kind sportscasters describe as falling off a table. While he groped for something appropriate to say, the woman rubbed the dashboard, as if she were dusting a dirty table.

"I was never too smooth at fielding bunts because of the type of follow through I have," Seth told the woman but she didn't know what he was referring to. He was thinking of an error he had made in his last game which had let in two unearned runs. Then he saw the flashing lights. Should he stop the car or keep pitching? He heard someone in the stands say, "I'm getting out of here, stop."

Seth stopped his windup in mid pitch and stepped off the mound. Had he balked? In the rearview mirror, he could see his manager walking toward the mound. Damn, was he going to be taken out of a game again? He turned to his right and saw the stands were empty, completely empty. How was that possible? he said to the angry manager, who seemed to be reaching into his pocket for something. Let me finish the game, he pleaded to the manager, but the manager said the game was over.

WHAT WAS THE ARGUMENT ABOUT
IN THE FIRST PLACE?

People had pretty much forgot-
ten about me, even after ten books of fiction, but then I haven't
had a new book out in fifteen years. I have been working on a
novel for those fifteen years. My *Finnegans Wake* book, I like to
joke, but no one thinks it's funny, or seems to appreciate that it
took James Joyce seventeen years to write. Mind you, years ago, I
used to call it my *Ulysses* book, but Joyce needed only seven years
to finish that one. Now people are talking about me, all because
an old friend's son who runs a reading series in his chichi art gallery downtown asked me to give a reading, a reading that has become more discussed than any of my ten books. In every paper I
looked at the next day, there was something about my reading,
including a headline that made me smile: LITERARY EVENT BRAWL.
It's been less than a month and I've given more interviews than in
the last fifteen years of being forgotten. Life, I've started saying,
sloshing the irony around in my mouth along with my coffee, begins at seventy-five.

So, how does this crazy miracle come about? I'm reading from
my ongoing novel, my fifteen-year growl at the world, reaching
back to the old days, and the disruptions begin, booming thun-
derclaps of words. In the second row were two large women, I'd
say in their late thirties. One of the women, the smaller of the two
large women, reminded me of an old lover, Edna, maybe fifty years
ago. Oh, when fickle memory embraces you, pushes away the de-
bris of time. I lived with Edna through the writing of my first novel,
then met dear Frances and married her. Frances, nine books of
enduring me, God rest her soul.

Thought for a second the woman in the audience might be Edna's reincarnation or daughter. But not when she thundered her words. Edna was soft-spoken, spoke in elegant sentences, or so I wrote in my first novel. The two large women would look at each other, shout something horrible, "You scuzzy degenerate" or "If you had a brain, you'd know how stupid you are" … lots of stuff like that, after being all snug and affectionate with each other when I first got in front of the audience. I kept reading, tried making a few jokes, but the two women sat there, insulting each other. I was scheduled to read for forty-five minutes, and I was determined to get through, even if all I was getting was a dinner and a bottle of wine.

Made it through my reading on pure stubbornness, and afterward I offered to reveal my deepest writing secrets, but most of the talk concerned the two cranky women, who had left together, still insulting each other. I said a few things about my fifteen-year unfinished novel, how I had recently written a touching love scene from decades-old memory. I could hear something was going on outside the art gallery. Several people were pulled toward the commotion and I followed along. There they were, punching each other like two frenzied prizefighters. The woman who reminded me of Edna was knocked down, her head hitting the sidewalk. Someone said they were arguing over my reading, another claimed it was over hockey or cooking, or God knows what. Another person was shoved, more punches thrown, a dozen combatants, dozens more of boisterous onlookers. The police came and the victorious woman, yelling what sounded like jumbled poetry, punched a boyish-looking policeman in the face – maybe she was angry at the whole world, not just her friend – and got herself arrested. An ambulance came for the woman on the sidewalk, and I thought about the ambulance that came for my father when I was a young man. Later I found out from the art-gallery owner that the injured woman was in critical condition, clinging to life, and I started thinking about writing a story called "Clinging to Life." It wouldn't be about the fight, but about my own struggling writing existence.

The next afternoon, refusing to let what happened throw me off my sanity-preserving routine, I have my out-of-work grandson

– we both live with my daughter and her husband – drive me to the subway station. Take the train to Bloor, do a little window shopping, have a few coffees – I've had at least fifty-thousand coffees in my life, such is my literary life's accounting system – then go to the library. After the library, maybe I have a beer or two, maybe I take in a dancer or two, maybe I remember when I was younger. But when I was younger I never went to strip clubs, not even for research or inspiration. It was my sixtieth birthday present to myself. Fifteen years of taking the subway downtown, fifteen years of visiting the dancers, fifteen years of working on my magnum opus.

First thing I do in the library, I look up my name on the Internet, pump those search engines. Only recent reference was to a master's thesis on the automobile in Canadian literature, which has a reference to a car-theft scene in one of my early novels. The budding little scholar even managed to find out about my brother's criminal life. I was fascinated by my older brother's stories of stealing cars and jail life. But he died at twenty-eight and I became the older brother.

A few days later, I visited the injured woman in the hospital, held her hand, read to her. What was the argument about in the first place? I asked. Her friend was infuriated that she had published a love poem ... about a former lover. Told her about my old lover, who she evoked in memory for me – the beauty of memory, changing pain to art. The ambulance that picked up my father; my brother who was stabbed to death; the lost love affair with Edna – the novels that were born from those events.

Getting ready for my next reading, a fat honorarium, media coverage, but let's see if something eventful happens. Frightening when you expect life to provide your inspiration. But I'm glad that at seventy-five I can still want to get frightened. Now, if I can just find the right vibrant words to describe the literary event brawl.

THE NEVER-AGAIN MAN

I WAS SITTING IN AN OUTDOOR CAFÉ, in Halifax, a beautiful autumn afternoon, going over the proof sheets for my first book of poetry. If everything goes smoothly, the book should be published right around my fifty-third birthday, in the spring, by a small press in Nova Scotia. And then I saw him, the Mountie who one of the poems is about. Not the first poem I ever wrote, but the first one I got published, about ten years ago in a literary magazine in Vancouver. What a national production, I thought: me sitting in Halifax, having a cup of Earl Grey tea, looking at a poem about me and a Mountie in Ottawa two decades ago, which first saw the light of day in Vancouver. I was tempted to call the man over, ask if he remembered me, when he walked over to my table and asked if I remembered him. The last time I beheld your face, I said, was the day my life was transformed completely. Because of him? he asked, and I said, not exactly. I was ready to show him the poem, tell him about my development as a poet, but instead I raised my left forearm and said, Because of this. I thought for a second he was going to touch my forearm, but he gave me a gentle smile, wished me well, called me "The Never-Again Man," and walked away. Neither one of us asked what we had been doing the last twenty years. I stared at my left forearm and thought about the last time I had seen the Mountie, thought about it as if it was that day that made me a poet.

THE RCMP OFFICER WALKED INTO THE ROOM a minute after the two Ottawa policemen had left, giving me only enough time to ponder a few possible scenarios.

"Ah, it's the Never-Again Man doing it again," the Mountie said as he stepped closer to me. "I wasn't expecting to see you so soon."

"Why don't you stick to your Musical Ride?" I said with listless sarcasm, not lifting my head from the small table in the centre of the room. I flicked a pencil off the table that one of the city policemen had been using to write notes. I was displeased to see this Mountie again, the officer who seven months before had first questioned me after I returned to Canada from Washington, D.C. On three other occasions the Mountie had questioned me about my involvement with militant Jewish organizations and my participation in less than peaceful demonstrations in Ottawa. The Mountie was not reluctant to declare that he found dealing with me the most distasteful assignment in his eleven years with the RCMP.

"Live in the present," the Mountie said to me, reminding me that the Second World War had ended a lifetime ago and that his own father was a decorated war hero, for Canada. "That war belongs to another world, before we were both born," the Mountie said before he had grown to detest me. "This is 1980, not 1940," he repeated when I talked too vehemently about the Second World War. We were less than a month apart in age, both thirty-two, but me with my long brown hair looked five or six years younger than the Mountie with his short, neatly combed reddish-blond hair and pyramidal, pink face.

"The War lives in my blood," I had told the Mountie during our first long interrogation session, but he didn't understand or want to understand. "Just forget World War II, for your mental health," was the Mountie's response that time. I had argued that Jews shouldn't forget – forgetting is the greatest crime for a Jew. When the Mountie merely smiled and scratched his chin, I informed him that there was a motto at the heart of the State of Israel: Never Again. "Without believing that lesson of history," I told the Mountie straight to his face, "I might have grown up to be exactly like you." It was at that exact moment, I sensed, that the Mountie started to hate me.

I had been questioned by the city policemen for forty-five minutes. Baffled by their concern and line of questioning, I kept prefacing my replies with "Why are you conscientious cops so curious about a harmless drunk?" The two policemen were persistent and imperturbable, unmoved by my sense of humour, acting as though they had heard my scornful wisecracks and wry comments countless times before. Their politeness was unshakable and their expressions disclosed not a single inner thought as I became more and more exasperated with what I regarded as their pointless questioning. In my best sarcastic voice, I had said: "One public binge and I'm a threat to the peace, order, and good government of the neighbourhood." The policemen revealed a knowledge about me that made me uneasy and feel that a silent eye had been hovering above me for years. They made several remarks about my politics and lifestyle and favourite brand of beer, but were most critical of my long history of social activism, as though being a Jew were irrelevant to the case. The policemen seemed to regard my behaviour as no different from the behaviour of the war criminals I pursued with increasing preoccupation.

157

"Why do you have to stir shit?" one policeman had asked as he sat down next to me. The policemen alternated making comments about things I had done years ago, that I believed the city police should have had no way of knowing. One policeman even knew that my wife had left me a few months ago, had recently applied for admission to a master's program, and had a wire-haired terrier named Gevalt. You know what *gevalt* means? I had asked, and one officer said he had a Jewish neighbour who used the word all the time, especially when things went wrong. Their remarks, as the questioning progressed, became more judgemental and critical. Soon they were rebuking me, not questioning me. In my tired condition I felt that these two policemen were judging not only my entire life, but the lives of every one of my family who had ever lived. Essential, fundamental issues were on my mind and I wanted to talk about the Nazis who were still alive and living in North America, about my need to locate and expose each and every one; I wanted to talk about the need for justice if there was ever to be even a semblance of sanity in the world, but the policemen were only interested in my penchant for causing disruption. They wouldn't even forgive me my three-days' growth of beard, I believed.

"I should have known," I said, when I focussed in on the Mountie, who was wearing the same grey suit he had on during each previous interrogation session. "My eternally vigilant keeper. I'd prefer it if you wore your scarlet tunic, so you can really look like Nelson Eddy."

"An educated man like you – what, you got two college degrees – should be able to stay out of trouble. In two countries yet," the Mountie said, shaking his head at me.

"It's a genetic defect," I said, diverting my eyes from the Mountie and returning my attention to the pencil on the floor.

The Mountie picked up the pencil and put it close to my face and then stepped away. I was fatigued and burdened with a stubborn nausea, my eyes now closed and my head resting on my folded arms on the table. I listened to the Mountie criticize me, at times a stern father berating a mischievous son, other times warning the reprobate wino that he was heading down the path to perdition if he didn't clean up his unsavoury act. When the Mountie announced that it was too bad that I had lost my job at the Archives, I lifted my head and looked at the Mountie's pink face.

"Did you compile some sort of dossier on me for my supervisor?" After my return from the demonstration in Washington and four months in jail for disturbing the peace and trespassing, the supervisor for Record Group 18 – Records for the Royal Canadian Mounted Police – began to refer to a mysterious dossier. I initially thought it was a dark joke; after all, we earned our living working among Mounted Police documents and reports dating back to the 1870s. The abundance of letterbooks, general orders, circular memoranda, daily journals, weekly reports, patrol reports, annual reports, and the like, made references to secret reports or dossiers, a common form of joking and teasing in the RG 18 section of the Archives.

The Mountie's half-formed smile proclaimed that the question about the dossier did not deserve an answer. He was studying me and seemed pleased to see me so dishevelled.

"You're a right mess. Collecting pogey yet?" the Mountie said, giving the pencil a slight spin. He moved away to a corner of the room, as though the interrogated might lunge at the interrogator.

I stood, weak on my feet, and took a few uncertain steps toward the Mountie. I stopped three steps from him and said, "I'm surprised you don't know."

"No need for you to be surprised," the Mountie said, making his expression serious, but I felt that the man was suppressing laughter.

"How do you know so much?" I asked in a nausea-muted rage. "You'd have a higher rank if you were omniscient, wouldn't you?"

"You look downright pathetic," the Mountie said, ignoring my questions. "How you going to catch any war criminals?"

Despite being nauseated and sapped of strength, I attempted to make my next question sound forceful: "What do you want from me?"

"The city boys want to charge you. They really want your ass in jail, but I said to cool it, you'd gone through quite an ordeal in the States and you'd lost a real good job, too."

"Why in the world did they call you? There must be some drug ring you could be wiretapping or infiltrating. Since when did drunkenness become a threat to the country?" I realized I had been snappier and more acerbic during my previous encounters with this Mountie, but a visceral dizziness was draining my caustic wit.

After a pause to study me closer, the Mountie said in an easygoing murmur: "The booze doesn't matter. It's your particular background."

"You bastards got me fired!" I shouted.

"You got yourself fired," the Mountie said firmly but without raising his voice. "Nice pension down the road and you screwed it up ..."

The louder I spoke, the more deliberate and restrained the Mountie's words became. I knew that the Mountie would tell me only what he wanted to, which was nothing of importance. Without a trace of eagerness or politeness, forcing myself not to lose my temper again, I asked if I could leave, I wanted to go to *shul*, that's synagogue, I explained.

"That's up to the city boys. They really think you should be charged, as an example. We certainly don't want to have one law for the uneducated and another for government archivists. You made

159

some ruckus in that hotel. You find a Nazi there or something?" the Mountie said, barely holding back a smile.

I remembered only the dream I was having when the police roused me, as if that dream was the only reality of the night worth remembering. In the dream, I was attempting to read books that described what had happened in Europe during the Second World War. But the books were written in a language I couldn't decipher, except for the occasional word in English.

"You have pleasant dreams?" I asked the Mountie. I didn't even ask what I had done last night. My hands felt sore and I could see that my knuckles had been bleeding. I touched the dried blood on my fingers like a wounded animal dealing with an incomprehensible injury.

"I just want your word that you'll behave yourself and be a good citizen, nothing more than that," the Mountie went on, making his expression serious. "I want reassurance that I won't have to be bothered anymore. I've got more important work to do than run down here and talk to a hung-over civil servant who doesn't know his ass from a hole in the ground."

"Ex-silly servant. Superannuated keeper of the public records now put out to stud," I said, squeezing a mock joviality into my delivery.

"I'll take your word for it."

"*Maintiens le droit*. Maybe you can write out my parking tickets. You might find that a challenging assignment, unless today is your day to go after counterfeiters."

"You should behave yourself and be happy to be back in Canada. There's no way you're getting back into the States. Jumping around an scaring people at the gates of the White House with your big bad signs can get you really screwed up. Aren't there enough Nazis for you here?"

"The problem transcends local jurisdictions. I'm not a common criminal. Why don't you at least concede me that point and then we can be respectful adversaries?"

"I'd say it's not a matter open to debate. You do break the law from time to time."

I took the final three steps toward the Mountie and collapsed at his feet. The officer didn't make a move but shook his head in affected disgust. I laboured to my knees but looked down at the officer's shoes, as if praying to faceless icons. I didn't want to stand up. Much more than tiredness or sickness immobilized me. I thought I would just kneel there for a few years and think, attempt to unravel the confusion and mysteries, prepare for the real battles. I had passed this police station hundreds of times as I walked to and from the Archives yet I had never attempted to imagine its interior or internal goings-on. I suggested to the Mountie that we go to *shul* together, if he wanted to get insight into why I acted the way I did. I liked the image of this Mountie dressed like a Hasidic Jew, *davening* away in a synagogue.

The Mountie stood silently above me and I wondered what the officer would do if I bit his leg. If Gevalt were here ... But the dog rarely listened to my instructions. It was my wife's pet. Instead I gave a taunting growl but the Mountie remained silent.

My nausea increased and I simply didn't feel like struggling to some remote washroom. The Mountie nonchalantly stepped away from me, not in anger, but as though stepping away from a regurgitating prisoner was a manual's prescribed act. The Mountie said it would take a lot of advanced study to get into my psyche. He obviously didn't want to get into my stomach. But he wouldn't go with me to a synagogue. He didn't even like going to church, he told me. Then the Mountie left the room without saying anything else.

I wanted an excuse, an explanation, for throwing up in this room. What would I say to the city police? The flu? Motion sickness? A wicked dybbuk stuck its tickling finger down my throat? I felt that my credibility wasn't worth much in that room. To me, it was a room for the guilty as surely as a coffin was for the dead. As I started to feel the oppressed martyr, I cautioned myself that my parents had endured much worse in Poland during the War; I didn't want to ennoble my predicament.

As soon as I had cleaned up my vomit to their satisfaction, the two city policemen allowed me to go with only a wordy warning and the cryptic declaration that they had my fingerprints and so did the FBI. I started to chant a prayer in Hebrew, but stopped a quarter of the way through.

SLOWLY, FEELING REPRIEVED, I began to walk to the hotel bar I had been drinking at last night, an automatist's search for clues. A cold November wind was biting into my face, and I pulled up the collar of my light-brown sports jacket. I couldn't remember if I had had an overcoat with me last night, but I thought so, always being such a practical dresser. The discomfort would not abandon me, but the wind seemed to stabilize my system. I was hungry and tired and desired a storm, a fierce storm, a wind so furious that it would obliterate all I didn't understand and leave only a tranquil justice in its wake. Feeling dirtied, my guts having been pried open and studied by unsympathetic surgeons, I wanted to take a shower and talk to my wife. The need to tell Claire all about my latest brush with the law was strong, but I didn't even know where she was living then, perhaps in Montreal with her parents or in Toronto with her older sister. I should have asked the Mountie for her address.

"Looking for Nazis is making you a crazy man," she had said a month before I left for Washington, my loving wife turned cold psychiatrist. Why did she want to forget what the Nazis had done to her family? "If we forget, Claire, we might as well be dead," I had argued with my wife. "If we don't forget," she had countered, "we are worse than dead." "Never again, never again, never again," I had screamed into her face. I cried in apology but she warned me that if I didn't start controlling my emotions and obsessiveness she would leave me. During our next argument about my obsessive search for war criminals I screamed louder, went into a worse rage. I offered to rip out my own tongue if she would forgive me. She moved out while I was in Washington trying to convince the American government that more strenuous efforts should be made to flush out war criminals hiding in the United States. I had already spent months lobbying the Canadian government and had even received a sympathetic letter from a government official informing me that the RCMP kept meticulous files on all known war criminals. I wondered now if my dossier and the RCMP files on war criminals were together in the same file cabinet, different drawers I could only hope.

I looked to see what time it was and realized that my watch was gone. How could I have lost that beautiful watch, my thirtieth-birthday present two years ago from Claire, and concluded it had been stolen last night. A check of my wallet showed my money was also gone but not my one credit card. I tried to imagine who had crept up on my senseless body and stripped me of my thirtieth-birthday present. Repulsion, like a garotte, strangled my thoughts as I visualized someone peering at me, the defenceless prey, the dead chicken waiting to be plucked, without protest, without resistance, without even the necessary scream of defiance.

It was only a watch and a lousy twenty bucks, I still had my magic plastic card, I told myself, slowing my pace, resisting the urge to sit down on the sidewalk. Sentiment was for bourgeois jerks, I consoled myself; my bourgeois days were over – I was determined to do something with my life more than earn money and accumulate worthless possessions. But since I had lost my job the matter had been taken out of my hands. I had enough savings for about six months of frugal living.

Saturday crowds of people were already walking around downtown Ottawa and I guessed it must be nine or ten in the morning. When I looked up toward a bank building's clock and saw it was three-thirty, I felt I had been robbed of priceless hours. First my job, then the watch and money, now the morning, as though a band of crazed thieves had descended upon me and stolen me blind. I could not rationalize the loss of the morning, only the loss of the watch and money. Pushing against my body's reluctance, I started to walk faster in an effort to combat my thoughts, trying to outrace the growing feelings of helplessness.

I walked to Lowertown, where the old hotel I had been at the night before was placed into the ground like a crude, grimy monument. The old hotel was an ill-conceived centre of the universe. I turned occasionally to make sure I wasn't being followed. Every single Mountie seemed to be on my tail.

163

Lowertown was a different topography to me. Not quite exotic, but hardly familiar. Through the six years of our marriage I had come with Claire to Lowertown nearly every Saturday morning during the spring and summer. Claire would eagerly head off to the market area, to wander among the produce stalls and produce sellers. Happy, carefree Claire would purchase vegetables for a week's worth of nutritional salads and I would bury the hour at Leviticus' Antiquarian Book Shoppe.

For years I had always carefully sidestepped the spiritless bustle of the area and hurried to the sanctuary of the bookstore. Before Claire had left me, I had neither interest in nor tolerance for Lowertown with its famous Byward Market and changing façades with new restaurants and abundant specialty shops. A portion of the old houses and the poor hung on somehow and I did not care for either the sandblasted newness or the clinging oldness. Leviticus' Antiquarian Book Shoppe made sense, was safe, and the old proprietor knew books better than any of the researchers or academics or archivists I used to work around.

The bookstore was a block from the old hotel and I headed for Leviticus' only after I had determined that I hadn't done anything terrible, after I had inspected where I had passed out the night before, the scene of my hapless arrest. "Where are you, Claire? Why are you staying away from me?" I quietly called as I crossed the street to Leviticus' Antiquarian Book Shoppe. Why didn't she understand?

I lingered in front of the large old building with its four decaying stores and anonymous upper-floor apartments in which I had never seen a sign of life. The renovators and developers hadn't yet clutched this ancient edifice. First there was the used-furniture store with its dead radios and bleak sticks of furniture in the window, and squeezed next to it was a greasy-odoured lunch counter at which I first found out about the Nazis in the city and was given the names of people who weren't going to rest until the score was settled, followed by Leviticus' and then a darkened tattoo parlour. I stared at the sign in the window of the tattoo parlour. The sign was old and faded and surely had been there since the beginning of time but I seemed to see it as though it had just miraculously materialized.

ALL DESIGNS AND CREATIVE MESSAGES ... TWELVE BRILLIANT COLOURS ... PAINLESS, EXPERT WORK ... SATISFACTION GUARANTEED OR YOUR MONEY BACK ... MAKE A PERSONAL STATEMENT.

The sign was between the smudged glass and a velvety purple curtain that, I thought, belonged in an exalted holy place.

A sudden pain inflamed me throughout my body and then I quickly felt inexpressible relief that was explainable only in mystical or religious terms. I had never realized this store was a tattoo parlour although I had passed it for years full of Saturdays. I had never thought about the tattoo parlour, the same way I had never really thought about the inside of the police station. It had been a blank, a too familiar sight lost in its familiarity; always directly to Leviticus' and the bookstore's old smells and endless shelves of books.

Now the tattoo parlour called to me, scolded me for my indifference, for my blindness. The mystical experience was sudden and overwhelming, like drowning or a savage blow to the face. You gasp for air or you check to see how many of your precious teeth have been knocked out. Soon the voice of the pain renders all else insignificant. The experience itself is all – not the antecedents, not the consequences, not the perplexing interpretations that a thousand minds will give in a thousand different lights. ALL DESIGNS AND CREATIVE MESSAGES ... For me there was only one design, one creative message, and that design and message bludgeoned my mind with its simplicity and necessity. Why had I never thought of it before? The idea of a tattoo made so much sense, was the act that would atone for all my mistakes and blunders. God, I yearned for a symbol, a simple handle on history and the innumerable deaths.

I tried to open the door but it was locked; still I turned and turned the rusted knob, hoping it might open with the proper magical twist. Yet no sleight of hand, no stolen incantation, no Mephistophelean subterfuge was adequate. I wanted to get the tattoo right away. All twelve brilliant colours flashed before my eyes, painted a sanctified, alluring picture. I knew exactly what I wanted

– needed! – as clearly as any inspired artist gripped by an artistic vision, and I craved to get it done immediately. Now! Before the volcano erupted; before the world ended in a blaze of complaints and unpaid debts and I was forced to meet my tight-lipped Maker without a creative message.

In a corner of the door was a frayed decal displaying the tattoo parlour's hours: MONDAY–SATURDAY, 10:00 A.M.–3:00 P.M. Better than an archivist's hours, I thought. *Now!* I needed to have the tattoo done before another thought crushed me. PAINLESS ... PAINLESS ... I didn't care what pain there would be. I who feared dentists and exaggerated little aches and fits into cancers and dementia, didn't care what pain was caused. EXPERT WORK ... The work of history, the vital inscription, the lifeline back through the years, disinterring graves, resurrecting the executed innocents. My parents' concentration camp tattoos darkened the window and I fought to dissolve them; stay in my nightmares, my nervous movements seemed to declare.

Flailing at my chest, attempting a physical, punishing retribution, I turned from the tattoo parlour. Sweating as though from hours of exhaustion, trembling with the joy of seeing a long-forgotten confidant, I entered the familiar bookstore and greeted the proprietor with an ebullience that erased the misbegotten events of the night and morning and cold afternoon.

The old man, hunched over some papers at a desk near the front of the store, was unimpressed with my entrance. He peered up at me, one of his best customers, and complained in an actor's resonant voice: "I can't stop peeing."

"See a doctor," I said, my euphoria evaporating with a soul-suctioning rapidity that made me actually gasp. Automatically I went to the middle of the store and the Jewish-books section. (It used to be part of the History section, but I convinced the old man to put in a special subsection for books related to Judaism. The books in his store were divided into several dozen precise categories.) The Jewish-books section was little different from last week or the week before. When I was in jail in Washington, it was this Ottawa bookstore that I described to my lawyer as the place I would take him first if he ever visited Canada's capital.

"Doctors I stopped going to. They're guessers," the old man said loudly in my direction. "I trust you more than a doctor. You know history. What do you think?"

"It could be lots of things," I said cautiously, touching some old books, not even reading their titles yet, their textures soothing medicaments for me. The old man never displayed a book published after 1940 – rubbish, modern rubbish, he would groan if you asked him for a more recent work – as though the printing presses had stopped then and the world ceased to utter meaningful words. I felt my usual comfort and serenity in the old bookstore.

"I'm thirsty, so I drink. But I pee more than I drink. I pee like I've been drinking gallons and gallons. I'm a professional urinator now," the old man said sadly.

Although my deepest thoughts were elsewhere, I turned toward the old man at his desk and smiled, telling him, "Maybe you have the clap."

"Don't I wish. If only it was so ordinary ..."

For fifteen minutes the old man and I talked about his various ailments and worries, he cursing the medical profession and discussing the ailments of the famous in history. The old man had an incredible knowledge of the medical problems of the famous, from epileptic Julius Caesar to syphilitic Ivan the Terrible to asthmatic Marcel Proust; he spoke with particular passion about the maladies of Napoleon and Søren Kierkegaard.

"Bad enough I can't make a decent living, now I pee every twenty or thirty minutes," the old man said and rushed off to the backroom toilet, leaving me alone in the bookstore.

Feeling the walls closing in on me, I hurriedly searched for a book to buy. It was my unalterable routine: I would not leave without buying at least one book. When the old man reappeared, I grabbed a book from a shelf and showed it to him.

"Add it to my account," I said and rushed out of the bookstore, just before my lungs were about to explode. I ran back to the hotel, wanting desperately to have a drink, to tell someone about the tattoo parlour.

That evening I got more drunk than the day before yet I remained conscious. The Saturday bartender didn't know about yes-

167

terday's incident and at first joked with me, even skimming through my latest acquisition, Cecil Roth's *History of the Jews in Venice*. I ordered a salad and a steak, and started to eat at the bar, not remembering the last time I had bothered to have a decent meal. I kept talking about the RCMP and war criminals and Jews and the concentration camps my parents had been in and about the tattoo parlour. I talked even when no one was listening.

When I thought I couldn't stand my own words any longer, I took my steak knife and carefully scratched a tattoo into my left forearm: NEVER AGAIN. In a pocket of my sports jacket I had the names of some of the Nazis living in Ottawa; I didn't need to go to the States, even if there were bigger fish there, more rotten fish. Tomorrow, I decided, I would get back to searching for the murderous vermin. It was good I didn't have a job to interfere with my real work, the work of history.

I raised my bleeding, tattooed forearm high into the air and before I passed out from the alcohol and pain and memory, I heard a man at the end of the bar ask, "What in Hell does that mean?"

I HEARD A WAITER ASK if I wanted more tea. How long had I been reliving what had happened so many years ago? I took a pen and stroked out the title of the middle poem in my manuscript, and wrote, "The Never-Again Man." Not only that, but I decided then and there to change the title of the entire collection to *The Never-Again Man*.

ZACHARY WAS BASICALLY A DECENT, hard-working soul. But he also spent a great deal of time following professional basketball, much to the dismay of his wife and two children. What his family didn't know was that Zachary liked to bet on basketball games, and lately had been having a run of bad luck. Yet he was an optimist, and was confident he would soon recoup his recent losses. At forty years old, he still had the fantasies of a promising high-scoring teenage basketball prospect. He had always been on the tall side – he reached his full height of six-foot-four at the age of fifteen – but he was not blessed with much athletic ability. Despite his gangliness, he did make his high-school basketball team, albeit as a second-stringer. (At university, where his grades were mediocre and he barely managed to complete a degree, the closest he could get to the varsity squad was as its popular animal-costumed mascot.)

Zachary's team was the Toronto Raptors, having attended the majority of their home games since they entered the NBA, and watching away games on television whenever he could. In fact, the only time he ever allowed his emotions free reign in front of other people was during basketball games, when he was able to yell and cheer with spirited intensity. His loyalty to the team was constant, whether they were winning or losing. (Before the Raptors had entered the NBA, he had followed the Boston Celtics, the team his parents, who had moved from the United States to Canada when Zachary was a little boy, were interested in most.) Except for the time he spent in a provincial-government office building, he was consumed by basketball. Even at his routine desk job, Zachary still

fantasized, made some of the most incredible dunk shots that imagination would allow.

Complain as his wife and children did, they learned to live with
Zachary's life-long obsession. Zachary didn't. He went deeper into
his unrealistic desires, prayed for a chance at the NBA, one lousy
game. One Sunday afternoon, during the fourth period of an exciting Raptors basketball game on television, a game he had a large
wager on, two-weeks pay, an average-sized man in a new basketball uniform (without any logo or identifying number), wearing
dirty street shoes and a wrinkled cowboy hat, appeared in Zachary's
living room.

170

"I don't want everything you own," the strange man said, "but
I do want something of value in exchange for that one big game."

"How did you get in here?" Zachary said, both startled and
frightened. He immediately thought of protecting his wife and children from this intruder, but realized they had gone earlier to visit
his wife's parents, whom he rarely visited because they criticized
his basketball-watching. In an occurrence that had long since taken
on the proportions of family legend, his father-in-law said in the
midst of a house full of relatives, when Zachary, in front of the
television set during a tense playoff game, refused to leave his seat
for a holiday family dinner in another room, that his son-in-law
had a shrunken basketball for brains. Maybe two shrunken basket-
balls.

The strange man in the living room, after giving a detailed history of Zachary's unillustrious life and a fascinating overview of
the NBA, topped off by an eerily accurate imitation of the university basketball coach that had cut him from the team, convinced
Zachary of his extraordinariness if not his power.

"Your sailboat, in return for the ability to score the most points
ever in a championship game, along with scoring the winning bas-
ket in overtime. A sensational dunk shot," the man said.

"*My sailboat?*" Zachary responded, completely unnerved.

"We're talking over one hundred points in the seventh game
of the NBA championship. Your name will be spoken of as long as
there is basketball on Earth."

"Are you telling me a hundred points in a playoff game?" Zachary said, one eye on the man and the other on the television screen.

"*More* than a hundred. The seventh game of the championship series. It will be the most phenomenal single event since the beginning of professional sports ..."

Zachary, while truly impressed by the strange man's basketball erudition, still had one foot planted in the rational, empirical world, but, feeling somewhat disoriented and mischievous, not to mention anxious over his big bet, nevertheless offered the thirty-two-foot sailboat, his family's pride and joy. He and his wife had saved for years to buy the boat, and planned to sail for an entire month this summer, along with the children, a family-enriching dream of a lifetime.

The strange man snapped his fingers, said several words that Zachary did not understand but thought sounded like a referee calling a technical foul on an unruly player, and created a small cloud of orange-grey smoke in the living room.

"As a token of my good faith," the strange man said, and pointed to the ten video cassettes that were now in the centre of the living room.

"Mess up your own living room," Zachary said, annoyed by the slowly dissipating cloud of orange-grey smoke.

"I do not take kindly to sarcasm," the strange man said, "but I understand you are under a great deal of stress in your everyday life. No substantial accomplishments in forty years of life is indeed a heavy burden."

"Not everyone can make it into the Basketball Hall of Fame," Zachary said, his sarcasm thickening, and walked over to the video cassettes. As he read the video titles, his annoyance disappeared. "These are some of the best basketball games ever played," he said.

"I don't care for any of the more recent ones. 1960 is my cutoff date. None of the ten videos, you'll notice, has a game played after that year."

"These are great games. I've seen clips or read about most of them." He tapped four of the video cassettes in quick succession,

171

calling out the teams and dates, and added, "I know for sure that these went into overtime or double overtime."

"Quite astute of you," the strange man said.

Zachary, noticing that one of the video cassettes had the film title *Tall Story* printed on the opposite side from the game information, declared, "Anthony Perkins was wonderful as a college basketball star in Tall Story." Zachary paused and smiled in recollection, then said, "My wife and I rented an Anthony Perkins movie early in our marriage."

"*Psycho*," the strange man said, and then he snickered: "You necked during most of the film. Very heavy necking, I might say. I think you missed most of the horrific shower scene."

"That scene wasn't very long, and I had other things on my mind."

"You also saw the remake, again with your wife. What a beautiful romantic symmetry. This time, however, you watched the scene in its entirety, your eyes wide open. You necking days, alas, were over."

"You a private detective in your spare time, when you're not sneaking into people's houses and filling them up with phony smoke?"

"There you go with the sarcasm again," the strange man said.

"Oh, I am profoundly sorry," Zachary said, balancing the sarcasm on his tongue as if it were a creamy, delicious dessert.

"On a serious note, for your information, both *Tall Story* and *Psycho* had their big-screen premieres in 1960."

"You have a psychological thing about 1960?"

"Jane Fonda made her very first film appearance in *Tall Story*."

"I'll take your word for it."

"This old cowboy hat I'm wearing," the strange man said, fingering the brim of the hat, "is the same one Alfred Hitchcock wore during his brief appearance in *Psycho*. How dearly Hitch loved to do those cameo appearances in his films."

"Now who is being sarcastic," Zachary said, noting that the Raptors had fallen further behind in the basketball game.

"Believe me, this was Hitch's cowboy hat. I picked it up at an auction of film memorabilia, just the other day."

Zachary pulled on the collar of his shirt, and said in a raised voice, "This was a shirt Norman Bates wore in the movie." Zachary looked at the television screen again and was relieved that the Raptors had scored two quick baskets. "*Nor-man*," he shouted out as sarcastically as he could.

The strange man closed his eyes, took a deep breath, and burst out refreshed and exuberant: "I shouldn't get all hung up on your sarcasm. Human frailty, nothing more. Forgive and forget, live and let live, on with the show."

"I do, without sarcasm, thank you for these," Zachary said, changing the order of the video cassettes.

"I did know you would be pleased with the 1960 baseketball film," the strange man said, opening his eyes and going through the motions of shooting a basketball. In mid-shot the imaginary ball turned into a real one.

"Another nifty trick there," Zachary said, his words again laced with sarcasm. "Try not to knock anything over, all right?"

"Do I look like an undisciplined shooter?" the strange man said, not a trace of insincerity or sarcasm in his tone. "I have a keen shooting eye and am most selective about the shots I take. The last thing I want is to look bad taking a shot from too far out. I'd rather pass inside and get an assist."

Zachary returned his attention to the video cassettes on the floor: "I remember watching *Tall Story* on television with my parents. It was late at night, and there was a real blizzard outside. Call me sentimental, but all three of us laughed and I dare say there wasn't a more joyous family at that time. My mother and my father were both basketball fans. Not a lot of kids in Toronto in those days could say that."

"Nor could many kids say that both their parents had gambling problems."

"There was always food on the table, good food, and a roof over our heads. We did live simply sometimes, but so what?"

"Made for an interesting childhood. On average, your mother did do better than your father."

"A few years ago, at my father's funeral, my mother and I talked about the night we watched *Tall Story*. She died a couple of months

173

ago, before we had a chance to go to any games together this season ..." Attempting to push away the sadness that was surrounding his thoughts, Zachary picked up the tenth video cassette and said, "I never heard of this game. And the Raptors certainly were not in existence in 1960."

"It will be the game you star in. The tape is still blank, but it doesn't have to be," the strange man said, and laughed loudly.

"What's so funny about a blank tape?" Zachary asked, tossing the video cassette up and down, as if it were a basketball.

"I had this image of your son and daughter bringing all their school friends to the game, and every single one of them wearing T-shirts with your name and number on the back, and cheering you on."

"My kids are bright, cheerful teenagers. And fine athletes."

"I understand your fatherly bias, but your son is not sports-minded," the strange man said. "He has never shown any basketball ability, thus depriving you of an opponent in backyard, driveway games."

"He is only thirteen," said Zachary vigorously, as if defending his family's honour. He coughed away a pang of sadness, and continued his defence: "There is time for him to mature. My daughter is a good basketball player."

"That she is," said the strange man. "She is a better free-thrower than you were at her age."

"I wouldn't go that far," said Zachary, recalling two important free throws he had made during his last high-school game, but his team was defeated when a minute later he fouled an opponent who then sank the winning free throw in the last second of play. (Zachary remembered that game not only for the shimmer of heroics he had briefly felt, but also because he got drunk for the first time in his life after the game.)

As the strange man promised that Zachary's mother and father would also be in the stands, but not wearing T-shirts, Zachary tossed the video cassette at him, more like a behind-the-back pass, but before it reached the strange man, he was gone, as mysteriously and quickly as he had arrived, and the video cassette hit the television set. The basketball game on television was already over and

Zachary realized he had lost his wager, two-weeks pay. Refusing to get too depressed over the lost money, there would be other games to bet on, Zachary inserted *Tall Story* into his VCR, wishing his parents were alive to watch the movie again with him.

The basketball season ended and Zachary concluded that he had been the victim of a peculiar daydream, until the next season when he found himself on the Toronto Raptors bench, in the seventh game of the championship series, seeing his mother and father in the stands, in the row above his son and daughter and the rows and rows of their school friends, all chanting his name. Zachary began to enjoy the experience, knowing that he would have the memory of only one game to carry him through the rest of his life.

On the tipoff, Zachary got the basketball, and in his nervous excitement, missed his first shot; missed shot after shot; missed every shot he took. Late in the game, the Raptors leading by two points, a small guard stole the ball from him, dribbled the length of the court, and scored a layup to tie the game, sending it into overtime. Zachary started to tremble at centre court, knowing his deal was irrevocable.

The small guard was a quiet, unassuming bachelor, whose summer cottage, which he and his brother had built with their own hands, would be reported burned down before the game's final buzzer.

PROPELLER-WHIRL ROMULUS AND GYRATION THE PERPETUAL-MOTION DREAM DOLL

CHRISTOPHER SLAMMED DOWN THE receiver and stood by the wall telephone in the hallway. "Darn it," he muttered and kicked at the wall.

"Something wrong, Christopher?" Megan called from the kitchen, busily preparing their one-month-living-together celebration dinner.

"Nothing to worry about," he said, his voice full of worry, "but I promised to do my mother a favour."

"How is your mother?"

He didn't answer or move. Megan repeated the question, assuming she had spoken too softly.

"You're fortunate to have your parents in another part of the country, Megan. Distance is conducive to sanity."

"I miss my folks. What's the favour?"

Christopher had promised his mother to go on a double date with his twin sister, Laura, who was visiting Toronto with her fiancé and staying at the fanciest hotel in the city. His mother just happened to have four excellent theatre seats to the latest mega-musical downtown, not far from her daughter's hotel, and had already made arrangements with "poor Laura."

"Why do you always call her 'poor Laura'?" Christopher had criticized over the telephone. "You know" was his mother's predictable and exasperating response. All his life, whenever there was a question she could not or would not answer, even when he asked why his parents had divorced when he was a child, his mother uttered "you know." He intended to engrave the two empty words on her headstone.

"Supper's ready," Megan shouted cheerfully. Christopher could hear the clinking of plates and utensils coming from the kitchen. The familiar sounds failed to comfort him.

"In a minute ..." His mother wouldn't stop pleading until he had consented to the double date. "Save her, save her," the woman had wailed in a tone more appropriate to a revival meeting, the Devil hovering nearby.

"Christopher, before the food gets cold ..."

His twin sister had already, at twenty-four, gone through two marriages and her mother wanted to make sure that her daughter wasn't plunging into a third disaster. Christopher's arguments that his sister was an adult and should be left alone to run her own life only worsened his mother's anxiety.

178

"Open the wine, please," Megan said as Christopher came to the kitchen table, unable to dispel his mother's words. He was certain his mother possessed supernatural powers to depress him.

"You want to see a play this week, Megan?"

"I'd love to. We haven't been to the theatre since our first big date."

"Oh no, the cork sank."

"You're always tense after talking to your mother."

"Do you mind going with my sister and her latest beau?"

"Your sister? Great. I was wondering when I'd finally get to meet her."

"She's *different*."

"What kind of different?"

"You'll see."

"She's your *twin* sister."

"*Technically* ..."

THE EVENING OF THE BIG DOUBLE DATE Christopher studied difficult legal cases for law school until five minutes before he planned to leave. He dressed hurriedly, switching to an old sweater and new jeans, moaning all the time that he wasn't in the mood to see a play tonight, and then complained as he and Megan rushed to his car that he was being sent to spy on his sister.

During the drive, Megan asking questions like an irrepressible talk-show host, Christopher offered a few childhood anecdotes about himself and his twin sister. Ordinarily he didn't talk much about his sister.

"We were extremely close until Laura started to untangle the perplexities and intricacies of sex. Then we began to drift apart. We were almost telepathic until then."

"How old were you?"

"Fourteen."

"I hope to God you didn't start untangling *that* young."

"No perplexities and intricacies until you came along," Christopher said, grinning smugly.

"Perhaps you should have started practising a little earlier, darling," she retaliated quickly.

"You're taking lessons from my mother," he accused and almost hit the back bumper of another car as he tried to park near his sister's luxury hotel.

Christopher hadn't seen his sister in a year, and that was for less than an hour at the airport. Her latest domicile was on the tenth floor of a fancy waterfront complex in Montreal that left her mother baffled as to how she could afford it on a secretary's salary. Her expensive lifestyle was the basis of all Christopher and his mother's telephone conversations lately. That and her new boyfriend, of course.

Laura warmly greeted her brother and Megan at the door, joked that Megan was much too good-looking for him. Despite not having seen his sister in so long, Christopher kissed her on the cheek indifferently. Megan had never seen a male and female look so alike facially. All she could say as they were led into the suite's large living room was, "Christopher, if your hair wasn't an inch longer than your sister's I couldn't tell you two apart."

On the thick beige couch in the room sat the stockiest, most muscular man Christopher or Megan had ever seen in person.

"Richie, this is my brother Christopher and his lady friend, Megan," Laura said politely.

Christopher gave a cautious nod and Megan smiled as if to a police officer stopping her for speeding. Richie did not move except for a simple head bob. Christopher and Megan sat down on a loveseat that matched the couch and was separated from it by a long, low coffee table.

"What'll it be? We have an hour to get silly," Laura said as she stood behind the couch and Richie, rubbing the top of his bushy-haired head, starting to itemize the abundant selection of beverages they had. The two guests both asked for wine and Richie ordered a large glass of apple juice. Laura simultaneously kissed Richie on the lips and smacked him on the shoulders before going into another room to get the drinks.

"Apple juice is the elixir of good health," the large man, caressing one of his biceps as if it was a loved family pet, said with a seriousness that made Christopher say, "I've always been under the assumption the elixir has to contain alcoholic to be beneficial to good health."

"I've never had a cold in my life," the large man said.

"Christopher had a bad cold last week," Megan revealed, in an attempt at polite conversation.

"As much apple juice as you can drink. That's the secret to staying healthy," the large man said passionately, the caressing expanding to both biceps, two loved family pets.

Laura returned and as she handed out the drinks, said to her brother, "Give us a toast, Christopher. You got the imagination in our family."

"To friendship and good companionship," Christopher offered, sneering as he spoke. Some people uttered maledictions in a friendlier tone.

Richie finished his apple juice before anyone else had taken more than a sip of their drink.

Laura, sipping a glass of brandy, and her current lover sat cozily squeezed together on the thick beige couch that should have been roomy enough for three adults. She announced that Richie was a professional wrestler, one of the best in North America.

"Come watch Richie wrestle tomorrow night," Laura suggested after a short, uneasy silence. Christopher was staring at a painting on the wall of an old car parked near a farmhouse and he thought of the row of porcelain antique-car figurines that used to be in their parents' house when he and his sister were children. One of the figurines was a Model-T Ford that looked like the car in the painting. Fifteen years ago, he had broken two of the twelve-car set and blamed it on his sister. He had the urge to apologize now, but didn't.

When her brother only frowned at her suggestion, Laura shook a finger at him and said enthusiastically, "You've never seen grappling until you've gazed upon Richie in the ring. His moves will dumfound you, not to mention his bright red, glow-in-the-dark, unbelievably sexy wrestling trunks."

"A wrestler like the wrestlers on TV, you mean?" Megan said.

"Richie's been on the tube a lot of times," Laura said, giving the large wrestler another kiss.

"Brawling doesn't interest me," Christopher stated contemptuously, having taken a quick dislike to the huge man. He had appreciated Laura's first two husbands much more; one, at least, was even skinnier than Christopher.

"Take my word for it, it's not plain old brawling. It's a competitive sport," Richie said with jovial conviction, as if narrating a fairy tale to a disbelieving child.

"Richie wrestles Toronto's Masked Terror tomorrow night. He's going to expose him. The Masked Terror challenged anyone to try to take his mask off and show the fans who he really is. Richie will put the big mouth where he belongs – under the mat and minus one fat head." Laura slapped Richie on his massive back and it sounded like a leather bullwhip being cracked.

Richie smiled joyfully, seeming to sink deeper into the couch. He made a fist the size of a large grapefruit and punched a pillow to demonstrate what he would do to The Masked Terror.

"Richie can give you ringside seats, Christopher. It's gonna be a sellout. You can contemplate the artistry up close. You'll be able to smell the wrestlers." Laura inhaled deeply to emphasize her point.

"Everyone's got tickets for me this week. Give them to Mom."

"I told her on the phone that Richie and me are engaged, and that he's a successful accountant."

"You're not engaged?" Christopher said.

"Richie doesn't believe in marriage."

"I *was* going to be an accountant once ... took a few courses and did decent at them. But there's more money in the ring. Anyhow, who in the heck asks an accountant for his autograph or turns on the tube to watch him do his moves."

"Probably other lonely accountants," Christopher said.

"Never lose that sense of humour, Christopher. Richie's not big on jokes," Laura said.

"You should hear some of the things I say during a match. Damn funny sometimes," the wrestler said, curling his lower lip in feigned indignation.

"Come to the arena tomorrow night and you'll see great wrestling," Laura said.

"Is that why you're in town, sis?"

"I had some time off, so I'm doing this trip with Richie."

"Six cities in three weeks," Richie boasted. "This is the roughest pro circuit around."

"One cultural event a week is all my system can tolerate," Christopher said, looking into his wine glass, searching for an escape route.

"It's a great card, besides Richie. There's going to be a tag-team match to end all tag-team matches," Laura said excitedly. "Wrestlers from four different continents."

"I've never quite cultivated an interest for tag-team matches, regardless of the geography. Oh, but believe me, I've tried and tried, sis."

"Why can't we go, darling? I've never seen wrestling live," Megan said, a child asking for permission to enter a toy store. She couldn't take her eyes off the man sitting across from her.

"I don't get off on grown men pounding each other, Megan."

"*Wrestling* ... scientific wrestling," Laura corrected her brother, giving the huge man next to her another powerful slap. "Richie wrestles scientifically and never loses."

"Please, Christopher," Megan begged. "I bet it will be good fun."

"Wait until you get a close look at Richie's body. It's the Eighth *and* Ninth Wonders of the World all by itself," Laura said, her rapture sincere.

"Like cuddly King Kong," Christopher whispered.

"Better than King Kong, my dear brother. Much better. Richie has the best stomach muscles in the business." Laura placed her glass on the coffee table and refilled Richie's glass from a pitcher of apple juice. This time he drank at a slower pace, forcing himself to observe some sort of unwritten etiquette.

"You could hit me in the solar plexus with a sledgehammer and I wouldn't give a burp." Richie stood for the first time since the guests' arrival and he seemed even huger. He wasn't that tall, less than three inches taller than Christopher and Laura, who were both five-foot-nine, but his overwhelming bulk made it difficult to determine what his real height was. He lifted his arms apart – still holding a glass of apple juice in one hand – and said, "Take a punch, Christopher boy ... hard as you want."

183

"I wouldn't want to ruin your career, Richie."

"Only thing you'd ruin is your fist. Not to mention your ego."

Looking at the huge man's midsection, imagining a flat but treacherous highway of muscle underneath the wrestler's shirt, Christopher folded his arms and said, "Houdini died from a punch to the stomach. Led to peritonitis."

"I ain't Houdini," Richie said, his arms still extended.

"As a matter of fact, he was in Montreal when he got punched by an overenthusiastic university student."

"This ain't Montreal. Give me a punch. Take as many as you want."

"Houdini died right on Halloween. In 1926. It's become a national holiday for magicians." Christopher recalled one Halloween when he and his sister had dressed up as magicians and attempted to make each person who answered a door disappear. He thought of Richie surrounded by a circle of skilled magicians, all of them frantically trying to make the huge wrestler vanish.

"Christopher knew more than our teachers when we were growing up," Laura said.

"Don't play trivia with him, not for money," Megan cautioned.

Staring with determination into Christopher's eyes, Richie said, "I'll buy you a gorgeous new sweater – cashmere – if you get me to flinch. Your hardest punch."

"Try it, Christopher," Megan encouraged, "you've never had a cashmere sweater."

"On next Halloween, how's that?" Christopher increased the number of magicians in his fantasy, but still no success.

Richie lowered his arms and said with disappointment, "I'll be waiting, little fella. You got yourself a hole in your elbow." He took another sip of apple juice and sat back down next to Laura.

Christopher unfolded his arms and rubbed the hole in his sweater, recalling when his mother had bought the sweater for him, as a high-school graduation present. He asked Laura if she still had her graduation-present sweater and she confessed she had worn it once and given it away. "A little too tacky for my tastes," she said, and quickly qualified her disclosure: "But it still looks good on you."

"Christopher, it would be something spectacular seeing wrestling in person," Megan said.

"I have no desire to go, Megan. Let's wait until the circus is in town ..." Christopher had always been self-conscious about his slender physique. What made Laura's figure attractive, made him appear frail. The sight of Richie's body caused him to feel almost invisible. An evening full of combative, scantily clad muscle men was not Christopher's idea of entertainment.

Richie shaped an offended expression and was willing to take off his shirt then and there to give the unappreciative guest a sneak preview, but Laura stopped him after two buttons: "Don't waste your talent, Richie. My intellectual brother wouldn't know a great body if it fell on top of him. He doesn't appreciate *physical* strength."

"I can rip a phone book in half," Richie declared.

"Christopher breaks chocolate-chip cookies in half," Megan said.

"I'm talking major metropolises – cities with over a million population – white pages, yellow pages ..."

Plucking two tickets out of his wallet, Richie handed them to Megan: "Here, maybe you'll find yourself another escort. A beautiful girl like you should never have to go anywhere alone."

"*Woman*," Christopher said. "Megan is a woman." Christopher wondered why Megan hadn't corrected Richie herself; she never allowed women to be called girls in her presence.

"Whatever you say. Megan, if she wants, should come to watch the boys," Richie said, smiling at Megan.

"Thank you for the tickets, Richie," she said, waving them in front of Christopher's face.

Richie picked up a local entertainment newspaper that was on the coffee table and turned the pages until he found what he was looking for. Carefully he ripped out the advertisement for the wrestling matches – with his and The Masked Terror's faces glaring ominously into space – and handed it to Megan.

"I can rip newspapers in half," Christopher said, moving away from Megan.

Continuing to wave the tickets at Christopher, Megan taunted, "Only the business section, dearest one."

Laura stroked Richie's smooth face as they waited for a reaction from their guests to the picture in the advertisement. Richie's head didn't look like it should belong to such a large man, but it was balanced on a wrinkled red tree trunk of a neck that appeared larger than Christopher's waist. Richie had a baby face and there was a gentle set to his clear blue eyes. His gestures and facial expressions were emphatic and frequent.

"You like Richie's ferocious picture?" Laura asked, as if she were a proud mother showing off a prize baby picture. She imitated the wrestler's expression in the advertisement, and Richie kissed her face until she started giggling.

"It took me five minutes and some nasty thoughts to get that ferocious look on my face," Richie said, and duplicated the truculent expression he had in the advertisement.

" 'Propeller-Whirl Romulus meets The Masked Terror in a death match,'" Megan read aloud, her face contorting in confusion.

"I gave myself that name Romulus," Richie said, with almost childish pride. "Heard it when I was in bed watching a late movie about the ancient Romans. Romulus was their first big boss. I added the Propeller-Whirl part. The propeller-whirl is the move I'm best

185

known for. I went through a lot of names early in my career, but I've fixed on Propeller-Whirl Romulus. Isn't it a terrific name?"

"The myth I read claimed that Romulus and his twin brother Remus were suckled by a she-wolf. Inter-species cooperation kept the abandoned twins alive," Christopher told the large wrestler.

"I don't remember that in the movie."

"My brother is an endless spraying fountain of useful information," Laura said.

Christopher flashed a chiding glance at his sister, then returned his attention to Romulus' namesake: "Years later one twin killed the other ... *ferociously*."

186

"I wouldn't dream of hurting you, Christopher, and I know some lethal holds Propeller-Whirl Romulus taught me."

"What about the Romulans from the planet Romulus, on *Star Trek*? Any relation to them?" Christopher asked, inspecting the wrestler's face as if he were a strange-looking Romulan.

"I thought about that later, but the name came to me during the late movie," the wrestler explained.

"Richie the Romulan," Christopher snarled as insultingly as he could.

"The ad says only one man will walk out of the ring conscious," Megan said.

"That's going to be Propeller-Whirl Romulus," Laura said. "The best name and the best body."

"You'll have to get a powerful and impressive name when you start your legal practice, darling," Megan teased, but Christopher's expression grew sad.

"Smarty-Pants should do," Laura said, blowing a kiss at her sad-faced brother.

"Laura tells me you're going to be a *lawyer*," Richie said to Christopher, the wrestler's face indicating that he might be about to discuss the symptoms of dysentery.

"I'm in my last year of law school."

"What kind of law?"

"Criminal."

"I could have occasion to use your services someday. I've been known to have altercations with the authorities." The huge wrestler released a booming laugh. Christopher could feel the wrestler's breath against his face like an ill wind. Then Richie added, "I can afford the best lawyers, so you'll be able to make some heavy dough on me."

"Maybe you could use Megan's services also," Christopher said. "She teaches Grade Six."

"You have any idea how many Grade-Six books Richie could rip in half?" Laura said.

"You're funnier than sin, sweetie," Richie said and gave Laura a hug.

"Christopher has the sense of humour in the family," Laura said, squirming free of Richie's hold.

"But he does get a tad too sarcastic, in case you haven't noticed," Megan said.

"I like to think of my wit as sardonic or caustic ... or trenchantly vitriolic," Christopher defended himself.

"Always straight A's and the biggest vocabulary in school. Christopher used all the big words for the dirty ones everyone else was using in the schoolyard."

"I didn't get bad grades myself, but in the ring you don't need no big words," Richie said, laughing again.

"Your mother told me you do secretarial work," Megan said to Laura, placing the picture of Propeller-Whirl Romulus and The Masked Terror on the coffee table.

Richie's laughter increased, to everyone's amazement. The ill wind turned into an irrepressible typhoon. Laura tried to shake her lover silent.

"Did I say something wrong?" Megan asked.

"Her a secretary?" Richie bellowed, pointing at Laura as his body shook in delight, the luxury suite shaking with the cadences of his amusement.

"Laura, what are you doing *now*?" Christopher asked, horrified by the possibilities that Richie's reaction implied. He still remembered when his sister, as a teenager, told him that working in a massage parlour was an honourable way to make a living.

"Keep your blood pressure down, Christopher. When are you going to learn to relax?" Laura took a step behind Richie and could barely be seen.

Richie ran into the bedroom and returned holding a glossy black-and-white photograph over his head. He kissed the photograph and then held it toward Megan and Christopher. "I wouldn't be without an inspirational picture of my sweetheart."

"Oh, Christ, no!" Christopher blurted out, slapping himself hard on the side of the face.

"Don't panic, Christopher, mother will never find out," Laura said, returning to her hiding place behind Richie.

"Tell me this is not you, Laura," Christopher said, a panic-stricken victim praying that what was happening was only a bad dream. The stage name of the woman in the photograph was printed along the bottom of the picture, and Christopher read it in disbelief.

Laura poked her head from around Richie and confessed meekly, "I am Gyration … the Perpetual-Motion Dream Doll."

"You should have told me."

"You'd only worry. You'll get enough ulcers being a lawyer."

"But a professional stripper of all things, Laura?"

"We rented a movie about a stripper a while back," Megan said lightly, attempting to ease the tension between the brother and sister.

"A movie about a stripper I can take," Christopher said.

"You fell asleep before it ended."

"I'd been studying for two straight days.

"When don't you study?

"I study with my clothes on."

"It's a great job, Christopher. The money's good and I'm independent. I get lots of healthy exercise," Laura said and then began performing a few of her less titillating dance steps around the room. "Richie calls me his heavenly little dancing damsel," she said as she danced.

"I fell in love with this picture. I have a whole wall at home with publicity pictures of Laura. Before I wrestle I kiss this picture for luck. Wet, juicy kisses." The romantic wrestler gave the photograph another kiss and tossed it on the coffee table as he started to pursue Laura. When she paused, he first hugged her, then lifted her effortlessly over his head. She didn't seem upset or surprised.

Christopher and Megan moved toward their hosts, and stood poised, as though to catch Laura if Richie faltered.

"I enjoy my work, Christopher. You should take in my act if you come to Montreal," Laura said from near the ceiling, as relaxed as her brother was tense.

"I should be thankful you're not a stripper here. If I do go to Montreal, maybe I can see Propeller-Whirl Romulus and Gyration the Perpetual-Motion Dream Doll on the same night: Beauty and the beast," Christopher said.

"Laura is no beast," Richie said, offering a mock growl, as he put his love gently down. For Christopher it had been a grotesque ballet by his sister and the huge wrestler.

"Stop being so damn protective, Christopher," Laura scolded as she repeatedly poked her brother in the chest, forcing him to take several steps backwards. Her sudden aggressiveness startled him.

"I enjoy being a stripper, okay. I never told you not to try being a criminal lawyer," she continued, the start of tears in her eyes. Then she sighed as if she couldn't say another word.

"I guess we're in the middle of a family squabble," Richie said amiably to Megan. He was blushing with embarrassment.

Suddenly Christopher embraced his sister and kissed her lovingly on the forehead and cheeks. "If you want to be Gyration, be Gyration." He recalled the time his sister had almost died in a car accident. Her first words to him, after surgery – she had been given a fifty-percent chance of surviving – had been, "Hurry up and be a lawyer so you can sue the bastard who hit me."

Richie and Megan clapped spontaneously at the show of sibling affection.

"That's the attitude. The only time I like to see meanness is in the ring," Richie said. "You ever wrestle, Christopher, my boy?"

"I was never the athletic type," Christopher answered, his loathing for the wrestler increasing.

"How much do you weigh?" Richie asked, inspecting the skinny law student. His movements comic and exaggerated, Richie started to go after Christopher, pretending he was preparing to wrestle.

"About a hundred and thirty pounds, I think," Christopher said as he moved away from the playful, brawny, immense wrestler.

"Dripping wet, I bet. Jesus, I'm more than two of you. Nearly three. I weigh three hundred and seventy-five pounds. That's one-hundred-and-seventy-point-four-five kilograms," Richie said proudly, the way Christopher told his mother his outstanding law-school grades whenever she asked. "I used to weigh over four hundred, but that's no good for your heart." Richie pounded a fist against his chest, and laughed. "In Jolly Ol' England," he added, sliding easily into an English accent, "I'm a smidgen under twenty-seven stone."

"Go tomorrow, Christopher. Ringside seats. And I guarantee you that Richie will win," Laura said as she resumed dancing around the room, much more sensually than before. Megan began clapping in accompaniment, smiling at Laura's total lack of inhibition. She genuinely liked Christopher's exuberant twin sister.

Richie put an arm around Christopher, and the one-hundred-and-thirty-pound law student pushed the three-hundred-and-seventy-five-pound wrestler away. Taking the fierce shove as an invitation to play, Richie lifted Christopher as easily as he had Laura earlier, and gave Christopher a single propeller-whirl.

"Put me down," Christopher commanded, moving his arms and legs as if he were a drowning man trying to tread water.

"Promise us you'll see Richie tomorrow, Christopher. You'll find out who The Masked Terror is. He's supposed to be a well-known Toronto celebrity," Laura said, chuckling at her brother's midair discomfort and helplessness. She abruptly forced herself to look serious.

"I have to study," Christopher said, his water-treading becoming more desperate.

"Please, darling," Megan called up at Christopher, also enjoying the ludicrous show.

"Richie won't put you down until you say you'll go. Richie can be very stubborn," Laura said.

"This is asinine," Christopher said.

"You can look at life as one big wrestling match, Christopher, my boy, and I know how to win," the wrestler stated with complete confidence, giving Christopher another propeller-whirl.

"Wrestling's phony, for heaven's sake!" the twirled law student said with a quaver in his voice.

Laura stopped her dancing and exclaimed, "Christopher, what you've said!"

"You tell me what's not phony in life. Tell me, Christopher, my boy!" Richie said, and gave Christopher three slow-motion propeller-whirls.

"Nothing's more phony and sham than professional wrestling." 191

"Wrestling is as real as lawyering."

Summoning all his oratorical strength, Christopher said, "You wouldn't have a chance in a courtroom, Richie, my boy, unless you want to rip law books in half."

"Make believe we're in a courtroom now, Christopher, *my boy*."

"We should be on our way to the theatre. We don't want to waste my mother's generous gift," the midair man attempted to say reasonably and confidently, but his voice was tremulous, his face pale.

Laura moved closer to her brother, and stretching on tiptoes toward his captive head, said, "We'll make it in plenty of time. Promise you'll come to the wrestling matches, Christopher. You'll see how real they are and find out the identity of The Masked Terror."

"I'll tell mother you're a stripper," Christopher threatened, touching the ceiling with his fingertips to steady himself.

"You that eager to put her into her grave, my dear brother?"

Richie slowly spun Christopher around several more times, Megan and Laura cheering the wrestler on. Richie felt like he was in the wrestling ring, enjoying himself as much as during a sweaty and tumultuous match.

"Getting all those A's and knowing all those big words won't get you out of Propeller-Whirl Romulus' propeller-whirl. A simple promise will," Laura said, forcing herself to sound as serious as possible.

"I'm getting sick ... nauseous," the rotating Christopher yelled. His face grew more pale as his dizziness intensified. He thought he heard his own death bell ringing in his ears.

"My brother always did have a weak stomach," Laura said, without too much sympathy.

"That's true," Megan confirmed, indicating with a twirling finger that Richie should keep on with his famous propeller-whirl.

"Oh, God, I'm nauseous," Christopher said, closing his eyes to the ceiling.

"My ears have to hear you swear you'll show up tomorrow before I can declare this match over," Laura said, taking the stance of a vigilant referee.

"I'll go to wrestling, I'll go," Christopher surrendered. Richie put Christopher down between Laura and Megan, and threw his arms victoriously into the air. As the three unsympathetic onlookers laughed and cheered and offered each other high-fives, Christopher bent over and vomited, making absolutely sure Propeller-Whirl Romulus and Gyration the Perpetual-Motion Dream Doll received a few emerging chunks of his discomfort and humiliation. Megan nimbly escaped her lover's reprisals. As his stomach settled and the room stopped spinning, Christopher experienced the glorious taste of triumph – triumph in the ring.

DIOGENES' LANTERN

IN A LARGE, WINDOWLESS ROOM A woman, wearing only a long, elegant silk robe, is sitting at her dressing table. The room is bright, exceptionally bright, but there is no visible source of illumination. On the woman's dressing table, along with a large assortment of makeup paraphernalia, are a mask lying face down and several illumination devices not giving off any light.

The woman, who if you surveyed ten different people as to her age would give ten different years, has a timeless quality to her features, comportment, and gestures. This unusual woman is looking into her large table mirror and humming happily. After some hasty preparation, she starts to speak aloud, as if to an invisible observer to whom she is responsible: "Lipstick, lots of lipstick. The next visitor likes glistening red lipstick and dark makeup, very dark ... sensual ..."

The woman touches the silk cloth of her robe and contemplates changing her outfit but decides against it, and resumes her preparation and happy humming. Then, as if caught off guard, she says, "I should check everything in the room before he arrives. I hope he's more interesting than the last visitor. Talk about the walking comatose. Deception and fear coming out of his ears, and not even the slightest comprehension of his confinement. The one before that wasn't too bad. He had some spunk, at least. There was quite an unpredictable fellow a few hours ago –" She cuts herself off by saying, "Enough of this silly analysing. I must get ready for the next visitor."

The woman looks dreamily at the mask and the illumination
devices on her dressing table: flashlights, candles, lamps, matches, a
lantern. She touches the lantern and laughs: "Like Diogenes looking for an honest man."

Gracefully the woman stands up and goes around the room, lantern in hand, seeming to do an inventory: "Old living-room sofa ...
drum set – nearly thirty years old ..." She picks up a drumstick
and taps at the drums. "Still has a good sound," the woman comments. At a wall rack of keys, she stops briefly and does a quick
count: "A thousand ought to be enough for the next one." Then
she moves toward a gun rack on the wall near the set of drums.
"These two pieces of handiwork haven't been used in twenty years,
but they're still nice old hunting rifles ..." She moves about the
room, swinging the lantern at her side: "The bed is ready ... fresh
sheets. I changed them after the last visitor. It's not easy getting
the room arranged for each visitor ..."

The woman moves past the wall clock and says, "He'll be here
any second." Suddenly there is a loud, enthusiastic knock at the
door.

"Ah yes, the desperate knock," the woman says, "that persistent, desperate knock. I can't begin to count how many times I've
heard it in my life."

There is another loud, enthusiastic knock, and another. The
woman returns to her dressing table, puts the lantern down, and
sits in her chair. After starting to brush her hair, she calls out loudly,
"The door's not locked."

A man, thirty-seven years old, six-foot-two, a few pounds be-
low two hundred, and neatly dressed in an expensive suit, opens
the door and enters the room. The woman turns her head without standing and says, "I am pleased to see you, sir. On time ...
yes, right on time."

The man is confused by the interior of the room but main-
tains his unruffled outward expression. His eyes take in the clock
on the wall, then he looks at his own wristwatch, and says, before
any greeting, "Your clock there isn't the correct time."

The woman puts down her hairbrush, stands up, and in an un-hurried manner goes to the wall clock. "This decrepit clock is a nuisance," she says, and turns it around.

"There was about five-hours difference," the man says, check-ing his wristwatch once more.

"No use worrying about time," the woman says, standing across the room from the man. "I want us to take our time ... make our stay together last." She extends her left hand and motions in front of her: "You like my humble little domicile?"

"This is a very large room, as far as rooms go," the man says. "You certainly have some odd things around."

"It might be a good idea if you closed the door," the woman instructs the man.

"Sorry ... sure," the man says, and quickly closes the door.

"Make yourself at home," the woman tells her visitor. "My place is your place."

The man takes a step away from the door, continues to inspect the contents of the room, and remarks, "I appreciate the hospital-ity."

The woman, looking directly at the man, says, "Share your most secret thoughts with me. Hold nothing back."

"I don't really open up until I get to know a person," he says, an enforced confidence to his words.

"Then get to know me," the woman says, her expression lively and engaging. "We'll become the most intimate of friends."

"Friendship takes time to cultivate."

"Time we have," the woman tells the man. "But what do we need this impersonal chatter for. Words interfere with true emo-tions."

The man appears annoyed by the woman's statement and re-plies from behind a wall of controlled formality: "Without words there is no communication. Without communication there is con-fusion, and confusion leads to nothing but problems."

"My, my, you possess a philosophical streak," the woman re-sponds with an easy-going rhythm. "You know who Diogenes was?"

"The name sounds familiar," the man says.

"See that lantern on my table. It was Diogenes' lantern."

"Looks like an antique."

"To say the least," the woman says, releasing an unselfconscious laugh. "Diogenes was a Greek philosopher. An extremely fascinating man. When he visited me I wasn't much help to the old chap."

"Wasn't he an *ancient* Greek philosopher?"

"I'd say about three or four centuries before Christ, but let's not get bogged down in chronology."

Rubbing the sides of his short, neatly combed hair, the man says, "You two must have had a memorable visit together."

Irritated by the man's sarcastic tone, the woman observes: "You look like a modern-day philosopher in your beautiful, expensive suit."

"I'm not philosophical at all."

The woman shakes her head in disapproval, and the man says, "That doesn't mean I don't think about the world around me. I pay careful attention to the news."

"Good, I like a thinker," she says.

Attempting to escape the woman's gaze, the man looks around the room again, seeing the gun rack and two hunting rifles – the woman notices a slight tremble to the man's mouth – but he quickly focusses his attention on the rack of keys on another wall.

"You certainly have a great many keys there," the man comments, dispelling the image of the two hunting rifles.

"I'm a key collector of sorts," the woman says and points to the centre of the cluttered key rack: "This is the one for the door."

"I locked the door," the man reminds the woman.

The woman takes a key from the rack and walks to the door, inspecting the man as she moves. She carefully inserts the key into the doorlock and says, "A precaution. So, now that we're safely locked in, tell me who recommended me to you."

"I'd rather not say," the man says, watching the woman return to the key rack.

"Say, please, or I'll pout horribly for days," she says, hanging the key back on the rack, then jingling out a cacophonous tune with her fingers over the other keys.

"I can't remember the name," the man says, straining his memory to recall who had told him about the woman and this room. "Isn't that strange?" he says with awkward embarrassment.

"Lapses of memory aren't that rare around here. To tell you the God's honest truth, I encounter them frequently."

"I'm sure it must have been an acquaintance of mine who told me."

"Not worth getting in a dither over," the woman says to the man. "Take several deep breaths. You're too tense."

"I'm always uneasy in a new place."

"You're safe here ... safe and protected as nowhere else. Believe me, there are no microphones or fancy hidden cameras in this room."

"I wasn't looking for anything like that."

The woman removes a small notebook and thin pen from a pocket of her robe and starts to write.

"What are you writing?" the man asks.

"Oh, a few notes ... for future reference."

"Future reference for what?" the man demands to know, his eyes narrowing in distrust and concern.

The woman puts the notebook and pen away, and says, "Let's forget it. You're not here to discuss my note-taking. You are here for pleasure."

"You don't know my motives."

"It's pleasure you're here for," the woman insists, then says the word *pleasure* as though it were twice as long.

"To avoid argument, that's as good as any other word."

"You all come here for pleasure. What else could you possibly desire?"

"Company ... relaxation ... maybe some conversation."

"Pleasure ... solely pleasure," the woman says emphatically. "That is a fact not open to dispute."

"Then I won't dispute it with you," the man says without conviction. "This is your room, after all."

"Keep looking around my room. Don't be timid ... Not the newest set of drums in the world, but they get the job done. Go have a closer look."

The man goes to the drums. He is reluctant to touch the set even though he raises his hands to do so.

"Pick up the sticks and have a go," the woman says.

"I can't," he tells her, lowering his hands.

"Of course you can," the woman encourages, and imitates the sound of drumbeats: "Rat-a-tat-tat ..."

"These are fine drums."

"Sit yourself down and let loose."

The man sits down behind the set of drums and cautiously takes the two drumsticks in his hands. "Unfortunately, I don't know how to play the drums," he admits.

"I think you can. Rat-a-tat-tat ..."

The man gives a single drumbeat, and the woman tells him to play more, not to be shy. He hits more drumbeats; the woman's encouragement grows stronger. Soon the man is drumming away, lost in a fantasy.

"See, my friend, you possess the talent to have been a great drummer."

With the man engrossed in his drumming, the woman abruptly shouts, "Enough!"

The man keeps on drumming and the woman shouts louder: "Enough! Concert over!"

The man stops drumming, and with a puzzled look, says, "I thought you wanted me to play."

The woman alters her voice and says, "My head hurts ..." She offers a mocking laugh.

"What are you laughing at?" the man asks, pointing one of the drumsticks accusatorily at the woman.

In her own voice, the woman says, "You've finally got your drums. A dream come true."

"What are you talking about?"

In the false voice the woman used before, she says, moaningly, "My head hurts ... My head hurts ..."

The man hits the drums hard with both drumsticks.

"Not in the house, my little son," the woman says in her false voice. Then, resuming her own voice, "Better late than never. Those drums are nearly thirty years old. *They're your drums.*"

"I never had drums," the man says.

"*Headaches* ... severe, incapacitating migraines," the woman says.

"How did you know?" the man asks.

"A well-informed birdie told me."

"Did you know my mother?"

"I know everyone ... and their mother."

"I couldn't have drums around my mother, not with the way she was," the man explains.

"Commendable to listen to one's mother."

"She couldn't stand any kind of noise around the house."

"You were born to be a drummer."

"I did without drums."

"It was your strongest dream."

"Only when I was a kid. I grew up."

"Yes, you grew up," the woman says. She takes out her small notebook again and flips through the pages. "Let me see, I have it written down ... Ah, here it is: thirty-seven years, five months, nine days old, you are."

The man, both nervous and antagonistic, says, "What's wrong, you don't have the hours, minutes, and seconds?"

"I could calculate them for you."

"Spare yourself the mental exertion."

"According to my notes, you've packed an impressive amount of accomplishments and successes into thirty-seven years."

"I get by," the man says. "I work hard."

"Well, now's not the time for work. Be comfortable, sit on the sofa," the woman instructs the man. "The drums won't run away. Later, a longer concert."

"That sofa does look comfortable," the man says. He leaves the drums and walks toward the sofa.

"It's from your parents' living room."

"I doubt it," the man says, but the familiarity of the old sofa frightens him. He hesitates to sit down.

"I need to ask you some more questions before pleasure-time," the woman says.

"I didn't come here for pleasure, I assure you," the man states firmly, attempting to avoid the memories associated with the old sofa.

199

"You want to talk about your family instead?"

"Not at all."

"Tell me about your mom and dad."

In exasperation, the man asks the woman, "What about *your* family? Tell me about your mother and father."

"Zeus and Hera conceived me ... during a heavy-breathing session on top of Olympus."

"You're being ridiculous."

"Horny Zeus slept around a hell of a lot. Like you."

Angrily the man says, "Keep your mind off my personal life. Stick to talking about sex on Olympus, something you know about."

"Actually, Adam and Eve are my real parents. Conceived me under the Tree of Knowledge. A big, juicy apple fell on Adam's cute bum during the act."

"You can keep your birth certificate hidden away. I don't care."

"You don't have to tell me anything you don't want to, not even about your wife and children."

"Good, then I won't."

The woman goes to the bed and sits down at the edge. Smiling alluringly, she pats the mattress in invitation.

"There's no rush," the man tells her.

"Why delay? You're here for pleasure."

"I'm not in the mood."

"You want a drink first?"

"I don't drink anymore."

"Holding on tightly to the rickety old wagon, aren't you?"

"My drinking days are behind me."

"But not your amorous days."

"I told you, I am not in the mood right now."

"Because I'm not beautiful enough for you?" The woman stands up from the bed and goes back to her dressing table. "I have the remedy for that right on my table. With some more makeup I can make myself look better for you. Like another woman, if you want."

"You don't understand why I'm here."

"Which woman do you want me to be?"

"I couldn't care less."

"How about Hippolyta, Queen of the Amazons? Or Cleopatra, Queen of Egypt? Perhaps Salome, dancer *extraordinaire*? ... If not the magic of makeup, I can put on a mask. It's simpler and quicker."

The woman puts on a mask that makes her look exactly like the man in the room, and turns around to face him: "Recognize me?"

The man, startled, asks in a raised voice, "Where did you get that mask?"

"It even has a little scar on the forehead. You fell down the stairs at your aunt's house ... when you were eleven."

"How'd you find out?"

The woman ignores the man's question and says, "I'm certain that you'd prefer if I put on the mask of a beautiful woman."

"A person's physical appearance is secondary to me. It's the mind that impresses me."

"Don't play the compassionate, sensitive, enlightened gentleman with me," the woman says, still wearing the mask of the man. Moving closer to the man, she says, "Those feelings don't fit you. You can't tailor your words like that expensive suit of yours."

"I don't *tailor* my words."

"Defensive, aren't you?"

"Take off that mask," the man orders.

The woman, inspecting the man's suit coat, says, "I hope we don't get your expensive suit dirty or ripped in the heat of passion ... when we're finding our pleasure."

"I'm not here for pleasure, I told you!"

"There, off with this mask. I was finding it hard to breathe properly. Besides, a mask would inhibit your pleasure."

"Why don't you let go of that stupid word."

"You came here for pleasure."

"Not at all."

"Didn't the person who told you about me warn you?"

"About what?"

The woman puts the mask of the man down on her dressing table. "Coy, aren't you? My insights, shall we call them."

"He didn't say anything specific."

"He must have said something specific. You need very good directions to find this place. My room isn't exactly your corner convenience store. Your acquaintance had to give you directions. Turn left, turn right ... up fifty flights of stairs, down the hundred-kilometre hall ... knock loud ... knock like your life depended on it."

"I'm here, so he must have told me how to find you. That's pretty basic logic."

"When your acquaintance told you about me, your heart dropped, didn't it? Dropped right out of your well-dressed body."

"I don't know where you get your stupid ideas."

"Does my imprecise phrasing disappoint your highly ordered mind? You know, logical lover boy, there's something about *your* mind that is uninspiringly crude."

Indignantly the man says, "I'm not here for insults."

"That's true ... and that's logical. Why would a successful, well-dressed, intelligent married man, father of two adorable children, go somewhere to be insulted. You're here for pleasure ... for what I and only I can provide to you. *Pleasure* ..."

The man shakes his fist in frustration at the woman and then starts to walk toward the door.

"How pathetic. Lost your passion and resolve. Don't you know that love is everything."

"Now it's love," the man says angrily. "You've made a remarkable jump from pleasure to love with the same effort it would take you to sneeze."

"Pleasure and passion and love are not mutually exclusive, even to a compartmentalized thinker like yourself."

At the door, the man says, "Coming here was a mistake." He tries without success to open the door.

"A lock needs a key, remember? Simple logic." The woman takes a key randomly from the key rack and warns, "Catch," as she throws the key at the man.

The man catches the key and the woman says, "Nice catch, logical, nimble-fingered lover boy."

The man forces the key into the lock but is unable to get the door open. "Wrong key. You gave me the wrong key," he tells the woman.

"Try this little charm," the woman says and throws another key at the man, which he also catches.

"Two clean catches in a row," she remarks in mock astonishment.

The man futilely attempts to open the door with the second key. "Give me the right key. This one won't even get into the lock."

"So many keys I have." The woman takes several more keys off the rack and begins to throw them at the man. "Try all of these ..." Some of the keys fall near the man while others bang against the wall before falling to the floor.

The man works frantically, key after key, to try to open the door. "You get off giving me keys that don't work?" the man asks without looking at the woman.

The woman, muffling a laugh, says, "I can't allow you to leave before I've provided you with the services only I can. It's my responsibility and obligation. We know what happens to those who resist their responsibilities and do not fulfill their obligations ... who fight, defy, disrupt, do not pray loudly enough to God. Try praying loudly to God that your next key will work."

"Damn, it's not this one ... Or this stupid one," the man says, growing more upset with each wrong key. Becoming more anxious, he adds, "Which cursed key is it?"

The woman takes more keys off her rack and throws them at the man, some hitting the floor and wall, others the back of the man. He shields his head from the rain of keys.

"Try them all. When you're done with those, then I have more for you ... boxes of shiny keys."

Overwhelmed by futility, the man stops trying to open the door. "You have no right to keep me here," he says.

"I'm not keeping you here," the woman says in a low, calm voice, then declares sternly: "*This is where you belong.*"

Defiantly the man exclaims, "I don't belong anywhere near this stupid place." With more intensity, greater determination, he picks up other keys and tries to open the door, this time from a kneeling position.

The woman goes to the bed and pats the mattress again. Remaining standing, she says, "Come to bed before you hurt yourself."

"I need to go home!" the man shouts.

"Your drums are here," the woman says. "Play and please your father."

"Leave my father out of this."

"Your handsome father visited me here years ago ... twenty years ago, almost to the day."

"You liar!"

"Relax ... feel at home."

"This is not my home!"

"You have no home."

204 "How can you say that?" the man says and pulls out his wallet from the back pocket of his trousers. With his hands shaking from anger, he removes several pieces of identification from the wallet. "I have all sorts of IDs ... I have an address ... proof I have a home."

"Put your wallet away," the woman says.

The man returns his identification and wallet to his back pocket but does not relinquish his argument: "I have all the proof necessary that I have a home."

"You are deluding yourself," the woman says and steps toward the man. She offers her hand to him: "Let me help you up."

"Get away from me," the man says.

"Everything you require is here in this room."

The man grabs more keys from the floor and says, "I haven't tried all the keys."

"Come away from the door."

"This key the one?" the man asks, and tries another key.

"So stubborn ... so deluded," the woman says, her voice a mixture of contempt and compassion.

The man picks up two more keys and tries them without success. "Goddamn keys!" he shouts.

"Raising your voice is unnecessary," the woman tells the man.

"Which key is it?!"

"No one can ever open the door from the inside. It would be against all the laws of science and Nature."

"Which key?"

"Think about love, not keys."

"Goddman you, I'm not interested in love."

"You came to this room expressly for love."

"You're confusing pleasure and love again."

"Love will give you pleasure ... pleasure will give you love."

"Shut the fuck up!"

Unperturbed, the woman says, "I look forward to getting close to you. To feeling you deep inside me."

The man picks up a handful of keys from the floor, decides against trying any of them in the doorlock, and then throws them angrily at the woman. "Goddamn useless keys," he yells at the top of his voice, but his words no more strike the woman than the keys he has thrown.

205

"What a mess you've made with my keys," she scolds.

"Let me out of here!"

"In time."

"When?" the man asks in a lowered voice, sensing that perhaps reasonableness affords him a better chance than anger.

"I liked your drumming. I want to tell you that before we have any more misunderstandings."

The man stands up, not far from the woman. "How did you know I wanted drums when I was a kid?"

"I knew," the woman says soothingly.

"I pestered and pestered my mother for drums. I could be a brat."

"But you gave up trying to get drums."

"My mother had terrible headaches."

The woman takes the man's hands, the first time they have physically touched, and begins to dance slowly around the room with him. "Don't be afraid. I only want to dance."

"I'm not afraid," the man says, and allows the woman to lead him dancing around the large room.

"Isn't dancing together better than arguing or being at each other's throat?"

"I guess so. It feels good dancing with you."

"You're as good a dancer as any man I've ever danced with, even Nijinsky. I waltzed with Nijinsky in this very room."

"That's great."

"From your eyes, I can see you don't believe me."

"Anything you say. Feels very good dancing with you, I can't deny that."

"I could dance with you eternally."

"Peculiar dancing without music."

"I do it all the time."

"I can't describe how good you're making me feel ... the sensations — "

"You want to play the drums again?"

"The dancing is fine ... I used to watch my mother and father dance in the living room when I was growing up ... almost every night."

"You'd sit by the record player, behind this very sofa, and change records for your parents ..."

"You know a great deal about me."

"Until the murder," the woman says without changing her tone or altering her dance steps.

The man stops dancing, but the woman holds on to him.

"It was an accident," the man says. "Let go of me."

"You like dancing with me."

"Accident —"

"Don't lie to me, not at this stage," the woman says into the man's face. "We were making such progress."

"Let go of me."

"You like me close to you."

"Let go!"

"Such progress."

"It was an accident ... that was the ruling. Hunting accident."

"Your rifle should have been empty."

"I thought it was."

"You didn't care for your father."

"I loved my father."

"You had never been careless before. You were a skillful hunter for a seventeen-year-old."

The man breaks away from the woman and rushes toward the gun rack.

"You're stronger than I thought," the woman says.

206

"These are guns you bought somewhere ... at a store around here."

"I was wondering when you'd acknowledge their existence."

"I knew they were there, big deal."

"The same guns. Your hunting rifle and your father's hunting rifle."

"That's not possible."

"One of them is loaded."

"No!"

"Show me how safe you can be."

With fear, the man says, "Those can't be the same guns."

"You're looking at the murder weapon."

"No!"

The woman goes to the man and embraces him. "I want to hold you. See how good it feels ... Lies will hold you back."

"It was an accident."

"You'll be able to walk away from here if you tell me the truth."

"It was an accident, I swear to you."

"The only way out is truth."

Regaining some of his composure, the man says, "What happened to pleasure and love?"

The woman releases her embrace of the man and commands him, "Undress!"

"You tired of holding me?"

"I told you to undress."

"I don't want to undress."

"Take off your clothes. I'll help you with the truth."

The man goes to the door again and says, "I'm going to smash this goddamn stupid door open."

"Come with me to bed now. The pleasure will be freeing. Then everything will be clear to you."

The man kicks the door – hard, angry kick after hard, angry kick – until exhaustion. The door, barely marred, remains solidly closed.

The woman leads the unresisting man to the bed. Weakly he says, "Please leave me alone."

"You're here. It's my responsibility to give you pleasure. My obligation."

Tearfully the man says, "Please let me out of here."

"Don't snivel!" the woman yells at the man, then tells him placatingly, "Get on the bed and I'll take care of everything. You'll be glad you chose to visit me."

"I didn't want to come here."

"And I suppose you didn't want to be born, too."

"I really didn't want to come to this room."

"Of course you did. I've been waiting for you all of your deceitful life."

Summoning forth all his defiance, the man says, "My life has nothing to do with you. My life is my wife and our son and our daughter."

"They'll be here ... eventually. It all gets sorted out sooner or later. Now, before I lose my patience, get undressed and get on the bed."

"You can't force me."

"For the love of God, don't you know yet? Everything's been spelled out to you in the most colossal letters possible. Don't be obtuse ... I'll have to undress you myself."

The woman takes the man's suit coat off, then his tie: "Isn't that better? ..." When she starts to unbutton his shirt, the man rushes to the gun rack and takes the bottom rifle off the wall.

"Come back to me," the woman says.

"Unlock the door!" the man orders, pointing the rifle at the woman.

"No use doing that."

"You better listen to me."

"Come to bed. Everything will be as it should."

"Unlock the door or I'll shoot."

"You're so obtuse," the woman says, and goes to her dressing table. She picks up the mask of the man and puts it on once more.

"You can wear whatever you want on your goddamn face."

"The texture of this mask is almost like real skin," the woman says, touching the mask. "The scar is identical to yours. Identical"

"Unlock the door!"

208

"Pleasure ..."

The man pulls the trigger of the rifle and only a clicking sound is made. Repeatedly he pulls the trigger, but the gun is not loaded, and the same clicking sound results each time.

"No accidents here," the woman says.

The man drops the rifle to the floor and starts to cry. The woman, still wearing the mask, takes the man by his hand and leads him back over to the bed.

"Down on the bed," she says.

The man gets onto the bed face down; amid sobs, he pleads, "Let me go home."

"Don't you want to try the other rifle? It might have a bullet in it ... like when you went hunting with your father twenty years ago."

"You have to believe me that it was an accident." The man, still sobbing, says, "Please ... please let me go home."

"Without pleasure? Without your full understanding of everything? ... I'll give you a little massage to relax you ..."

The man screams when he is touched by the woman.

"You're as bad as the rest. I thought you might be different. Too many lies. Too little truth ... I should know by now ..."

She gets on the bed next to him. "We'll have a wonderful time. I will enfold you completely ... completely ..."

The man tries to scream again but the sounds which leave his mouth are little more than whispers.

"Building a life of lie upon lie, deception upon deception, you lose control. But that's no reason you can't experience pleasure. Pleasure will dissolve you ..."

When the woman stands up from the bed, the man is lifeless, an expression of absolute fear on his face. She takes off her mask and soon is humming happily, in the same manner as before the man arrived.

"I spent more time with him than I should have, but it couldn't be helped," she says, as if to an invisible observer. She places a sheet over the man and suddenly the body vanishes, the woman paying no attention to what has happened. "I have to straighten this room out quickly ... Keys all over the place ... Drums, gun rack with

209

rifles, old sofa, I have to get them all away ... These new things, ah, they look interesting: Old tricycle ... books – quite the collection of erotica ... old portable typewriter – novel never written ... a pair of crutches – didn't go off to war ..."

There is a loud, enthusiastic knock at the door.

The woman sits down at her dressing table, moves the old lantern over, next to the new mask she has placed down, and starts to brush her hair.

Another knock ...

Loudly the woman calls out, "The door's not locked ..."

Earlier versions of some of the stories in this collection have appeared in the following publications: *The Antigonish Review, Jewish Dialog, The New Quarterly, Origins, Tabula Rasa, TickleAce, Waves, Windsor Review,* and *Writer's Block Magazine.* "Anton Chekhov Was Never in Charlottetown" is based, in part, on an earlier short story, "Sanity Hearing," from *Unmapped Dreams* (Crossed Keys, 1989) by J. J. Steinfeld; "Sanity Hearing" first appeared in *TickleAce.*

The text of this book was set in Bembo and printed on
acid-free paper made from fifty percent recycled fibre.

Published, printed, and bound in Canada by Gaspereau Press.

Gaspereau Press acknowledges the assistance of the
Canada Council for the Arts for its publishing program.

1   3   5   4   2

Canadian Cataloguing in Publication Data

Steinfeld, J. J., DATE

Anton Chekhov was never in Charlottetown

ISBN 1-894031-28-8 (pbk)
ISBN 1-894031-27-X (bound)

1. Title.

PS8587.T355A75 2000   C813'-54   C00-950111-8
PR9199.3S7824A75 2000

GASPEREAU PRESS
POST OFFICE BOX 143
WOLFVILLE, NOVA SCOTIA
CANADA BOP 1XO